HACKER LAWRY

The Lonely Heroes Series, Book Four

SAM E. KRAEMER

This book is an original work of fiction. Names, characters, places, incidents, and events are either the product of the author's imagination or used fictitiously. Any resemblance to actual persons, living or dead, business establishments, events, or locales is entirely coincidental.

Copyright ©2018 by Sam E. Kraemer
Rerelease Copyright ©2021
Editor: Beau LeFebvre, Alphabitz Editing
Cover Design: Arden O'Keefe, KSL Designs
Proofing: Mildred Jordan
Formatting: Leslie Copeland, LesCourt Author Services
Published by Kaye Klub Publishing

These characters are the author's original creations, and the events herein are the author's sole property. All rights reserved. No part of this book may be reproduced, scanned, or distributed in any form, printed or electronic, without the express permission of the author. Please do not participate in or encourage piracy of copyrighted materials in violation of the author's rights. Purchase only authorized editions.

All products/brand names mentioned in this work of fiction are registered trademarks owned by their respective holders/corporations/owners. No trademark infringement intended.

THEIR STORY

Lawrence 'Lawry' Schatz -
Heartbroken? Check.
Unemployed? Check.
Homeless? Check.
Self-medicating? As often as possible.

My life has been upended with a three-word text, and a meeting with my boss's boss nearly finishes me off. I'm in a downward spiral, and I have no intentions of pulling out. My brother Hank has other ideas. He's called in a big gun, Gabriele Torrente, who drags me to New York and pushes me to get myself together.

At a family event, I hook up with the hottest guy I've ever met, intending to just relieve some tension. The guy turns out to be more than I could imagine. He's sassy, opinionated, and he completely sets me on my ear. I can tell Maxim Partee won't put up with my crap. I made a huge mistake with him, but he still agrees to be my friend, and that is precisely what I desperately need. I live under no illusions he'll ever need me in return.

Maxim 'Maxi' Partee -

Sexy? Check.

Successful? Check.

Lonely? Very much so.

Power bottom? You bet your... bottom.

I have a successful business—two of them as a matter of fact. I have friends I cherish, and I love my life. I keep telling myself it's more than enough for me. I choose the men I spend time with, and it's always on my terms.

An unexpected hook-up at a birthday party leads me down an unanticipated path where I meet a man who has been crushed by a mountain of disastrous events, and he's doing his damnedest to push everyone away so he can quietly self-destruct. Why in the hell can't I just walk away?

This fictional story is approximately 86,000 words in length. It is the fourth book in "The Lonely Heroes Series." TRIGGER WARNING: Discussions of suicide and a description of an attempt.

LAWRENCE SCHATZ

Prologue

August 2019

"Agent Schatz, the Assistant Director wants to see you." I was sitting in my three-by-three cube—well, it was bigger than that, but it was still like a shoe box, nonetheless.

I turned to see Paula Gore, the Executive Assistant to Assistant Director Mallory who was head of the Dallas Field Office, standing at the opening of my cubicle. I was a third level agent for the Central Intelligence Agency—or the Spooks, as the other agencies referred to us.

I was an expert in monitoring cybercriminal activity and breaking coded messages that were transmitted among criminal enterprises, and I enjoyed my job. I could tiptoe through anyone's information without leaving a footprint, and it pissed off most of the agents with whom I worked because they weren't always so successful, but I just laughed at them when they complained. I was doing something for the good of the country, but I wasn't *actually* in the field doing it, which was never my thing, anyway.

My work was something I took seriously, and I was proud of the fact I'd reached a level of expertise that set me above my CIA colleagues and my peers in other agencies. I wasn't gloating. I was just better at my job than the rest.

"What's up?"

Paula Gore was the kind of woman who minded her own business, and I liked her. When Julien had gone to the Assistant Director and asked to transfer from the Directorate of Science & Technology—Cyber Surveillance to Clandestine Services—Anti-Terrorism, we both learned Paula had kept quiet about the fact she'd caught us making out in the hallway near the break room two months earlier. I'd be forever appreciative for her discretion.

"I'm not really sure, but he said he wants to speak with you immediately." Paula turned and left the area without another word. I sighed as I looked around, seeing a bunch of people staring at me, which made me uneasy. I pulled on my sports jacket and locked my laptop, following the trail Paula had blazed back to Mallory's office. Once I was on the express elevator to the AD's office, I pondered what the fuck the man might want from me.

I'd been following up on communication intercepts for a number of suspected terrorist cells in the Southwestern United States with possible counterparts in Mexico and Central America. It was my job to confirm they were credible before passing on the information to field agents for follow-up investigations. The work was tedious and time-consuming, tracing out all of the connections, but it was what I did best. I couldn't imagine the request to report to the AD had anything to do with my work product.

One possibility for being summoned could be that AD Mallory learned about my moonlighting job for Gabe Torrente, or Gabby as my brother Hank referred to his good friend. They were Army Rangers once-upon-a-time, and Gabby had gone on to start up a U.S. subsidiary of his uncle's private security agency in Italy. When I had down time, I did research for Gabby. His IT guy, Johnny Chang, had left him after being shot during a protection assignment. The primary, Dexter Carrington, was being hunted by members of the Mangello crime family because he was hiding his niece and nephew to keep them safe. Turned out they were Frankie Mangello's grandkids.

I'd followed up on several leads for Gabby and had confirmed one of the guys he'd asked Julien and me to check out for him, Royal Conway, hadn't been affiliated with any agency or bureau under the U.S. umbrella. The other one had been a Drug Enforcement Agency operative, but it seemed there'd been an internal investigation into his activities, according to a red-flagged file on their server, which I'd known better than to open, regardless of how tempting it had been.

Had the DEA beefed up their security and detected me taking a stroll through their network? Was that what got me called up to the AD's office? Would my Supervisory-Agent-in-Charge Wendell Robb be there waiting as well?

I couldn't blame Gabby's IT guy for wanting out of the security business—it was dangerous. With all of the crazy shit I'd been privy to in my time with the Company, everyone didn't have the stomach for it. My older brother had been a sniper in the Army, and he'd seen his fair share of unholy hell that had left him with scars—a few external, but most of his damage was invisible to the naked eye.

Hank handled his inner demons with the help of Cosmo, his service dog, and Reed Bayless, his husband. My big brother had met and married a wonderful man, an educator of children with special needs, and Reed and Hank were recently granted foster guardianship of a ten-year-old boy they were hoping to adopt.

My new nephew was on the autism spectrum and had some difficulties I suspected would have caused most potential parents to shy away. I knew for a fact Hank and Reed would help Brock through the difficulties he'd encounter as he grew up in their home because failure was never an option for Hank and Reed. All in all, I wouldn't say I was trying to live up to the tall shadow cast by Henry Schatz-Bayless, but *maybe*?

Paula nodded for me to knock and enter, so I did. Assistant Director Ian Mallory rose from his chair and stepped around his desk, extending his hand. "Agent Schatz, thank you for coming so quickly. I, uh, you are friends with Supervisory Field Agent Julien Renfro, correct?" he asked.

I shook his hand and took a seat, worried about the way the conversation was starting. Julien had been my boss when I was promoted from a junior grade analyst in Intelligence & Analysis to a

Field Agent in Science & Technology. With his recommendation, I got promoted to a Senior Field Agent within eight months, and that was before we ever really got to know each other. Julie, as I called him, told me I had excellent skills and often teased me about a sealed juvenile record that must exist somewhere, because there was no way I didn't hack into shit when I was a teenager.

Obviously, Julie didn't know Maureen and Gene Schatz very well. They would have killed me if I'd pulled anything of the sort. I hadn't learned to hack systems until I'd started my training with the CIA, unlike Johnny Chang. That kid was a natural at it, but he'd taken risks I'd been taught to avoid by the Company. I was a programmer at heart and went about entering my target in a different fashion than a natural-born hacker like Johnny. Neither of us were wrong in the way we went about gathering our intel, we just had different styles, and from what I was learning, we were both proficient at acquiring what we wanted without being caught.

Before I met Julien Renfro, I'd identified as mostly straight... okay, at least bisexual? There had been a few guys at Washington University who'd turned my head during undergrad and graduate school, and my interest and reaction to them had had me confused in the beginning. As I'd further considered things, there weren't really many women who'd caught my eye since high school when I lost my virginity to Molly Ingram. I'd arrived at the conclusion maybe I'd slid up the *Kinsey* scale long before I'd been willing to acknowledge it?

"Yes, sir, Director Mallory, we're *friends*."

Of course we were friends. We were more than goddamn friends if one counted all the nights I spent with my cock buried in Julie's ass, but I was currently pissed at him. Julien Renfro had left Dallas without a goodbye, kiss my ass, or go fuck yourself. The bastard had even left me in the middle of the night, adding insult to injury. Three weeks later, I'd gotten a text from him, before he went dark.

GET OUT NOW!

I had no idea what the fuck his message had meant, and since I'd been paying half the fucking mortgage and my name was on the goddamn deed and loan documents, he could just go straight to hell. I wasn't going anywhere until he came home to explain himself to me face-to-face. I had hoped I meant more to him than just being his roommate and booty call, but the way he'd behaved before he took off? I feared he was done with me, anyway. Things hadn't been going well with us before he left.

"I'm not in the mood, Lawry. Take a fucking hint," he'd snapped at me one night when he was crawling into our bed in a pair of sweatpants and a t-shirt. He'd been late getting home from an assignment that took him out of the country for a few weeks, and he was in a horrible mood. I'd saved him a plate in the fridge, which I happily heated for him, only to learn he'd gone out for dinner with his SAC after his debriefing. I behaved like an adult by throwing the plate and food into the trash, but I calmed down and wanted to reconnect with him. I'd missed him.

Julie had stopped talking to me about what he was working on, but I wasn't surprised. After he'd left my department, we hadn't really talked shop at home. In fact, it was almost as if we didn't have much to talk about at all any longer. I'd been optimistic it was just a phase in our relationship. Mom had told me a relationship was fluid—it ebbed and flowed. I'd believed we just had to get to know other things about each other, and I was looking forward to doing so. I'd foolishly believed Julie would be, as well, once we discussed it, but that was my midwestern gullibility showing its ignorant head.

The director looked nervous, which didn't alleviate the tempest rolling around in my stomach. Finally, I couldn't take it any longer, so I went with the obvious. "What's happened to Julien?" My head was spinning. Julien Renfro was the example of an agent I wanted to measure up to, though I doubted I ever would. The man was flawless at his job.

"He committed suicide. He put himself into a situation he shouldn't have, and he couldn't get out of it any other way, or so we deduced from messages found on his phone and documents in his possession at the apartment where he was residing at the time. I can't tell you any more than that, Agent Schatz. I know you were a friend of his, so I pulled you in as a courtesy before you heard it from anyone else. I'm sorry for your loss. Take a few days off." Mallory's voice showed no more emotion than a person would offer before flushing a fucking goldfish down the toilet.

I couldn't believe what I was hearing, so I chuckled before I stood in front of his desk. "I'm sorry. *What now?*" The director looked uncomfortable at my reaction but come the fuck on. He *killed* himself? That was all the fuck they had to offer me about the man I loved? That was fucking ridiculous.

"I'm very sorry for your loss, Agent Schatz. His remains were recovered and have been sent to his listed next-of-kin in Boston. Of course, his identity will be expunged from the records, as is protocol in a situation of this kind. Seriously, son, take some time off.

"Unofficially, I know the two of you were in a romantic relationship. When Julien came to me and asked for a reassignment, I didn't want to approve it at first. He told me the two of you were seeing each other, and he confirmed you were too valuable to Cyber Surveillance to transfer elsewhere, so I changed his assignment as he wished. I swear, I never imagined for a second that he'd end up dead or I'd have... I don't know what I'd have done, but I'd never have assigned him to Anti-Terror. You have my deepest sympathies, Lawrence. If there's anything I can do for you, please call me." And, just like that, it was over.

I nodded, unable to speak. I was stunned silent, waiting to awaken from the nightmare. *What the fuck did I eat that brought this into my subconscious?*

As if on autopilot, I went to my desk and grabbed my shit to go home. I logged out of my computer and left the building without a word to any of my fellow agents. I got into my SUV, heading straight to our home in Dallas where I parked in the garage of our townhouse and walked up the back stairs and into the mudroom. I removed my shoes as Julie had insisted since the first time I'd gone over to his home. It was how he'd grown up, shoes off at the door, and I respected it even if his parents were total pieces of shit.

I stepped into our kitchen and looked around, seeing every scene from our time together replaying in my mind's eye as if I was watching a video. We'd cooked up culinary disasters and had laughed until we'd cried or peed our pants before he'd thrown a frozen pizza into the oven once the smoke cleared.

I was able to make simple dishes because Maureen Schatz insisted Hank and I learn to at least feed ourselves before we left the nest. The man I loved couldn't boil water, but he tried so fucking hard, it brought a smile to my face even now.

For Julie, I ate a lot of burned or undercooked food, but the proud grin on his face was enough to help me choke it down and secretly eat handfuls of antacids while we watched movies. As I looked back on those times, there were signs I'd chosen to ignore. Signs we had more differences than commonalities.

Julien had grown up with a nanny, cook, housekeeper, and gardener, so he didn't learn to do shit on his own because nobody had cared enough to teach him. Hell, I had to show him how the fuck to sort his laundry to wash it at home instead of taking it to the cleaners. But to me, Julien was still the brightest star in my sky.

His parents were venture capitalists, running their privately held corporation and being quite successful at their trade. They'd had no time for caretaking the son who had been an accident, as he'd heard them refer to him during arguments when he'd barely been old enough to comprehend the meaning of the words. They'd hired people to provide Julien with the necessities of life while they'd traveled the world to further their fortunes without worrying about what had happened to Julien at home or school on any given day.

It had broken my fucking heart when Julie had told me some stories from his childhood on our first date when we'd finally decided to give a relationship a try. Of course, we'd slept together that night, and I'd held him in my arms after I sucked his cock, and then we'd fucked because he'd seemed to need it. After that, I'd always held him when we'd slept because he'd missed out on being bonded to anyone as a child, and I'd wanted him to bond with me. Julien had believed he was meant to walk the world alone, which was why he'd seemed so disconnected from everyone around him. I refused to believe for a minute it had been his destiny.

It was also why he'd worked so goddamn hard to be the best of the best. He'd wanted to prove his parents wrong in the worst way. He hadn't been a mistake; he'd been born for a reason, which I hadn't doubted for a minute. Julien Delaney Renfro had been a born leader, and he'd been loyal to his agents, his friends, and to me, the man he'd said he loved. I sat wondering what he'd gotten into that had cost him his life, but I had no idea where he was sent for his last assignment, so trying to find out anything from anyone who'd been with him would be impossible. Hell, they'd already erased him from the records.

So, the greatest romance of my life would end with his death, and the last words I'd seen from him would be a text message telling me to *"GET OUT NOW!"* for no rhyme or reason. I was only left to assume he meant out of our home and his life, and it left a sour taste in my mouth. The future was pretty bleak as I faced it with a shattered heart.

Many, many times I attempted to contact his family, but the Renfro's never acknowledged me in any way. I wasn't able to find any information regarding when or where the funeral would take place, nor was I informed where Julie had been laid to rest. The only thing I could confirm was his parents hadn't bothered to purchase a headstone because there was no record of purchase at any of the monument companies in or around Boston. I'd hacked each and every one of them myself. I had to finally accept I'd never know the physical location where Julien Renfro, one of the most beautiful people on the planet, had been placed to spend eternity. That news broke my fucking heart.

I received an eviction notice about three months after his death, which didn't surprise me, really, considering who had filed it. His parents challenged my status as a co-purchaser of the townhouse in Dallas, stating I'd coerced their heterosexual son into a relationship and then into adding my name to the mortgage and the deed. They wanted to stop me from making an illegitimate claim of entitlement to half of his estate, as if money would take away the hurt I felt at losing him.

I didn't give a flying fuck about those bricks and the mortar holding them together. Julie was dead, and I didn't buy that he'd committed suicide. He'd told me to get out of our house, so maybe he was ready to end our relationship, and when I didn't respond or get out, he decided to commit suicide to get away from me? It sounded far-fetched, but if it was true, that might account for the Renfro's fury at me. Had I inserted myself into his life when he didn't want me there? I had no idea, but they claimed he wasn't gay, and I wasn't about to dispute it publicly.

I had the memories of the wonderful nights we'd spent together, naked in the bed we'd shared. On the other hand, some nights Julie wanted it really rough when we'd fucked, and it had made me uncomfortable. Call me a romantic, but I wasn't the aggressive type. Silly me, I'd thought when you loved someone you were happy to be with them. You counted yourself lucky they were yours. You were theirs. You showed each other *that* love when you were together. We'd had those nights, but then, we'd had *other* nights.

There had been times it had seemed as if Julie had hated the fact he'd rather be with a man than a woman, and he'd wanted me to be rough with him, almost like a punishment, so he felt—hell, I hadn't known what he'd wanted to feel when he'd begged me to hit him and had pleaded for me to choke him while I'd fucked him hard, sometimes without lube at his insistence. I'd staunchly refused to do anything of the sort because I fucking loved him. There was no way I'd agree to do anything that would have put him in physical danger. It had been a sticking point between us, which I had to consider might have been one of the reasons he'd wanted me gone.

After I'd met Julie's parents, which had only happened once, I'd been able to understand why he'd been so broken and had wanted to feel the physical pain manifested on his body that he'd felt in his soul. His mother and father had never made him feel worthy of their love, and he'd never known how to channel that hurt. One night, after several drinks, he'd explained to me that the physical pain he needed during sex had felt like it cleansed his soul enough that his parents might find him worthy of their love, but that hadn't been anything I could comprehend. Maureen and Gene Schatz had never raised a hand to Hank, Jewel, or me. All we'd known from them had been unconditional love.

The one time we'd visited Boston when Julie had introduced me as his boyfriend, his parents had lost their shit. They would have never accepted the fact he might be gay, so they'd circled the wagons and had gone on the offense. They'd said I was a money-grubbing whore, and that Julien should have had me arrested for fraud. We'd left their home and had gone to a hotel near Logan Airport until we had been able to get a flight out the next morning. Julie had kept telling me the whole time it had been a mistake for us try to talk to his parents about our relationship in the first place.

Before I met Julien Renfro, I had settled myself into the happy illusion that any interest I might have had in a member of the same sex had been merely a curiosity for what made one attracted to one person versus the other. In high school, I'd looked at guys to compare myself, but I'd been sure I was still looking for the right girl to date. That had never happened, so I had to believe maybe I was a little bent back then. I'd only thought of guys when I'd jacked off as a teen, but I had likely been too dumb to figure out those fantasies probably had meant something else.

After I met Julien, I'd told myself I had an odd attraction to a handsome guy with a wonderful personality. It had been the same story I'd told myself in college and grad school when I'd find myself attracted to guys I'd seen on campus. I'd been secure enough in my masculinity to admit Julie was gorgeous, just as I could have admitted the models gracing the pages of GQ had been fine specimens of manliness. I'd been a fool, but it had taken me some time to figure that out for myself.

When the idea of Julie being gone forever settled in my mind, I concluded I had no reason to live, either. After nearly an entire fifth of bourbon, I went to the drawer in the motel room where I'd been forced to move after his parents kicked me out of our home, having come to a final decision. I reached into the dresser drawer and pulled out the "emergency" .45 revolver Julie and I had at home, which I'd taken with me when I'd left with my sparse belongings.

I wrote a note to my family and left it on the table with my identification because I knew Maureen and Gene would want to give me a proper burial in the family plot. I wrote to Jewel that I loved her more than anything, and I would be happily watching her grow up from heaven, even though I didn't believe in it. I told Hank I knew he'd make a great father, and he should fight for Brock because the little boy would bring joy to their lives, and they would bring love and understanding to his.

After I made sure my affairs were in order, I sat down on the bed, removing the safety latch from the metal door of the room so the motel staff, or the cops, didn't have to destroy it to get inside. As I considered it, I was guessing the spatter would be a bitch to clean up. Hell, as I looked around the room, I decided the place could use a makeover, so I put the gun under my chin and looked up at the ceiling as if I actually believed there was heaven above and hell below.

I closed my eyes. "I love you, Julie. I hope you're waiting for me." I felt the tears cascading down my cheeks as I hooked my finger over the trigger, held my breath, and squeezed, hearing a click. I pulled it again and was surprised when there was a loud click and turn of the cylinder, which surprised me.

I pulled the pin to open the cylinder, seeing the fucking thing was empty. Not one cartridge in the flute. Why hadn't I thought to check for bullets? Surely, I was smarter than that? Or, under the circumstances, I'd have to say—*not!*

MAXIM PARTEE

May 2021

"Okay, my doves, listen up. We have a fortieth birthday party to plan for Gabriele Torrente. Dexter wants it to be a surprise, so what are we thinking? We know he's not really a renaissance man, though he is quite proud of his Italian heritage. The party we planned for his son, Dylan, seemed to capture the spirit of the event, so let's try to channel that energy again." Hopefully, I sounded encouraging. I was attempting to get the creative juices flowing in my staff as I spread baby lotion on my hands. Just because it was spring didn't mean my skin didn't need hydration.

"Theme?" Toni Williams was my rock and my left hand because my right hand was used for self-abuse since I couldn't find a decent guy to date. I didn't even know my type any longer, so I didn't pursue romance. I was a man, but I could have a full life without romantic entanglements, *right*?

In all honesty, without Toni at my side, I'd still be filling balloons with helium at the party store Sale-A-Bration Nation where I'd worked during high school. I met my best friend at that little brick building in a strip mall when she was picking out supplies for her own high school graduation party back in Lafayette, Louisiana, and we'd hit it off immediately while deciding her party colors definitely shouldn't be her *school* colors. They should be her favorite colors—chartreuse and magenta. Not my pick, but she'd loved the combo, so that had been our inspiration, and the party had been a smashing success.

We became friends, and when I'd graduated from the University of Louisiana-Lafayette with a degree in Hospitality Management, I'd been able to get a job working at a banquet facility where I had discovered my life's true calling. I was made to party, or at least plan them for others. I couldn't help but drag Toni along with me, because that girl was crying out for escape from the hell of working for an insurance agent and the cloying stench of living in a small town with even smaller minds.

Toni had the unhappy misfortune to be named Tawny at birth. The name belonged to the actress from that Whitesnake video that had been popular in the eighties. The actress had been a favorite of Toni's father, who'd been granted the option to name the last child in the family of seven.

They'd been very Catholic and hadn't believed in birth control, but the man had named his youngest daughter after a half-naked woman writhing on top of two Jaguars, and he'd believed it was okay. *Some people's parents... Tawny* wasn't a person's name; it was the color of a spray tan, so we'd changed her name on the way out of Lafourche Parish where we'd grown up in the small burg of Thibodaux.

At the time, Toni had been working as a receptionist at her father's insurance agency, which she'd hated. She'd had absolutely no fucking ambition to look for any other line of work in Lafayette, and the fact she hadn't known how to dress had led me to an intervention.

I'd known it would break her heart when I'd told her that she didn't look good as a blonde, but over the years, we'd worked out the kinks of her look *and* my business plan simultaneously, and we'd moved our Dixie asses up to Yankee-Central... New York City. We'd worked hard and had finally made our way to the top of the heap, though I knew for a fact I couldn't have done it alone. Toni was definitely my grounding rod.

The woman kept all of the facts straight in her mind regarding our customer base and upcoming events so I could allow my creativity to flow freely. I was able to envision the parties and events I planned for the paying public—who generally had horrible taste—because I didn't have to think about how many dinner napkins were necessary. Toni handled all of the details like it was a job she was born to do.

I didn't fault my clientele for their general lack of imagination, because without their inability to formulate an original plan for a wedding or a party, I wouldn't have two businesses—parties and weddings. Toni was a godsend, and she kept me anchored to the ground because on my own? I'd flit and fly right into the sun.

"Hmm. Gabe is a fan of sports. Should we plan a sports-themed party? Take the emphasis off the big 'four-oh' so as not to bruise his ego?" I joked with two of the people who made up my event planning team. I had many other people who worked to make our occasions fabulous, but I had five in particular who I depended upon the most. Those five would see the thing to fruition because I wanted Gabriele Torrente's birthday party to be flawless.

For Dylan's birthday in January, we'd planned a *Vikings-and-Dragons* themed party, complete with a castle-shaped bouncy house and a balloon sword fighting ring. It was all a hit. For Searcy's birthday, which was in late March, they'd taken their family to Disney World, asking me to assist with adding a little something extra for Dylan.

Those two angels nearly lost their minds with the special events I'd helped Dex schedule with the assistance of an event planner at the happiest place on earth, though I had other ideas what would constitute a happy place for myself. The Torrente family had a fantastic time, sending me pics for my website to showcase my tagline, "No event too big or too small."

With Gabe's fortieth, Dex wanted it to be equally as spectacular, especially since they were stuck at home because Gabe was busy with work. I loved the Torrente family, every one of them, so I was determined to do my best. Parties by Partee had a reputation to uphold, after all.

My little businesses had moved from my brownstone on Seventh Avenue to the first floor of the building where my dear friend, Shay Barr, had his spa and salon, DyeV Barr. Dexter had alerted me that the lady who owned the yoga studio on the first floor, Kitty Rae, was closing her business, and the whole building was available for purchase. It seemed Kitty had fallen madly in love with a yogi, Ramesh Singh, and the two of them had decided to move to upstate New York and open an ashram.

Kitty referred all of her yoga clients to Dexter Torrente who had his studio on the first floor of a beautiful blue and white Victorian conversion, where his husband's offices occupied the remainder of the building. Kitty sold her twenty-three-hundred square feet of prime real estate to me at a very economical price, making Shay Barr my new lessee. My purchase of the building provided a more convenient situation for both of us, and it was a joy to be able to pop in for chats with each other on a more frequent basis.

Planning the party for Gabe was my way of returning the favor to Dexter for alerting me about his friend's desire to sell the property and putting in a good word for me with the quirky woman. I had four weeks to whip up a magical celebration, and I was excited at the prospect of what our collective mind could create.

"Well, we could go that way, but he's still going to be forty, and he *does* have two kids. Maybe something a little more sophisticated that celebrates his accomplishments without using the 'over-the-hill' approach? How was your date on Friday, by the way?" When I looked up, I saw the smirk.

Friday night. That was something I'd rather have forgotten, but since Toni had been the one to create a profile and sign me up for the goddamn dating site without my permission, I wasn't pulling any punches. I wanted her discouraged from trying that shit again. The date had been such a fucking disaster, she deserved to hear every painful detail. I appreciated that she was trying to get me to focus on other aspects of my life to keep me from being too work-centric, but she picked the wrong loser from the tree to make that happen.

Besides, giving the woman a play-by-play also seemed the best way to proceed to get her to leave me the fuck alone regarding the way I went about seeking a little *sex-u-al healing* to keep me from being too fucking lonely and disagreeable. I used a reputable agency for my sexual needs, and yeah, I paid handsomely, but there was a price for happiness. Hell, some of those guys were the three 'S's': strong, sexy, and stupid. They still rung my bell quite nicely, and they were on the clock, so I could kick them out when I was through.

"Friday night was a fucking tragedy, Toni. The guy's attending NYU, and he's studying Economics. He decided it was his mission in life to explain the *market basket,* as it pertains to my business. What the fuck do you have on my profile, and how can I take it down?" I took a dramatic sip from my cappuccino, which had grown cold.

"Blah!" I pushed away the saucer and scooted closer to my desk.

"Harley gave notice." Toni was changing the subject to keep me from ranting, and I was actually grateful. The past was over. Move on.

Harley Brown was a stunning man who was Persian/Caucasian. He had dark hair and big, soulful eyes. His vanity job was working as a drag queen, a/k/a Blaze O'Gloryhole. He'd worked for me for a year now because he was so fucking entertaining when we met at a fundraiser I'd organized at The Bone Yard, a club in the area. I simply couldn't resist hiring him. He was also chock full of ideas, which I used to my advantage.

The event where we met had been for the benefit of the Bay Ridge Health Center, a free, queer-friendly clinic in the neighborhood. Teens over sixteen, LGBTQA+, and straight could get tested for STDs and pick up condoms without hassle. The place provided counseling services for young people who were dealing with various issues at home —anything from coming out to an unplanned pregnancy to physical or mental abuse in the wake of either scenario. It also offered support for those in the community who were HIV-positive. It was a multipurpose shop for everyone under the rainbow (or not), and I'd been eager to support the cause.

I did not, however, like Mr. Jeffrey Oswald, the owner of the club that had hosted the party. He seemed to be a total fucking douche, and I hated the fact he was the owner of the venue where the fundraiser was to be held. I'd almost backed out when I'd met Oswald, but the event had been for a good cause, and Harley Brown had talked me into going through with it in spite of the horrible owner. Harley possessed a true gift for the work, especially when it came to tolerance of the public, and I'd offered him a job at the end of the night. It didn't hurt he was a beautiful man.

"Why? Is there something more we can do to keep him?" I truly hated the idea of him leaving.

Toni laughed as she stood from the table in the conference room and walked into the open area where everyone had working space. It wasn't cubicles or offices. It was fortified with conversation spaces filled with couches and chairs so people could freely exchange ideas. Music played throughout the space, and I believed it was an ideal arena where my staff's inspiration could be fueled.

Toni walked over to Harley and said something, pointing to the conference room where I was still sitting with Kenzie Imari, my graphics guy who handled the creation of all banners, signs, invitations, place cards, etc., for all of our events. Kenzie chuckled as we both saw the look of fear on Harley's face as he nodded and followed Toni back to the room. She opened the door and motioned for Kenzie to follow her out as she pushed Harley inside before walking away to leave the two of us alone.

I pointed to a chair next to me, which Harley took quickly. He looked really worried, and I didn't want that. "Harley, love, I'm just surprised you're leaving because you have so much to offer to this business. Do you not enjoy being here any longer? I mean, you're one of the best hosts I have on staff. Is there something I can do to make it more desirable for you to stay?"

That sweet smile came onto his face, and I knew I'd already lost him. "Look, Maxi, I love my job here and enjoy working with everyone, so thank you for giving me this chance. I'm a performer, through and through, and I've been offered a contract to travel and perform in drag, which is my dream come true. Since I was a little kid, I've loved to entertain. I'm never going to get a recording contract because my voice isn't that great, but I can dance. This man, Grandon Slade, he's seen me perform a few times, and he'd like me to sign on for a summer tour he's organizing.

"I don't *want* to quit, but this new opportunity is something I've wanted my whole life. I know I'm leaving you a bit short-handed, but I'll stay until you find someone to take my place. I'd love for us to continue to remain friends, Maxi. You've honestly changed my life, and I don't want to lose the connection." The sincerity came across, especially when his beautiful brown eyes began to leak tears.

I stood and pulled him up from his chair, wrapping him in my arms. "Oh, honey, you have a friend for life. Maxi Partee never abandons a sister. I'm always here, and if you have downtime or you decide you need a break from the travel, maybe you can come back to help out sometime. I want you to have the most wonderful life of your dreams, but if something doesn't work out, you'll always have a home here with us. Now, you call me and check in every now and again, ya hear?" My southern accent came out when I was emotional.

I never wanted to sound like a hick because that wouldn't take me far in my profession. I was from bayou country…Lafourche Parish, Louisiana. I had family who still lived in Thibodaux, but they didn't want anything to do with the likes of me. That was the past. I'd moved on, and I damn well would maintain the image of an erudite gentleman, even if I were still learning how to pull it off.

I'd had enough willow-switch beatings to decide it was for the best if I worked to get beyond my past. I couldn't mire down in that cesspool because it would suck me under, and I wasn't about to let that happen. I was better than the life I left behind, and that I would remain. Fuck. Them. All.

The bell over the door rang, so I stepped out of my office to see it was Shay Barr, one of the sweetest guys in the world. Shay and I had become great friends, and I loved sharing the building with him because he was as particular about his workspace as me, and he didn't hesitate to alert me of any repairs that were too much for him to handle alone.

"What's up, sugar?" I greeted, allowing the drawl to surface. Shay was from Arkansas, as I'd discovered when we first met, so he worked as hard as me to maintain the chic mystique that drew our elite clientele. He also would admit to me it wasn't always easy.

I met Shay one day when I desperately needed a haircut and

walked into the old salon where he worked in Manhattan. I'd waited an hour for him to be free to cut my hair, because I'd watched him through the large window a couple of times when I was working at a florist shop across the street from the fancy ass salon in Chelsea.

I could tell he was good at his trade, and I wanted the best—well the best I could afford. Shay was the best they had to offer at that little hen club, so I waited for him to be free. I told him he needed to get himself a salon because the woman for whom he worked was using him and wasn't paying him his worth. We became fast friends after that first encounter.

Shay was about five-six, and he had beautiful medium-red hair. It was a bit wavy, and he'd let it grow longer and pulled it back in a ponytail, though of late he'd branched out to the *mun,* which I thought was cute...selectively. Some guys could pull it off, but some guys couldn't. My friend, the adorable stylist, could work that mun.

Shay wore a subtle stubble, because if he didn't, he'd look about thirteen. He was slight of build, even lighter than my *burly* frame of five-eight and one-hundred fifty-eight pounds. One couldn't always help the fact they were slight of build and had a hard time putting on weight. I had my mom's metabolism, and even without the drugs she consumed on a regular basis when I was young, I was pretty sure she'd still have been thin.

Shay walked over to me and kissed both of my cheeks. I hugged him because it was what we did, he and I. We only had each other, but Dexter Torrente was becoming a part of our group, or we were becoming a part of his family, I wasn't sure which. I was happy at the prospect of either.

I truly loved Graciela and Tomas Torrente, Dex's in-laws. They were absolutely the most fabulous people in the world, and they welcomed Shay and me to all family occasions. That was why the birthday party was so important. It needed to be perfect.

"I'm bored. We're busy, but I've been locked in the office getting the tax shit ready. Do you have an accountant? I think I might need one because I'm not really good at bookkeeping." Shay took a seat across from me, his face matching the tension I'd heard in his voice.

Toni walked by the door and knocked, holding up her fingers to mimic drinks. "You want a coffee or something?"

"Cap, please." I held up my cup and two fingers. Toni laughed and spoke to one of the younger people who worked for us, sending him off to the pantry.

"How was your date?" Shay taunted, the jackass. We'd had drinks on Thursday night as usual, and I'd complained about how much I thought the blind date Toni had forced me into the next night would suck. Shay had told me I was putting out too much negativity into the universe, and I was swamping my possibilities of meeting my soulmate. I'd told him to go square to hell.

"Awful. The guy was a fucking grad student. All he wanted to talk about was his goddamn dissertation. Thankfully, he gave good head, or the night would have been a total waste." If I'd said it to Toni, she'd have scolded me for having a one-track mind, which was a theme she'd latched onto lately. It was driving me crazy.

Shay, however, laughed with me. "I should have known you'd make lemonade from the lemon. So, what are you working on these days? Another wedding?" His tone was eager, but of course, I knew why.

Shay Barr was an astounding hair stylist, and I recommended him to my brides and my grooms since he'd started cutting and coloring my mousy brown hair. He'd convinced me to let him bleach it to a beautiful sunny blonde, which he said made my eyes pop even more than the kohl eyeliner I used every day. In turn, I referred his salon to anyone who would listen, because the man was a wizard with scissors and a styling brush.

Shay had done the hair and makeup for Gabe and Dexter Torrente's wedding party, and the day had been perfection. He was the master of his domain, sweet Shay, but why he couldn't find a decent man to love him was a mystery to me. I wasn't actively looking, though Toni wanted me to be. I got by fine. She needed to worry about herself and maybe poor Shay.

"As you well know, we have three big weddings coming up over the next month, each of which is flawlessly planned. Key has the Burk's. Toni has the Pembrook's, and Fredrik has the Dawson's—all of whom, I believe, have already booked your services. My focus at the moment is on Gabe Torrente's birthday party in late May. I'm lost regarding anything other than a sports theme. Thoughts?" Leon, the new intern, came into the room with a tray and his toothy smile.

Leon Gilbert was mind-numbingly gorgeous, and he had a sultry vibe I wished I could master. Shay couldn't take his eyes off the beautiful man from Trinidad, and I had to stifle the laugh because my friend was nearly salivating onto the front of his shirt.

"How are things going, Leon?" I couldn't help fucking with Shay. The quick flick of his middle finger in my direction made me laugh.

"Things are great, Maxim. I'm getting ready for finals, but you know that because you've given me a week off with pay to study. Can I bring you anything else, gentlemen?" His voice was oozing that lovely accent I could tell nearly had Shay coming in his tight, black jeans.

I glanced at my friend, who gave me a stern look that radiated his desire for me to shut the fuck up. "No, but thank you, Leon. We appreciate it." I lifted my china cup in his direction. Leon swept his dreadlocks over his shoulders and grinned as he left the room.

I watched Shay as he stood and bent forward to watch that man's amazing bubble butt disappear into the kitchen. I finally let go of the laugh I'd been stifling. "Why the fuck won't you just ask him out?"

Shay laughed. "Maxi, he's looking for a top, just like me. He's pretty to look at, and that ass? Incredible. We aren't compatible, and he doesn't even give me a second glance."

"He's crazy if he doesn't." Yes, Shay was a bottom, just like me, but I got the attraction. Leon was beautiful, and the timber of his voice? Lordy, it almost made me wish I had the skills to rock his world.

I was a man who enjoyed a thick cock up his ass, but not just any dick, because I wasn't just any bottom. I wasn't a simpering twink—too old—and I got what I wanted when I went on the hunt. I needed a strong partner who could take direction because I didn't submit to any man. I might like a dick up my ass, but it was my choice of when, where, and how. Plain and simple.

Shay laughed. "My dear friend, we are as different as we are alike. You want control, but you don't want a wimp. That's probably why the economist didn't measure up. How the hell did you even let Toni talk you into that dating site? The guy wasn't enough of a challenge, right?"

I sighed because he was right. "Yeah. He honestly reminded me of my seventh-grade science teacher, and I always hated Mr. Wingate. He had a weak personality, and you know I'll just run over a guy like that without a second thought. You know me. I'm just not cut out to go down without a hell of a fight." I offered the wink for emphasis.

He laughed and nodded. "My prince charming comes in a large package…not unlike Dexter's husband. That man is sublime…" Shay released a starlet-style sigh that made me laugh.

"I think if you say that to Dexter, he'll kick your ass, *and* you'll lose a bunch of clients. He's a happy housewife, but if you tell him you're lusting after his husband, he'll make your life a living hell." There was no need to tell him that Gabriele Torrente had been an Army Ranger because that would only fuel Shay's fantasies, I was sure.

I didn't know if they'd shared that information, but I'd gotten it out of Dex at the spa on the wedding day. When I looked at Gabe again, I saw it. The big man had the posture and finesse of someone who exuded the confidence only a trained killer could pull off. It was sexy and dangerous, which would put the heart to flutter. It wasn't, however, the only thing I was looking for in a man.

Shay laughed as he finished his drink and glanced at his watch. "I've got to go. New customer coming in. You want to do anything this weekend?" He stood and smoothed out the white, broadcloth shirt that was his uniform. That and the black jeans he wore so very well. If we were different people…

"Definitely Sunday brunch, and I'll call Dex because I need more information on this birthday party. Cactus, okay?" It was a new Tex-Mex place in the neighborhood, and I'd heard good things about it. Their tequila flights were supposed to be incredible, and I didn't work on Sunday or Monday. It was a great way to end—or start—a week. Life was pretty good, except for the lonely parts. I could do without those.

LAWRY

"Get the fuck up!" It wasn't a kind greeting at all. My head was pounding, and I didn't exactly remember why. I opened my eyes to see myself in my sister's room at my parents' house. When I remembered why I was there, I felt the urge to puke, but I quelled it. I'd learned very well how to handle my liquor over the last two years. I had no reason to care what happened to me anymore, and the alcohol helped blur the lines. My reason for giving a shit about anything was gone like the wind.

"Go fuck yourself, Henry!" I rolled over and pulled the pillow over my head to block out the light. I had no idea what day it was, and I vaguely remembered how the fuck I ended up in Washington, Missouri, again. I'd lost my fucking mind and drove home to try to get my head on straight. At least I was somewhere familiar, which was more than I could say for the past two years.

After I tried to put myself out of my misery and then realized I had no goddamn bullets, I decided to go on a road trip. I got into my SUV and drove for almost two years. I checked out on my family and just drove around the country with no destination in mind. I had accumulated enough money in my 401(k) to get by after I quit my job with the Company, and the SUV allowed me the opportunity not to stay in motels.

I drank. I fucked people I didn't know—thankful I always used a condom. I'd definitely seen the seedier side of America, having stayed far away from the northeast. Julien had been buried somewhere in Massachusetts, and if I couldn't visit his grave, I wasn't going anywhere near that part of the country.

When I tried to pull up my pants one day and they slipped off my hips, I noticed I'd lost a bit of weight. I'd also missed Christmases, birthdays, and any number of other holidays, and the last time I spoke with my brother on the phone, he ripped me a new asshole because Jewel had a concert I hadn't attended where she won a scholarship or an award of some kind. I tried to explain she'd have many more of the same, and I'd be there for every one of them, but Hank let a litany of curse words fly and hung up on me. That was when I decided to go home.

My family let me slide and behave poorly because they didn't know what to do for me. Reed and Hank had tried to talk to me about shit when I checked in while on the road, but when I asked them how they would feel if one of them committed suicide to get away from the other? Yeah, they both shut the fuck up pretty quickly. I wished to hell I could bleed out and become an insignificant speck of dust, but the God my parents and sister believed in hadn't seen fit to be that kind to me.

There was a kick to my ass, so I turned over and saw it *wasn't* Hank who was there to torment me. It was Reed, my sweet brother-in-law. "Oh, hey. You sound like Hank, you know?" I rubbed my eyes, trying like fuck to shake off the headache.

Reed sat down on the side of the bottom bunk next to me. Jewel had taken over the guest room as her new domain, and my ass got shoved into the bunk beds I'd had to share with my brother when we were kids. They still weren't fucking comfortable, but I was guessing the whiskey I drank every night made me impervious to the lumps in the mattress.

"Yeah, I guess I might, but I've been married to the man for two-and-a-half years. It's a known fact the longer people are married, the more alike they become, just like with pets. We'll both morph into Cosmo any day now. Get up, Lawrence. This traveling hippy shit you've been pulling for the last two years needs to end now. You're becoming a degenerate, and Mo and Gene don't deserve it. You're coming to St. Louis with us." It wasn't a request, and I wondered what

Reed commanded of my brother in bed. Then, I had to fight not to puke.

Reed had a job as a deputy director at a school for kids who had severe special needs, and the man had that teacher voice down. "I don't think, Doctor Bayless, that it's in my best interest to go with you to St. Louis. Your adoption just finalized, and I'm not exactly a role-model. I'll leave here, but I'm not going home with you guys." I sat up and held my head in my hands, trying to figure out if it would be better to have blown it off to keep it from hurting so fucking bad.

There was a soft knock on the door, and I wondered who the fuck was there to bother me now. "Come in," Reed invited quietly.

The door opened, revealing Brock, their adopted son who was now twelve, standing nervously in the hallway. He glanced at me before stepping into the room, closing the door behind him. He wrung his hands and rocked back and forth on his feet, not looking at either of us, which had me worried. He was the sweetest kid in the world, and I didn't want him to be afraid of me. Clearly, my scraggly beard reminded him of someone who had done him harm a few years earlier while he was in foster care, and I hated myself for the fear I saw on his innocent face.

"What's going on, Bud?" Reed asked as he sunk to his knees and took Brock's hands, stilling him in the process. I watched as a sweet smile came over Brock's face, even though he didn't look Reed in the eye.

"Poppa said Mr. Gabby is here to take Uncle Lawry home," Brock stated as his eyes looked at the ceiling, not focusing on me and my vagrant appearance. I was guessing it was for the best because I knew I looked like shit.

I cleared my throat. "Brock, will you tell Mr. Gabby I'll be down in a little bit. I need to take a shower and pack. Thank you." I spoke quietly to my new nephew, who startled at loud noises or shouting, but not when Cosmo barked, which was a surprise.

Brock then stepped in front of me and leaned in, allowing me to hug him for the first time. He ducked his head away to avoid the fucking beard I should have lost long ago. He pulled back from me and snapped his fingers, which was something I'd taught him to do, or so I was told when I sobered up on occasion. He glanced at me with a smile before he left the room.

I didn't remember teaching him to do anything because I was drunk most of the time, and my brother, Hank, was too pissed at my behavior to even speak to me. Apparently, shipping me off with that big fucker he'd served with in the Rangers was his idea of how to handle me. I supposed I could do worse. Gabby was a decent guy. Maybe he'd wring my fucking neck and put me out of my misery.

I leaned back as I sat on the side of the bed, hitting my head on the fucking springs of the top bunk. Reed put his hand on my back and rubbed over my t-shirt. "Lawry, I can't imagine the pain you've suffered, but brother, you need to get to a place where you can handle it. Drinking yourself into oblivion isn't healing. Hell, it isn't even coping. It's numbing, and that's not productive. If I had my choice, I'd take you home with us and put you through the most intensive fucking rehab I could find, but Hank thinks you need to be busy with work.

"Johnny Chang didn't come back to work for *Golden Elite Associates-America* as Gabe hoped, and they're in the middle of reorganizing their business plan, so they need a tech guy. Gabe's here to take you back to New York so you can help them out until they can find someone permanent," Reed explained.

I turned to look at him, seeing his genuine concern for me in his eyes. Hell, they had their hands full with Brock, and I definitely wasn't helping out my parents' state of mind because they had my sister to look after. Reed was right; I needed to go. "Yeah, I get it. Do Mom and Pop know I'm leaving?"

Reed smiled. "Your mother and Jewel want you here where they can keep an eye on you, but Gene believes it's for the best right now. I'm sure your peace of mind is totally trashed, but Lawry, drinking or smoking yourself into oblivion won't bring Julien back. Would he have wanted this for you? Self-medicating?"

Under other circumstances, I'd have said no, but the fact he'd kicked me out of his life without more than three words had me assuming he didn't give a shit before he'd died. Reed had a point, however. Julie Renfro had been done with me, so my destructive behavior wouldn't have impressed or upset him. I needed to get my shit together and fast. My family pitied me, and I hated it. I owed more to them than to become a total, fucking waste of air. They expected more from me, and I'd been taught to expect more from myself. It was time to prove it.

I stood and went to the paper bag I was using as a suitcase. I'd left almost all of my shit in the townhouse I had shared with Julie just to be a pain in the asses of his parents when they'd evicted me. I'd tossed some jeans, t-shirts, sweatshirts, and tennis shoes into a handled grocery sack with a barbeque joint's name printed across the front of it from where I'd ordered food the night before I learned Julie was dead.

"Tell Gabby I'll be down in a few minutes, will you? I definitely need to shower and shave. I'm going to leave my SUV here with Mom and Pop, but if you guys need it when that ancient fucking Jeep finally dies, it's all yours. Thank you, little brother," I teased as I stood, pulling up the shorter man and hugging him.

I was pretty sure I smelled rank as hogshit, but Reed was too kind to mention it. I honestly loved the man like a brother because he loved the man I looked up to nearly as much as our father, and he kept Hank sane. With young Brock in their lives, I was sure my older brother was going to be just fine. I had Reed to thank for that.

Reed laughed and pulled away, wiping his eyes. "Hey, I'm older than you," he joked as he poked me in the ribs, making me laugh.

"I called you *little* brother, not *younger* brother. I know you're about ready to ride off into the sunset of your thirties. Have you picked your nursing home?" I asked as I gathered my clothes, seeing a lot of them were missing. I didn't have much, but more than half were gone, and I couldn't remember where they were. That was a problem.

Reed laughed, likely at the puzzled look on my face. "Your *mommy* did your laundry. It's downstairs in a basket." He popped me upside the back of the head like Hank always did. Reed left the room to give me space so I could get ready to leave. I had decisions to make, and I owed my parents more respect than what I'd given them since my arrival. I had to straighten up my shit before I was too far down the fucking drain and lying in the gutter where I belonged.

"He's been drinking a lot, Gabby, and that's not like Lawry." It was Hank telling his buddy about his degenerate young brother.

The deep laugh that big fucker had down to a science echoed throughout the house. "Bull, men will drink for a variety of reasons, but that doesn't make them alcoholics. He's in love with Julien, and Julien is missing. I'd probably drink a lot myself if I couldn't find Dexter."

I stepped into the kitchen with my paper sack in hand and cleared my throat seeing both of them jump. "Julien is dead. He committed suicide while he was on the job, or so I was told. His parents buried him somewhere, and I can find no record of it anywhere. Don't fucking pretend like I'm the same person I was before he died, Henry. You don't know how it feels—," I began to rant before Maureen stepped into the dining room with a tray of coffees.

"Lawrence Eugene, I don't like that language. You don't know for certain he's dead." Mom, always the bearer of a silver lining, served Gabby and Hank drinks, placing a cup of coffee on the table in front of me.

"Mom, he took his own life, likely to get away from me. His parents refused to tell me where they buried him, and there's no marble headstone on a grave anywhere in Massachusetts because his parents don't want me to know where he's laid to rest. It's the ultimate *fuck you*. Anyway, I'm sorry for the trouble I've caused. I'll call you." I loaded my bag with the clothes in the basket by the doorway to the living room before I took my shit outside and sat down on the front steps to wait for Gabby.

Fifteen minutes later, the lights flashed, and the horn sounded on a rental SUV, so I hurried to get inside, actually relieved not to see my sister around. I didn't like goodbyes. I just wanted to be somewhere else without her seeing me cry like a fucking baby.

Gabby climbed in and started the vehicle without looking at me. He drove around the circle drive my father had put in because Jewel wanted to learn to drive and backing up wasn't her thing, or so I'd been told. I didn't know if she could even get a driver's license, but my parents were set to let her try, god love them. I hoped she was successful, but I still worried.

We headed toward the highway in silence to get back to St. Louis Lambert International Airport. There was no music playing in the vehicle, so I reached toward the radio, surprised when Gabe Torrente had the balls to slap my hand away.

"Nope. You don't get out of the discussion, Casper. Are you a drunk? I won't have you on my staff if you're a drunk, because we owe it to our clients and to the men and women who work with us to keep them safe and healthy. If you're a drunk, I can't use you. I *won't* use you.

"I came to pick you up because Bull and Reed were there for me when I desperately needed them to care for my family, and I owe them a lot in return, especially when Brock came into my life and they came to New York to meet him. That little boy was brutally assaulted in his foster home, and he needed a family. His new dads need their focus to be on him because Brock deserves all the love they have to give, and Dex and I couldn't think of two better people to offer him the life he doesn't know he should expect.

"You should have a great life, as well, but you got screwed over by fate, and you're in a bad place right now. I get it. Been there myself a time or two, but I won't allow you to drink around my son and daughter. You're staying with us, but if you get fucked up? I'll put you out on the fucking street in a body bag." His threat wasn't idle.

I turned to look at him, not really surprised at his tough-love approach. "There's a White Castle burger place in Fenton. Let me out and go home. You owe *me* nothing, and I damn well don't want to be your millstone. I'll be fine."

Gabby drove for a minute without speaking, and then... He did. "I'm sure you've heard about Zeus and Scout, our former unit members who are both dead now. Zeus was K-I-A, and we were with him when it had happened. There'd been a kid in a village who had a gun almost as big as him. Your brother had seen him before the rest of us. Bull had busted ass to get to the kid before he'd pulled the trigger, but he hadn't made it in time. Zeus hadn't known what hit him.

"Scout had seen the whole thing and had decided he couldn't live without Zeus. It was a fucking waste of two good men.

"That look is in your eyes, Casper. I fucking know you tried the same goddamn trick when you found out Julien was dead. You've got it written all over you. What would that have accomplished?" He shifted into the left lane and passed a tractor-trailer.

Hell, I should have taken up driving a truck. It was solitary work, and I could have probably been good at it. For a minute, I thought about diving out of the SUV and under the truck. Would have solved a lot of problems for me and everyone I knew.

I exhaled, releasing the urge to jump, more for Gabby than me because I was sure he'd wreck the fucking vehicle to save me and end up dead himself. I'd then be beholden to his husband and kids because it was the Ranger way, as I'd learned from Hank.

"Julie sent me a text after he left our goddamn home in the middle of the night to go on an assignment without a goodbye. He told me to get out because he was fucking done with me, and I don't know why. I don't know what the fuck happened to make him want to be away from me, and the only reason I can come up with is that he didn't love me in the first place. He took the ultimate step to be rid of me forever.

"I was a convenient person for Julie to fuck around with, I guess. I fell head-over-heels for him without Julie having to do very much to encourage me. At the end of the day, I think he didn't feel lovable because he was an angry gay man, which was something I guess had been ingrained in him as wrong by his parents, those assholes.

"I did my best to try to convince him that he was extremely lovable, and I loved him, but he couldn't believe me because of the way he was brainwashed into thinking gay was wrong. Fuck, I suppose he hated both of us, and without me around as a constant reminder he was honestly loved and deserved to be in a relationship with a man, he felt it more necessary to tell me to get out—of our home, his life, I guess. I just don't know what changed.

"I mean, was he so fucking desperate to be away from me and put our life together out of his mind that he took the irreversable *out?* How am I supposed to feel about that shit? I feel like a piece of my soul got sliced away. He's gone, and I have no answers to any of the questions, which will probably haunt me for the rest of my fucking life, so I'd rather it be short. Just let me out in Fenton," I demanded, feeling I'd given him enough of an explanation for my behavior.

I didn't know shit about Gabe Torrente, only the persona my brother believed to be godlike. I was yet to be convinced.

Gabby laughed a bit. "I wish it were that fucking easy, but you met my husband at the wedding. Dexter thinks you're a great guy and has determined you need support right now, and he's not one to give up on anyone, so you're totally fucked. He's fixed up a room for you at our home where we live with our *children*. If you have an ounce of respect for me, or yourself, you won't upset my kids, because I *will* end you. I love Bull, but I'll tell him you just took off as I bury your corpse in the flowerbed in our backyard where Magic will likely piss and shit on your grave. You got it?"

I looked at the man, not surprised to see he was totally serious, and the fact he'd come to Missouri to get me touched something inside me. I'd been a total dick to my family, even though they'd only tried to offer me love and kindness. Hank had taken a step I was sure had killed him because he wanted to save all of us, but with the hell he'd lived through in the Army, he had to admit to himself I was too much to take on. He gave in and called one of his best friends to ask for help.

Determining he couldn't help me must have been a hard pill for Hank to swallow, but he still did it. My brother called someone who had trusted him with his family when Dexter and the kids stayed with Reed and him for a few weeks a couple of years ago because they were hiding from some bad people. My brother and the big fucker were *family*, and Gabby was reaching out to me, offering me a place in that family. I had to start over somewhere. Why not with the Torrentes?

⁂

"I think we need to make it a dry party," Dexter whispered as I came back from a run and slipped into their mudroom to take off my soggy shoes. It had rained hard that morning, but I loved to run in the rain, so I went, anyway.

I'd been in Brooklyn for a month, staying with the Torrente family and actually enjoying their company. I'd heard Dexter on the phone making plans for a surprise party for Gabby's fortieth birthday, and I had a feeling he was allowing my situation to influence his decisions.

He and Gabe had done enough for me since I'd shown up at their place. I wasn't about to allow him to get away with changing their plans to accommodate my bullshit.

The laugh that followed was unexpected. "You're going to punish a hundred people because you have one friend staying with you who is in recovery? I bet if you told him that plan, he'd be pissed. If he's trying to stay sober, then he's realized he has a problem and has probably called attention to himself in the past. He probably won't want to do it again, especially in a situation like this. Where is the man, anyway?"

I stepped into the kitchen, dripping on the floor, and cleared my throat. I saw a damn sexy guy sitting at the table with what appeared to be books and drawings scattered in front of the two of them. From what I could see, it looked like it would be a fun party and a lot of work was going into it. "*I'm* the drunk, and you're right. I'll be pissed if you change the plans for Gabe's birthday because of me. I'm ashamed that you'd even consider it because I'm staying with you.

"I'm twenty-eight days sober, and I go to a meeting almost every evening. I can control myself, Dexter. I'm not a fucking animal." I was trying not to chew the man up and spit him out, not being used to tempering my emotions because I hadn't given a shit about anything for two years. Dexter had been so damn kind to me that I simply couldn't be mad at him. The fact he was going to make Gabby's party a dry affair because of me—I didn't like it. I wasn't the center of the fucking universe.

Dexter shot me a look that should have left me dead in the floor. "Oh, I'm sorry, Lawry. Was all that shit I heard Gabe talking about just a fairytale?" I stifled the smile. He was prepared to take me on, and I appreciated it. My family let me get away with too fucking much! Dexter Torrente was made of much stronger stuff, and I appreciated it.

The guest in his home stood and offered his hand. "I remember you from the wedding. I'm Maxi Partee. You're Lawry Schatz?"

The guy had me a bit speechless as I took in the sight of him. His hair was a dark blonde with flecks of gold woven through it, which set off his gorgeous features. He was wearing a white button-down shirt, jeans, and had a blue and white scarf draped loosely around his slender neck. The blue eyeliner rimmed around his eyes picked up the blue in the scarf and made his eyes pop even more. The guy looked like a rock star, although a petite one as I towered over him. I didn't like the things happening in my mind—and body for that matter—as I took in his appearance.

"Resident alcoholic, according to everyone I know. I'm having a hard time accepting it, but I've yet to walk the twelve steps. I'm pretty sure *denial* is the starting point for this type of situation. Anyway, I'm not exactly certain how I wronged anyone when I went on my binge, so it's taking a while to come up with my amends, but they say I have to do it." I extended my hand to shake his, as was polite.

Maxim looked me square in the eyes without one ounce of hesitation. "Why'd you go off on a bender?"

I didn't hesitate to respond, even though Dexter began protesting. I held up my hand and smiled at Dex before I turned to Maxi Partee. "I was in love with a man who took his own life rather than make a new one with me. I decided to undertake a mission of introspection to try to figure out why. It involved alcohol, marijuana, and a little peyote at a sweat lodge in Taos, New Mexico. I never came up with any answers, sadly." I had resolved to be honest with people going forward.

The smaller man laughed. "Do you miss the alcohol?"

I chuckled in return. "I don't miss the headaches, but I honestly never cared much for the taste of alcohol in the first place. At the time, it was a means to an end—numbing me from thinking about shit I didn't want to remember. Now, I'm trying to adjust to a loss, and I need to be sober for it. What's your deal?" I grabbed a bottle of water from the fridge.

The guy giggled. "I'm an event planner, and since you've been to an event planned by me, you know I'm superb at my job. If we have liquor at Gabe's party, do we have to worry that you'll start stalking the waiters who are passing champagne and end up on the tables doing a striptease? Though, on second thought, I sure wouldn't mind seeing that."

I chuckled. "Champagne isn't exactly my drink of choice. Hell, I miss the peyote more than the liquor." It was a joke, but it wasn't far from the truth. I held up three fingers and stood to my full height in a Boy Scout pose. "I promise on my brother's life that I won't drink at

Gabe's party so you can have as much alcohol as you'd like. I'll be a good boy," I vowed, giving the party planner a wink.

The gorgeous man laughed again. "You're hardly a boy, trust me." Maxi turned to Dexter and smiled. "Good enough? The man seems to have his shit together. I've got the same servers lined up for your party as we had at the reception. It'll be fine, Dex," he stated.

I laughed. "Give the bartenders and waiters my picture and tell them not to serve me if it'll make you feel better, Dexter. Anyway, nice to see you again, Maxi. I've got to shower and get to the office," I stated as I hurried upstairs to the room I occupied, grateful to have been welcomed into the Torrente home in the first place.

The two men had been very kind to offer me a place to live while I tried to acclimate to my new circumstances: single, sober, and no longer working for the Company. I knew I needed to stand on my own two feet and relearn how to play nice with others since I'd basically secluded myself for a significant amount of time except for the company of strangers about whom I cared nothing. I didn't believe myself to be an alcoholic, but I had depended on many different substances to get me through a painful time in my life, so I guess people had a basis to make the judgment.

If I had to give up liquor, I concluded I'd be fine. It wasn't really a vice for me, but the one meeting I had attended was helpful in a way I hadn't anticipated. Hearing people tell their stories about what caused them to turn to the bottle in the first place made me feel like I wasn't the only person on the planet who had a broken heart. I needed to get into my head to work through the pain so it didn't fester and infect my life for the rest of my days. I wanted to be better than that, honestly.

I liked my new job at GEA-A. I liked the guys with whom I worked, now that I had faces to put to names because I'd spoken to most of them over the phone more than once. Abra Prinz and my predecessor, Jian Chang, had left the job because of their little girl, Vivien. I'd seen pictures of her, and the child was beautiful, just like her mother.

Abra and Johnny had started a tech-security consulting business in California, and they were doing well from what I'd heard around the office. I'd spoken with the two of them regarding the intelligence they'd cultivated over the last few years regarding Frankie "Man" Mangello for an ongoing dossier we kept on his comings and goings between the U.S. and Italy. I was yet to get briefed regarding why we kept an eye on him, but that wasn't anything to which I wasn't accustomed. I had worked for the biggest secret keeping organization in the world. If Mangello ever did anything that concerned us, I was sure I'd be told why at the time. For the time being, I had enough on my plate, which was exactly the distraction I needed.

I did my best to stay busy and in positive spirits so I could live up to the expectations of the people who hadn't done a damn thing to hurt me, namely Gabe, Dex, Dylan, and little Searcy. That was a change of pace as I thought about Julien and how his actions had devastated me. I could push the pain down for a while and look out for all of the people in my new orbit. It would be a welcome respite from the two-plus year status quo in the third circle of hell.

MAXI

I tied my black tie into a Pratt, pushing up the knot only to pull it a little looser again so as not to choke myself before I slid on the new sports jacket I'd bought for the occasion. It was a brocade, red and silver with a black velvet collar. I was wearing a black dress shirt and black jeans, so the pop of color was the jacket, which I'd paid a pretty penny to have handmade. I loved it and saw it as an investment, and that's what kept me from eating ketchup sandwiches to recoup some of the money I'd spent on it since I could write it off as a business expense.

The doorbell rang as I fastened my watch onto my wrist as if preparing for battle. I grabbed my loafers and made my way to the front hallway of my brownstone, opening the door to see Shay standing in front of me, looking quite sexy.

He'd cut his hair, which surprised me. The sides and back were very short, and the top was long, sculpted into a dramatic swoop. He was wearing brown eyeliner to emphasize his gorgeous amber eyes, and the champagne-colored silk shirt with the saddle-tan leather jacket made his eyes pop even more.

"Well, well, look who got a makeover," I teased as I stepped back and invited him inside.

He laughed. "The bun thing was so 2017, and really, I wore it because I was too damn lazy to do anything with my hair. I was also afraid to try a new look, but I finally got tired of the same reflection in the mirror. I had Ari, the new guy, chop it off this morning. He did a good job, don'tcha think? He even gave me a straight-razor shave, which you should experience, my friend.

"Anyway, I took more time with it today, but on any given day, I can just slick it back out of my face. Far less troublesome," Shay stated as he walked inside and followed me down the short hallway to the living room. "You look quite elegant," he commented as he popped the shoulder seams on my jacket from behind as if straightening them.

I turned and smiled. "Not *too* much, right?" Why the hell was I nervous? No, I couldn't lie to myself. Lawry Schatz was going to be there, and I found the man to be incredibly gorgeous and a little bit of a bad boy. After listening to Dexter talk about the man's situation, I'd felt sorry for him, but when I looked into his beautiful, green eyes? *Bless Madonna!* That man was fine!

Shay leaned forward and sniffed me, which was a bit disturbing. "Ah, so you brought out the *Sauvage* for the occasion? It doesn't work for me, but it smells good on you. Anyone, in particular, you're trying to lure into your web, Black Widow?" he teased.

I laughed at him as I retrieved my keys and wallet from the coffee table where I'd left them when I returned from the party venue. Gabe's cousin, Rafael Bianco, was providing the catering for the event. The man had recently opened a restaurant, Blue Plate, in Bay Ridge, and it was quickly becoming popular and hard to get into, not surprising to anyone who'd ever tasted the man's food.

Luckily, I knew the new head chef at Blue Plate, Parker Howzer, because he was dating one of Dexter's friends, Shepard Colson. Colson was a fine specimen of a man, but he and Parker were so freaking cute together, I couldn't be jealous they were in love. They were both sweet, sweet men, and perfect for each other.

"Maybe? I'm still interviewing for the position—any position he might want to try. Anyway, what about that bartender at Cactus? You invite him to be your plus one?" I asked, remembering our brunch a week prior. The bartender had been very good looking, and the conversation among Shay, Dexter, and I had ceased when the gorgeous Teddy had approached our high top in the bar area to take our order. We'd settled in on the bar-side, because the place was crazy crowded that Sunday afternoon, and Dexter had to pick up Searcy from a birthday party for a schoolmate by three.

"Teddy? Mother issues. No fucking way," Shay informed as we went down the back stairs to my garage where my baby waited for me. I had recently purchased a used 2017 Nissan GT-R Nismo, and I was extremely proud of her. Less than fifteen-thousand miles, which I confirmed with a good mechanic before signing the check for the sleek automobile.

Even with it being a certified, pre-owned, two-year-old vehicle, the price of the car still choked me. Fortunately, I'd had a few successful years, and I'd always reinvested in the business. I was due one splurge, and it was that damn car. It was a sunburst color, a mix of gold and orange metallic, and it was stunning.

"This is something else. My poor Volt doesn't hold a candle to this," Shay complained as we climbed into the car while I pushed the button for the garage door.

"I've never had my own car. I remember being in Thibodaux and seeing people driving beautiful cars and cool pickup trucks around town, but I didn't dare imagine I'd ever be one of them. I have vans for the transport of supplies for parties, but I never bought myself a car. It seemed decadent while I was trying to build the business. I figure after I get this fancy girl out of my system, I'll settle into something more economical, but just once, I wanted to go a little crazy," I confessed as we both buckled into the supple, tan leather seats.

Shay chuckled and touched my hand on the gear shift. "You go for it, Sugar. You deserve to treat yourself." I nodded in agreement. We both did.

Fifteen minutes later, I pulled into the garage under the building where the party space for Gabe's fortieth birthday was situated. It was in DUMBO—Down Under the Manhattan Bridge Overpass—which worked for the friends of theirs coming from Manhattan since it was just over the river. I knew the party would be perfect. I just had to get everyone to embrace my vision.

It was a stark, white space that we'd transformed into a Tuscan vineyard. It would be a wine tasting party with heavy hors-d'oeuvres from the recipes of Bianco's Manhattan restaurant, Mangia Con Me. All of the wine was coming from Gabe's Uncle Luigi Torrente's vineyard in Siena, Italy, and I was certain the party would be incredible because Uncle Luigi had brought prosecco with him for the wedding, and it was sublime. I didn't hate the grappa, either.

There were flowers, grapevines woven into faux trellises, olive branches decorating rows of tables and other natural elements in the space, which made it look nearly as incredible as their reception had been on Long Island. That party had unquestionably been one of my masterpieces, and the birthday party was set to be another.

Shay and I rode the elevator to the second floor, and when we exited, I was happy to see my people were rushing around. I had an hour to get things in order, so I took off my jacket and handed it to Shay. "Hang onto that, will you? I'll be back, but you go to the back room and get yourself a drink if you'd like. Thanks for coming with me."

Shay laughed. "I'll find my way home, Sugar. Hopefully, you'll get lucky," he stated as he walked over to a table in the back and settled my new jacket on the back of a chair. I grabbed an apron from a table behind the green-curtained screen and got busy. I had a party to put on.

The event was in full swing when the man I was waiting for walked into the venue. He was with a guy I knew worked for Gabe, and I thought his name was Raleigh Wallis. He was a muscular guy with an easy smile, which was the exact opposite of what I saw on Lawry Schatz's face. He looked worried, and I knew he had the potential to wreck the party if he started drinking, so I decided to approach the man and check his temperature, more or less.

I walked over to the two men and smiled, offering my hand. "Mr. Wallis, I believe? I remember you from the wedding. Mr. Schatz, it's nice to see you again. Please, feel free to get yourselves a drink. I'm afraid you missed the wine tasting portion of the party, but there's plenty of food and drinks for you. Toward the back of the room, there's dancing and a few tables if you're not in the mood to mingle. Help yourselves to the bar," I suggested, holding my breath.

"I'm starving. Let's get some food and something to drink," Mr. Wallis stated as he headed toward the bar in the back of the space.

Mr. Schatz turned to me and smiled. "Don't worry, *Partee* Planner. I'm not going to fuck up the birthday masterpiece you've created here for Gabby. Hell, I'd rather fuck you," he stated as he walked away and took the path his friend had traversed without looking back.

I was stunned silent for a second because the man didn't strike me as the aggressive type, but he seemed tense. I saw the bartender fill two, pint glasses with ice and then fill them from a pitcher of iced tea, which allowed me to exhale. The men left a tip in the jar and walked toward the steam tables in the other room where I'd put the buffet.

Dexter had decided to forego passing waiters, much to my dislike, but he'd said he didn't want it to be too pretentious. After he explained the mix of guests, I concluded he had excellent judgment. Everyone, including Gabe's family, seemed to be having a good time, and I would chalk it up as yet another excellent party planned by Partee.

I made my way back to the kitchen where Parker Howzer was working his magic with the timing of the food. I walked over to him and smiled. "I'm impressed. When Dexter suggested the restaurant, I wasn't sure because I'd never worked with you, but I'll eat crow. Can I use you again?" I asked as he handed me a plate with two, small cannoli on a paper doily. I bit into the cylinder of deliciousness and couldn't hold the groan. It was too fucking amazing to deny.

"Mr. Bianco is very sorry he couldn't be here tonight, but he was called away at the last minute. I'm glad you like the food. I made it with my crew, but these cannoli are my *own* creation. I'm a pastry chef at heart, but I went to culinary school and can hold my own at a stove. I'm sure we'd be more than happy to work with you again, but it's really up to Mr. Bianco," the guy replied, his face turning a little pink as he spoke. He was cute, and I instantly liked him.

Just then, a well-built man slowly walked into the room. He was wearing a pair of snug-fitting jeans and cowboy boots, which surprised me. When he turned to look at me, I saw it was Shepard Colson. His hair was longer than the last time I'd seen him, so I didn't recognize him. "Hon, you about done? I'm ready to get you home," he asked Parker as he pulled him into a hug. I didn't miss the kiss he gave the man on his neck just above the chef's jacket.

"One more refill, and then I'm finished. The crew can clean up. Shep, you remember Maxim Partee from Dylan's birthday party?" Parker asked as he turned the man to look at me. I could see he only had eyes for Parker, and it made me smile.

"Great to see you again, Mr. Colson. I'll leave you two alone. Good job, Parker. Thank you and Mr. Bianco for doing such a fantastic job tonight. I get together with a few friends for coffee sometimes—Dex and Shay Barr. Maybe you'd like to join us if you have time? We go to a place in Bay Ridge not far from Dexter's studio," I told him as I shook both of their hands and left the room. I glanced back to see the larger man kissing the living shit out of Parker Howzer. They were both lucky, lucky men in my opinion.

I was headed to the restroom when I felt a large hand on my shoulder. I turned to see Lawry Schatz standing near the entrance with a sexy smirk on his face. "Do you get to have fun?" he asked.

I chuckled. "What makes you think I'm not?" I asked him, hoping I could hold my bladder and not make a fool of myself. I'd been drinking mineral water all night, and I absolutely needed to pee.

"You're too *all business*. Speaking of which, go ahead. I'll wait here. I wouldn't mind a dance," Lawry stated while gesturing toward the men's room.

I nodded and hurried inside, feeling my stomach flutter a little. The man was gorgeous, and he was exactly my type—alcohol issues aside, though he claimed it wasn't truly a problem. I did wonder about him, but I still had that twink inside me who loved a bad boy. I hadn't had sex in a few months, not counting the blowjob from Mr. Wrong I'd met through the dating app. If Lawry Schatz was down for a little dirty dancing, who was I to protest?

I hurriedly did my business, expecting him to follow me into the bathroom. When he didn't, I wondered if I'd misread his signals, but finding him leaning against the wall when I walked out assured me I hadn't. "You could have come inside. I'm not a virgin," I joked.

He looked into my eyes and placed a gentle hand on my neck. "You're better than that." He then proceeded to skim his lips over my neck without making a direct purchase, his warm, moist breath lighting sparks in its wake. It was heated, and it was... voluptuous. His lips were full and warm on my body, and his grip was all-encompassing. I was off guard for a moment, but then I tilted my head to grant him access to my throat. The guy was tall—well over six foot—and he had muscles. His frame was lean but solid. He was sexy as fuck, and hell if I wasn't down for a good time.

He nipped at my jaw before he kissed his way to my Adam's apple biting a little which lit my bones on fire, nose to toes. His hands found their way to my ass, and he squeezed, turning me into the wall so he was blocking me from the line of sight of the people in the room. *A gentleman?* That was surprising.

Lawry kissed his way across my cheek to my ear. "I, uh, I don't have my own place yet, as you well know, but I can get us a room at the hotel across the street. That is, if I can get away from my handlers. That appeal to you?" he whispered, his low-pitched voice vibrating in my ear and nearly causing me to hyperventilate.

I couldn't speak, so I nodded and handed him my phone. "Give me an hour and text me a room number. You got supplies?" I asked, not having come prepared myself because I never imagined I'd be getting laid that night. The walk of shame the next morning would be well worth it if everything came together.

Lawry punched in his number and took a selfie before he handed the phone back to me. "I'll see you in an hour," he told me as he kissed my neck again. He pulled back and winked, making my stomach sink to my feet. He was a sexy mother fucker; I'd give him that.

I returned to the party venue after Lawry headed to the men's room. I found Shay laughing with Gabe's mother, Grace. I kissed her cheeks and hugged her, remembering how lovely she'd been when we were planning the wedding and reception. She was definitely good people. "How've you been, Grace? I'm sorry I was busy and couldn't sit down to catch up with you. Anything new on the family front?" I asked her.

She chuckled. "Two divorces in the works, thank goodness. Gabriele has been talking like a Dutch uncle to Lucia about Gio for years because she refused to even consider...," Grace began explaining, but I tuned out as I watched Lawry approach Raleigh Wallis. The two men spoke briefly, shaking hands before Lawry left the room without looking back. Ten minutes later, I received a text as I hugged Grace and Tomas Torrente before walking away.

Room 326. Went to store. All set. Knock twice. Oh, bring more of those pastry things if you can. They were amazing. LS

I swallowed hard because I hadn't really expected him to follow through on our plan to fuck. I rushed around the space to see everyone was still enjoying themselves, seeking out Shay, who was talking to Dexter and Gabe's kids. "Can I interrupt you?"

Shay nodded, and we stepped to the side. "Would you take my car home? Feel free to spend the night if you don't feel like going home. I'll be there in the morning," I whispered in his ear as I slipped the key fob into his hand and rushed back to the kitchen to fill a box with the leftover cannoli I found on a silver tray. Things were undeniably looking up for me.

॰

I took the elevator up to the third floor of the hotel, pastry box in one hand with a large bottle of water in the other. Hydration was important for what I had in mind.

When the elevator opened, I rushed down to the end of the hall, finding the room across from the emergency stairwell. I knocked twice, cursing myself for my nerves and my easy virtue.

The door opened slowly, and I saw Lawry Schatz wearing only his jeans. His feet were bare, as was that sculpted chest, and I was immediately sprung. I shoved the pastry box toward him, offering my sultriest grin. "These are for *after*." He nodded and pulled me into the room, closing the door and locking the deadbolt.

He took the box and placed it on the credenza entertainment

center before he took my hands and pulled me away from the door. "You are hot as fuck. Anyone ever tell you that?" he asked as he gently removed my jacket and hung it over a desk chair.

The tall man returned to me and leaned forward, swiping his tongue over my lips, which sent my body spiraling into the abyss. I felt his long fingers reach up and loosen my tie, whipping it from around my neck and draping it over his own. I opened my eyes to see a seductive smile on his handsome face.

"Too many clothes," he stated as he began unbuttoning my shirt. When he had it off, he worked the button on my pants and shoved them and my briefs down my legs as I stepped out of my loafers. Before I could catch my breath, he had me naked and in his long, muscular arms.

He swept the bedspread onto the floor before he pushed me onto my back on the sheet-covered mattress and grasped both of my wrists into one large hand. He leveled his mouth over my sternum as he moved to my left nipple, gently lowering himself over my body while sucking and biting the hard peak, bringing a sharp pain I wasn't expecting to feel.

When I felt him wrap my tie around my wrists, I started to object, but he kissed his way down my body too fast and had my weeping cock into his mouth before I could say a word of protest. "Oh, fuck," I gasped as he bobbed up and down before I felt slick fingers at my entrance. I placed my feet on the mattress and let the man have his way with my ass.

He devoured me before he moved up my body, reaching to the nightstand to grab a condom from the strip he'd already pulled from the new box. He tore it open and glided it down his rod, applying lube as he swallowed, looking into my eyes. "I love you."

I had no idea what the fuck that meant before he pushed himself all the way inside me in one full thrust. I lost my breath, but then the magical burn filled my body full of sparks, and I was ready to go.

He was a man of action, not a talker. I wished he would tell me what he was thinking because I'd have loved to have known what kinds of things went through his mind when he fucked. Unfortunately, he closed his eyes and pounded me into the mattress before he pulled out and flipped me over to my stomach like a ragdoll. "You okay, Julie? You ready for me to go harder? I know what you want, baby."

I froze at his words, but before I could respond, he shoved his cock inside me without giving me a chance to catch my breath. I tried to work the tie off my wrists because the fucker must have been a goddamn scout when he was younger, and I couldn't get loose. He was going to town, but it wasn't *me* Lawry Schatz was fucking. It was someone else, and I didn't need that shit.

A few seconds later, he stilled his thrusting and kissed my neck before he pulled out, trying to roll me onto my back. "You okay, baby?"

"Untie my hands, right now," I demanded.

He hopped up from the bed, seeming to be stunned silent, so I turned over, taking my tie into my mouth and untying it with my teeth until I could free my hands. He went into the bathroom and closed the door, so I quickly dressed. I didn't know if the fucker was high or if he'd been drinking that night when I wasn't watching, but I wasn't anybody's surrogate fuck. Him pretending I was *Julie?* Fuck him.

I left the room before he came out of the bathroom, having tossed two twenties on the nightstand to reimburse him for the condoms. I also left the tie. I didn't have an issue with being tied up because I'd dated a guy who liked rope play. With Quinn, it was always fun, never dangerous. What I didn't like was that Lawry Schatz had sex with someone else and used my body to do it. That crossed a line I didn't even know I had. He could go fuck himself for all I cared.

LAWRY

I'd sat in that fucking bathroom, crying like a goddamn baby once my mind finally cleared and I'd realized what I'd done. I didn't even know what the fuck had happened in my head until Maxi snapped at me. Had I experienced a break from reality? I hadn't smoked anything nor drank a drop, so my behavior was inexcusable.

The sound of the bedroom door slamming closed was justified and appropriate in light of what the fuck had just happened. I couldn't blame the man for his anger. It was the first time I'd had sober sex in nearly two years, and I remembered why I'd started fucking under the influence of whatever the fuck I could get my hands on. My heart hurt too much during sex when I realized it wasn't the man I wanted to be with forever. I honestly didn't care who I fucked post the worst day of my life. The words had slipped so easily from my mouth, *"You okay, Julie? You ready?"*

Maxi Partee wasn't like Julien in looks nor demeanor, and I had no idea what the fuck had happened inside my brain. I'd just lost myself in the fantasy I was with Julien again, and I was pretty sure I'd even told Maxi I loved him. That was so fucking wrong, I couldn't even imagine how the man must have felt when he'd heard me. I owed him an enormous apology.

The party had been a very good time. I hung out with Nemo and Smokey, shooting the shit and gossiping about the people at the party. Smokey had a few beers as he continued to survey the room as if he was on duty, Nemo and me laughing at his smartass comments about some of the people in attendance who didn't work with us.

Nemo then turned his teasing to Smokey's boyfriend, Parker, the chef who had made the most incredible food I'd had in a long time. "You fucking wish you had a guy like Parker to go home to every night, Frogger," Smokey teased in return, which had Nemo nodding in agreement. They were great guys, and I counted myself lucky to have them as co-workers. Hopefully, someday, we could be friends.

When I'd seen Maxi Partee headed toward the bathroom at the banquet hall, I hadn't been able to help myself. He'd been so fucking sexy, and I'd wanted him. I had proceeded to follow him, propositioning him right there in the hallway. Surprisingly, he'd accepted.

I'd shot out of the banquet hall like a ballistic missile and had stopped at a drugstore to get supplies before I'd secured the room, showing up at the hotel like a dog in heat with only a paper bag for luggage. I'd then texted the man with the room number, pacing the floors until he'd knocked—and had brought along treats.

The last time I'd had sober sex had been with Julien, and for whatever reason, being inside Maxi's warm heat took me back to that night, which I hadn't thought about for a while. It hadn't ended great because Julie wanted me to hurt him—choke him—and I wasn't down for anything of the sort. I was stupid enough to think we could make love, because I loved him, but I'd finally concluded Julie had nothing but contempt for our relationship. It hurt worse than anything I'd ever felt in my life, and the realization of his feelings had shredded my heart.

I owed Maxi Partee more respect than to insult him by calling him someone else's name or saying things to him that didn't fit the encounter, but I had no idea how the fuck to redeem myself in the man's eyes. The hole in my chest at losing Julien had opened again, but I knew I didn't want to numb myself the same way I had in the past. I needed to do something else, and the only thing I could settle on was to find out everything I could about Julien's death—the assignment he was on, and who he was working with at the time—in an attempt to get myself some closure and put the whole thing behind me where it belonged.

Assistant Director Ian Mallory had told me Julien had been erased from the servers, as was protocol if one died during a mission, but I had to find out what the fuck he'd been doing that had convinced him suicide had been his only option. Julien had never struck me as the type of person who would decide he had no one to talk to about things that had troubled him, so why hadn't he talked to someone—or me? Sure, I'd have been heartbroken if he'd actually manned up and told me he was finished with me, but I'd liked to have thought I'd have gotten over it... eventually.

What had really disappointed me in myself was the idea I'd been selfish enough not to consider the damage I could have done to my family if I'd pulled the same thing. At least, after my two years of self-abuse while on the ultimate binge, I'd realized how destroyed my parents, my brother, and my sister would have felt had I succeeded. During those few moments of clarity that I had every few days, I had wondered if I'd intentionally not checked the revolver for bullets? Maybe my subconscious—or natural instinct to survive—had saved my life?

My former lover had checked out without offering any explanation to the people who had loved him, leaving the rest of us to suffer the never-ending guilt of not having done enough, not having seen how much pain he'd been in and stepping in to help him in his time of need. Forever I would be asking myself what I could have done differently, but there would be no answers. No closure. The only person who could have given them to me had been silenced forever.

All of my regrets aside, I owed Maxi Partee a huge apology for my behavior the previous night. I'd used him, and I was pretty sure I'd offended him. He didn't deserve the way I'd treated him, and I would do anything imaginable to express my remorse for my actions. I would have said, unequivocally, I wasn't the type of person who would easily bring pain to others to relieve myself of the paralyzing ache I felt inside, but I'd done just that the previous night, hadn't I? The bullshit had to stop, if not for me, then for the sake of those around me.

I showered and dressed, seeing the tie I'd used to bind Maxi's hands the night before. Julie had always wanted an element of kinky pain in our sexual encounters, and I shouldn't have assumed it was the same way for everyone. I'd only ever had Julien as a male lover, having been with a few women who weren't into the sorts of things Julie had wanted in bed. I could absolutely admit that having him as my sexual mentor in the queer world may have skewed the views I had regarding what other men believed to be stimulating and what lines shouldn't be crossed.

Julien wanted to be made to crawl, called a dirty whore, and spanked when we were fucking. He didn't want me to prepare him for sex, "*Just shove it in, hard and fast*," and sometimes, he asked me not to use lube—only saliva. Sex was fucking, not anything romantic, and while I loved him, he'd refused to say he loved me. I believed he did, but his behavior at the end of our relationship was leading me to accept I'd been a fool.

Julie had told me there had been a time when he'd been into hardcore BDSM with his last partner. I'd told him that just wasn't me, and we'd reached a compromise on how far I'd been willing to go with it because I couldn't get into the debasement he needed for reasons unknown to me. Julien had always said he let me off the hook because I had a big cock, his words, not mine.

I'd believed I had enough sense to know not everyone had the same sorts of proclivities as Julie, but my actions the previous night had proven me wrong. I had no fucking idea how I'd ever unlearn that shit and understand what a man might want from me as a partner. It honestly seemed like a lost cause, which was really sad.

I shoved the tie in my pocket and tossed the keycard on the dresser before I left the room, leaving the condoms and lube. Just as the door closed, I saw the white box of those delicious desserts, but I left them. I didn't deserve them. I owed Maxim Partee the begging for forgiveness I was girding myself to do; however, I had no idea how to deliver it because I was pretty sure he'd never want to see me again. Hell, I couldn't blame him. I was a piece of shit and not worth his time.

I decided to go to the office on Sunday, hoping to have some time to myself with access to the network I'd been rebuilding after Johnny and Abra left the organization. I needed the ability to hack servers anywhere on the globe without leaving a trace, even in government servers, foreign or domestic.

Safe, unfettered access to necessary information would grant me the capacity to help my colleagues protect those who sought our assistance, plus, it would also give me the ability to attempt to find my own answers. Information was the light on the pathway to recovery for me. Without it, I knew I'd continue to flounder in the dark.

Gabe and Dexter, along with Searcy and Dylan, were headed out to Long Island for the family celebration for Gabby's birthday. I'd avoided them at the official party, but I could see Dexter giving me the evil eye that night at having isolated myself again, just as I'd tried to do when I arrived in Brooklyn. I'd wanted to duck him at all costs until I could get my head out of my ass because I was sure he, much like my brother-in-law Reed, had an opinion regarding my behavior of late, and I didn't need any more scrutiny or advice.

I needed to figure shit out for myself, by myself. Sending Searcy to beg me to come along that morning had been a cheap shot, which was why I left while they were upstairs getting the kids dressed.

I went into the building through the back door using the new fingerprint scanner I'd installed, which recorded the comings and goings of all of the employees. It also controlled the lights in the building, turning them on when someone entered and off when they left. I hadn't had the opportunity to test it because the Victorian was generally occupied during business hours, but I was relieved to see the place was dark except for the emergency lighting. Dexter's yoga studio was dark, as well, because only his or Gabby's scans would turn on the lights in the space, so the system was working as I'd promised. It appeared I had the place to myself when the lights flickered on, which was great.

I rushed up the stairs and down the hall to my office which was next to the server room. At Johnny Chang's suggestion, Gabby had upgraded their computer system just before I came on board. Golden Elite Associates-America had acquired top-of-the-line servers and a

VPN to ensure secure connections for employees while outside the office. The entire system had been kitted out with next-gen security—some of which I'd designed when I came on board—to keep others out.

Fortunately, it wouldn't keep me from going around our firewall to hack into the NSA to search for anything they might have on Julien. They ran maintenance programs on the weekends, which was when they were the most vulnerable to infiltration, and I was going to take advantage of the time.

The country was still scared shitless after the Russian hacks during the 2016 election, so I used it to my advantage and tagged a server in Pushkin outside St. Petersburg during my dance around the globe to disguise my misdeeds.

Once I was inside the NSA's mainframe, I decided to take another route aside from strictly searching for traces of Julie, especially since their protocols were similar to the CIA in that agents who were KIA were expunged. Instead, I went looking for his handler, Walker Anderson.

Walker Anderson was the Senior Supervisory Agent in Charge of the Special Operative Group, or SOG as they were called, of whatever mission Julie had been on, and I knew Julien was required to check in with the man at least once a week.

What "check in" meant for them was anyone's guess, but it would have been necessary for Julien to give a sitrep—situation report—for the record. Anderson would need to file it with the Associate Assistant Director over the SOG. Those reports were forwarded to the Secretary of State and the Department of Defense as necessary for risk assessment going forward and to establish criteria for threat level determination. If anyone knew what was going on with Julie before he'd died, it would be SSAC Walker Anderson.

The lights in my office flashed, which a notification to the occupants that someone had scanned in for entrance through the back of the building. Before I started working for GEA-A, Johnny had mounted a keypad outside the backdoor for the employees to use for entrance instead of a regular key. The keypads were too easy to compromise with the tech advances that had been made since he'd installed them, so I'd replaced them, adding in additional alerts such as the flashing lights when someone entered through the back entrance instead of the front. Fingerprint scanners were the next generation, though who knew for how long because technology was a never-ending work-in-progress.

I was surprised someone was coming in that early in the morning, especially on a Sunday. I hadn't heard anyone talking at the party about working over the weekend, but then I heard two sets of footsteps ascending the stairs, confirming there were additional people inside the building. I quickly logged out of the network and turned off the desk light in my office, slipping to the floor where the lower wooden panel of the door would hide me. For whatever reason, the top panel of the door was frosted glass with my name painted on it in bold, black letters. I didn't hate it, but at that moment, it was a pain in the ass.

I heard footsteps moving around the hallway and then a laugh. "I told you it was empty, dumbass. The lights automatically come on when your finger is scanned for entrance. Don't you listen to anything I say, you idiot? I was right about Gabe and Dexter, so you owe me dinner when you get back."

I crawled under the couch to the left side of my desk and held my breath as the door opened. "Fine. I didn't think Gabriele would actually take the weekend off and stay in Long Island with Uncle Tomas and Aunt Grace. Work your magic and hurry the fuck up. I've got a plane to catch in a few hours," I heard from a voice I didn't recognize.

"The monitor is warm. We must have just missed someone," a man said, but I couldn't distinguish the other male voice from those I'd heard in the office previously. The sound of hands gliding over the keyboard gave me a chance to exhale without detection, but I wasn't about to show myself. Clearly, one of them was in our system because they got into the building, but I hadn't been the one to scan them when I'd gone around the office to add everyone to the system based on the fact I didn't know either voice. I wondered who the fuck they were and what they were doing, but I wanted to live to see the afternoon, so I stayed put.

"Okay, here it is. Giancarlo Mangello. He's confirmed to fly back to Venice tonight. Don't get killed, or I'll never hear the end of it. Call me when it's over. You owe Gabriele an apology for not coming to his party last night. It was a good time," a man stated with a smile in his voice. The printer churned and paper dropped into the print tray, and then they left, closing the door behind them. I had no fucking idea who they were or what they were after, but I didn't give a shit. I had my own agenda that made me nervous.

I did pull up the last thing accessed on my computer to see it was a flight itinerary for Giancarlo Mangello, and that the man was, indeed, flying to Venice. I didn't know who cared or why, but they got into the office without tripping any of the alarms, so they had to be operatives who worked for Gabe of which I was unaware.

I made a note to keep my ears open to determine if other people worked for GEA-A that I was yet to meet. I'd met Mathis Sinclair recently, and he seemed like a decent guy. London St. Michael was on assignment, but I'd briefly met him when he first came on board while I still worked for the Company. As far as I knew, I'd met everyone, but maybe Gabe had some aces up his sleeve? It wouldn't surprise me.

I got back into the NSA and pulled up the archived files, going back to 2010 when I started working for the Company as an analyst. I searched for my name, seeing my file was sealed when I officially left the organization in 2017, but with a few keystrokes, I was able to crack it and see the information regarding my career trajectory displayed for anyone to find with nominal skills. The organization needed a security overhaul to be sure.

I used my file to search the organizational structure, seeing the link to Julien Renfro which pulled up his file. It was supposed to have been eradicated from the servers, but someone fucked up. If I still worked for those assholes, I'd have brought it up with them. What they deemed to be expunged could still be found pretty easily.

Julien's linear timeline stopped when he allegedly committed suicide, but there was a footnote with the name "Delaney Cartwright." When I clicked on the link, it kicked me out of the system. It was probably for the best because I'd been in their VPN for two minutes. Three minutes was when the backup started recording keystrokes and searching for the location of the ISP of the invader. It also notified the tech analyst on duty, who would report it to security. I'd have to keep a closer eye on the clock going forward.

It had taken me ten minutes to get in through back channels. I was confident they couldn't trace it back to the office, but I wanted to take no chances. I didn't want that shit following me back to GEA-A because Gabe didn't deserve to have his business plundered by the Company due to my quest for knowledge. Besides, I needed to find Maxi Partee to try and explain myself. How? I had no idea, but it was necessary because he was a good friend of Dexter's, who I liked very much. I honestly didn't want to cause any trouble between the friends.

I looked up Maxi's information and found his home address, which wasn't far from the Victorian. I took an Uber, having the driver stop at a florist shop on the way to pick up a gardenia plant with several blooms. I was more of a flowering plant person because plants were more sustainable, while fresh bouquets died in a few days. Plus, gardenias smelled incredible. Mom had a few she babied in the house and loved the smell of them. I didn't mind them either.

Once I was out of the car, having tossed a ten over the seat to the driver for his patience while I was in the florist shop, and I walked up to the brownstone. I pushed the doorbell, seeing it was one of the popular ones that had a camera connected to one's cell phone. "Yeah?"

I turned to the small camera and smiled, swallowing down the nerves because I'd been a bastard to him and needed to apologize for damn sure. Unfortunately, this time I couldn't blame it on alcohol because I hadn't had a drop that night. It was just my stupidity at play. "It's me, Lawry Schatz. Seems I have some amends to make, Mr. Partee," I offered, hoping it came off as cute, not creepy.

The door opened a minute later, and I was happy to see Maxi standing there in a pair of loose shorts and a tank top. His hair was going in ten directions, but he still looked incredible. He opened the glass storm door, not smiling at all. "I haven't showered, and I'm pissed at you. Unless you have a good explanation as to why you called me by some chick's name and tied me up, you need to leave me the fuck alone," he snapped as he gave me a death glare.

"Peace offering," I told him as I handed over the gardenia, which I'd tied his tie around like a bow. He took a sniff and smiled, which I took as encouragement to continue, though he pulled off the tie and tossed it into a trash can by his front door.

"I'd like to come inside and explain my abhorrent behavior, if you'll allow. I have an explanation, though it's up to you if it's credible. I'm sorry I treated you badly," I offered as Maxi continued to stare at me, his expression blank.

The sexy guy glared at me for a minute before he stepped back and granted me entrance to his home. I was immediately impressed. It was shades of white, beige, and taupe, with little pops of Granny Smith green or poppy red here or there in vases, throw pillows, and a gorgeous rug under his glass coffee table. It was classy and relaxing, and I immediately admired his taste. The entry hall with its light gray hardwood floors and large, black lacquer table under a beautiful iron chandelier gave off a welcoming vibe to be sure, and the rest of the house didn't disappoint.

I followed him into his galley-style kitchen and leaned against the white, quartz counter as he put a pod into his single-cup coffee machine, yawning. He turned to me and raised an eyebrow, which alerted me it was my turn to speak. "I'm sorry. I, uh, I barely have an excuse for what happened last night, and it might not even be enough to garner your forgiveness, but here goes," I offered.

"Coffee?" he asked as he pointed to a caddy next to his coffee maker while his navy mug filled. I nodded and retrieved a coffee to my liking, sheepishly handing it to him. He picked up another navy mug and placed it under the stream as he replaced his spent pod with my selection.

"You want anything in it?" he asked as he opened the fridge and pulled out non-dairy creamer, soy milk, and a small carton of whole milk like I remembered drinking in grade school. He retrieved a container with white sugar packets along with raw sugar and sugar substitute, placing them on the counter. I'd never seen such an elaborate set up in my life, but he was damn sure prepared for any coffee emergencies.

"Black is fine," I explained as I removed my mug from under the spigot once it finished dispensing and followed Maxi into the dining room, taking a seat to his left at a beautiful antique quarter-sawn oak dining table.

He pushed his hair back before he emptied three large, raw-sugar packets into his cup. "I'm waiting," he stated as he closed his eyes and took a sip of the diabetic coma in a mug. I took a swig of my own, hoping I'd find the right words to repair the damage I'd done to the man. When he turned to me and gave me a wicked brow, it didn't look promising.

"I, uh, I lost a long-term partner recently, and I got caught up in the memory of my time with him, which I know makes me sound like a cruel bastard. Julie was my *boyfriend*. His name was Julien. We've been apart for almost two years, which isn't recent, but I guess I sorta had a flashback because I haven't completely dealt with our separation. See, I haven't been attracted to anyone like I was to you. I wasn't drunk or high last night, if that's what you thought. I was sober, and the last time I had sober sex, it was with Julie—Julien. I'm extremely embarrassed by my actions, but I'd like us to be friendly because you're a friend of Dexter's, and I believe we'll run into each other on occasion. I don't want it to be awkward," I offered.

Maxi rubbed his eyes and took another sip of his coffee before he looked at me again. "I'm sorry for your break-up, but I'm not giving you a pass on the way you treated me. I'm not into BDSM or whatever the fuck you and your ex-boyfriend did in bed. I enjoy sex a lot, but I don't like being tied up or hit or fucked hard unless I'm asking for it. I didn't ask you for any of it last night because we don't know each other enough for me to trust you with something like that," Maxi responded.

I nodded and stood from his table. "I apologize, Max. I'll get out of here so you can go back to bed. I won't bother you again," I offered.

He grabbed my wrist and stopped me as I started for his front door. "I think breakfast would go a long way to smoothing my ruffled feathers. Give me ten minutes and try to come up with a better explanation for being a dick last night. I understand that he committed suicide and it did a number on you, but that doesn't explain what you did last night. You seemed like a decent guy when we met at Dex's. What changed?"

"I'll try to put together an intelligent answer while you get ready," I promised. Maxi squeezed my wrist as he released me and walked up the stairs, disappearing from my sight.

I sure as fuck wasn't ready to give him the lowdown on my sexual relationship with Julien, but I wanted to provide some type of rational response, because I liked him. He was sexy, generally upbeat, and funny as hell. He deserved to be treated well, and I wasn't going to disrespect him. He was worth much more than any of that shit.

MAXI

I hopped into the shower and did a quick wash up. I'd climbed into bed earlier that morning after I left the hotel, humiliation coursing through my body at the encounter I'd shared with Lawry Schatz. It started out with a lot of promise before it went to hell when he called me "Julie," apparently his old boyfriend's name, as I had just learned.

I wasn't ready to let him off the hook about it, but him telling me that he hadn't had sober sex in a long-time kind of struck a chord of empathy in me. Lawry was hurting. I understood it completely. Two years was a long time to mourn the loss because maybe he loved the man with all his heart? It was something I aspired to have in my life someday, so I'd let him feed me a good breakfast, and I'd listen to whatever he wanted to tell me. He did seem like a decent guy (the previous night aside), and I knew Dexter thought a lot of him. Another chance for the man was a reasonable reaction.

I combed my hair back and secured it with an elastic headband before I pulled on a t-shirt and a pair of cargo shorts. I slipped my feet into my suede Birkenstocks, and I walked out of my bedroom to find Lawry Schatz in the kitchen, washing his mug and placing it in the dishrack on the left side of my sink. He'd put away the coffee accompaniments, and he was drying his hands, looking quite worried as he heard my footsteps enter the kitchen.

"I'm starved. Do you have a favorite spot for breakfast?" I asked.

Lawry glanced at the floor before he looked up and offered a small grin. "New kid in town. You name the place. It's on me," he stated.

I grabbed my keys off the hook and headed out through the laundry room and into the garage, seeing my baby was tucked in, bless Shay. I was surprised he hadn't spent the night at my place, but considering how the evening went to shit, I was relieved he'd gone home and not witnessed my walk of abject humiliation.

I hit the garage door opener and unlocked the car. "Get in," I instructed as I settled into my seat and started Mona, as I called her. She purred like a lioness, and I couldn't help my smile. I was grateful to have some of the good things I had in my life.

I drove us to Bud & Freda's Diner, which was closer to my place of business below Shay's salon than to my home. I parked in my parking lot and headed down the block, not checking to see if Lawry was following me. When I reached for the handle of the door, a large hand shot out and grabbed it, pulling it open as I felt the gentle touch of fingertips on the small of my back. It was a start.

We settled into a booth, and both perused the menus. "What's good here?" Lawry asked.

I closed mine and flipped over my coffee cup before I spoke. "Everything, really. Gerard is the cook, and breakfast is his specialty. He's no Parker Howzer, but he's great with the most important meal of the day. The French toast casserole is like your momma would make, as is the BLTC omelet. It's bacon, leeks, tomatoes, and cheese. The taste of the leeks in the thing is so subtle it's addicting. Pancakes are great, but they're huge," I offered, admiring his muscular form. Based on the previous night's activities, I knew there was a six-pack under that polo shirt, and at that moment, I wished to fuck he hadn't ruined things. There had been a lot of potential for us until he called me by his ex's name.

After our coffee was poured and the orders were placed, I turned to Lawry Schatz. "I'm waiting."

Sundays were the days I usually hid out from everyone. I slept in, turned off my cell phone, lingered in a bubble bath while reading a trashy novel, and gave myself a facial. It was my *me* day, and I'd broken my routine for Lawry Schatz, so the fucker was going to cough up an explanation.

"I used to work for a government agency," he began.

"CIA, yeah, I know. You don't keep many secrets with this group of queens around. Continue," I ordered, seeing a little smile on his face. It was actually kind of sweet.

"Okay, uh, I made the mistake of falling for my boss, which is cliché as hell. We were both in cybersecurity, but when we decided to start a relationship, Julien transferred to antiterrorism.

"Things were great for a while with us not working together. That was, until he was sent away on an assignment, and, of course, he couldn't share the details even though I worked for the same organization. I know he left the country, but I don't know why, and I still can't find out where he went. I shouldn't be telling you any of this, but my behavior last night mandates that you're owed an honest answer.

"We spoke once on the phone, and I received one text before he went dark. As he was preparing to leave, he became distant and seemed to be pissed off a lot of the time, but I chalked it up to pre-mission jitters, which is something most agents suffer before they go undercover. Anyway, the last I heard from him was the text when he told me to get out of the home we shared. No follow-up and no explanation.

"Long story short, I was notified he'd killed himself before I left the Company. His parents had me evicted from the home we'd shared in Dallas, challenging the legitimacy of the paperwork we had signed when Julie had refinanced the townhouse and had added my name to the deed and the mortgage. I didn't contest their suit because it was no longer a home for me without him. Oh, and I went crazy, traveling the country and living like a hobo—although I did my fair share of drinking and drugging to earn the rep as a drunk and a junkie.

"Finally, my family had enough of my vagrancy and insisted I get sober, as I told you previously, but I don't really crave alcohol or the drugs I gave up. I won't test the theory that I'm not an addict, but it's what I believe. I was more addicted to the detachment they provided, not the taste of liquor or the feeling of the high. I just wanted to be numb.

"Julie had sexual tastes that I wasn't exactly on board with all of the time, but I gave him what he wanted because I loved him. You had the misfortune of being the first time I had *sober* sex since I was last with Julie. I had a lot of drunken or high sex, but I was always safe about it, I promise you. Anyway, I fell into an old routine I'm not particularly proud of, and I suppose I had a flashback, which was why I called you *Julie*," he offered.

"And, the '*I love you*'? What was that?" I asked, not yet letting him off the hook.

He sighed. "Julien used to get lost in his head when we were having rough sex, and I used to whisper it to him, but not loud enough so he'd really hear it because he would get pissed when emotions came into our relationship. He didn't believe gay men were capable of falling in love, and I could never mention the possibility of marriage someday without him going intergalactic.

"What we had was as much as he would ever give me. I shouldn't have been surprised when he left me, but it bugs me that I don't know what happened or what caused him to become so cold. I'd have given him anything…" Lawry trailed off as our meals arrived at the table.

I had a lot to chew on, aside from the beautiful omelet in front of me. Part of me wanted to feel sorry for the man because he looked positively done in, and really? He didn't have to seek me out to apologize. I'd dealt with my fair share of fucking douchebags over the years, and I'd written Lawry off as one of those guys before he showed up at my brownstone with a goddamn gardenia that smelled amazing.

I wiped my napkin against my stubble, hoping I didn't have egg on my face as I watched him pick at his meal of eggs, bacon, and French toast casserole. "Eat the food. It's really good. I'll forgive you, okay? Nobody ever knows another person's story until they hear it from the source, and I appreciate the fact you felt bad and wanted to make amends. Consider yourself forgiven. Besides, I don't go back to the well—sexually. We can be friends, Lawry, because that seems to be what you need the most right now," I offered.

"Can I ask you something?" he stated quietly. I nodded as I took another bite of my omelet.

"Julie was the first male lover I ever had, and he had some, uh, kinks, I guess you could call them. A lot of his preferences weren't things I was comfortable doing, but I went along with him. Are all gay men into BDSM?" he asked, which nearly had me spewing coffee across the table all over his blue and white striped polo shirt.

I gulped the liquid down before I coughed a bit as the waitress refilled our cups. She smiled as she left the table, which made me wonder if she'd heard him or if she was just happy. Who knew? "Didn't he give you a handbook?" I joked. When he didn't laugh with me, I realized he really was worried about it.

"Uh, no. All gay men aren't into that shit. I've had partners who get off on tying people up just because they read it in a book or saw it in a movie and thought it was cool to have someone at their mercy. I'm not down with that shit with a casual encounter like we had last night. I wouldn't even consider it with someone I didn't know well. Things can easily go wrong unless you know your partner and have established trust, which I don't have with one-night stands. I'm not a man who will ever be submissive, which is a misnomer to a lot of guys because I'm a bottom. My preference to receive my sexual partner doesn't make me weak, okay? Men who believe that are fucking idiots.

"I'm a power bottom. I like a strong man who knows how to take instruction because I *will* please a partner, but they gotta give it back the way I want it," I explained to him, seeing him for the "toddler" gay man he appeared to be at that moment. It wasn't his fault, honestly. The guy he'd fallen in love with was fucked up, and Lawry didn't seem to have gay friends he could talk to about day-to-day issues in the queer world. The man needed a mentor, and I was one to give back to my community. I'd step up and offer some advice if he needed it.

"Okay, so how about this? If you don't have anyone else to talk to about this stuff, we could spend some time as friends. I can try to help you with questions you have about how gay relationships really work. I think with a little guidance, you'll be fine. If you need my help, consider me your fairy godmother?" I offered.

Lawry offered a deep, sexy laugh. "Why not? I've finally figured out

I like men more than women, so I might as well go to gay charm school. What's next?" he asked with a smile.

It was a smile that made my heart flutter, so I'd have to remind myself he wasn't for me. Lawry Schatz was destined to meet a lucky twink or five. He was sex on two very powerful legs, and he was tall, which always revved motors among the masses. *Hell, it might even be fun to get to know him better before I turn him loose on the world.*

∽

The next Tuesday found the girls and me gearing up for our usual hangout day. Every Tuesday, I took a yoga class at ten-thirty at Dexter's studio before we ventured to DyeV Barr for a mani/pedi or a haircut/color, after which Dexter, Shay, and I met for lunch at twelve-thirty. A new twist was that Parker Howzer, Shepard's boyfriend, had agreed to join us since we'd all gotten to know him better at the party he'd catered for Gabe's fortieth. Blue Plate, where he was the head chef, was closed on Mondays and Tuesdays, so he took those as his days off.

Parker had explained to us that Monday was chore day. He spent his time doing laundry, shopping, and house cleaning at the home he shared with Shepard Colson. Tuesday, however, was his day for fun. The four of us had begun planning activities for future adventures, all of which I was excited to experience with my friends.

I was sitting in the swivel chair while Shay was touching up my roots and applying the foils to my hair when I felt a hand on mine, turning to see Parker standing next to me. "How've you been, Maxi?" He'd missed the previous Tuesday because he had a prescheduled meeting with Rafael and some vendors to see about consolidating something or other. I didn't get involved in people's business, literally. I had enough troubles with Parties by Partee and Weddings by Maxim.

"I'm good, dear one. How've you been? Recuperating still?" I asked, referring to Gabe's party for which he'd worked like an indentured servant to ensure its success. Parker's food was delish.

Parker laughed as I handed Shay a foil. Dexter was sitting next to me getting a trim. "Hey, I don't think the crowd was that tough," Dex snapped at me, making Shay and I laugh.

"You have that cast of Neanderthals who work for Gabe. They eat like wolverines, darling. Back me up, Parker. Have you ever made so many canapés and hors-d'oeuvres for such a small group of people?" I teased.

I turned to see Parker blushing, which was adorable. "Well, they are all very athletic, and their jobs are taxing. They train together and work hard to protect the people they work for. Smokey comes home from work exhausted when he's not on a job because they work out for hours. It's no wonder I've never prepared so many salmon mousse toasts or bacon-wrapped bison bites. They're not small men," Parker offered with a soft giggle.

The rest of us laughed because when anything made of meat came out of the kitchen to refresh the buffet trays, it was like calling a pride of lions to a fresh wildebeest carcass. "I think Nemo ate his weight in those cucumber and curry shrimp things," Dexter stated as he adjusted himself in the seat where Aristotle Davis, Shay's newest barber, was conducting business.

"I wasn't invited, so I can't weigh in on the current topic," Aristotle snapped at us. We all laughed because he was just bitchy enough to fit into our little group.

"It's a shame you just started here, but it won't be the last party. Join us for lunch?" I suggested as I looked at the reed-thin man with a gorgeous head of golden curls and a full sleeve of colorful flowers tattooed down his left arm. He was good at his craft. I'd succumbed to a straight-razor shave by him when he'd first started at the salon, and my face felt as soft as a baby's bottom. He'd spoiled me for my safety razor, damn him.

"I'm on a restricted diet, but thank you for the invitation," Ari stated curtly. I had my theories about that one, but I kept them to myself. Thin was one thing. Blown away by a puff of wind from a hair dryer was completely different. The man was fighting time, I was sure. His twink days were nearly behind him, so he was trying to push back. It only made one look older to be so thin, but you couldn't tell that to those who didn't want to hear the truth.

An hour later, everyone had finished with their particular procedures, so we were ready to go. "Sonya, I'll be back in a while. Call me if anything comes up," Shay stated with that big grin as he walked toward the front door and past the reception desk where the woman, Sonya Torres, ruled the roost.

"Gotcha, *jefe*," the beautiful Latina responded with a wink. We went down the stairs, and I looked into the office, seeing Toni speaking with a stranger.

"Gimme a minute, dolls," I offered as I stepped into the shop.

"Toni, I'm going to lunch. Everything okay?" I asked. Toni knew the routine. My boys and I got together on Tuesdays at Watercress, a delightful little spot a block away from my showroom. The staff at the restaurant knew to expect us and reserved us a table. The food was incredible, and the service was divine. Toni knew I wouldn't be back until late afternoon, so she handled everything in my absence.

"Uh, Maxim, if you have a second, I think you might want to speak with this lady," Toni suggested.

I held up my finger and opened the door to speak with my friends. "Go ahead without me. Order me a green tea with mint and a cobb, green goddess dressing on the side, will you?" I asked. Shay nodded, and they walked out of the building, heading down the street.

I stepped into my office where Toni was sitting behind my desk and took a seat next to the mysterious redhead. "I'm Maxim Partee," I introduced as I offered my hand for her to shake. She didn't.

"I'm Celeste Myers-Norman. My divorce will be final at the end of the month, and I'd like to host a party in celebration. Is that something you *do?* I got a recommendation from Natalie Sommers. You helped her with Miles' birthday party in Southampton last summer," the woman offered.

I recognized her immediately, and I remembered that fucking party. Those party-planning queens in the Hamptons don't take kindly to a fabulous interloper from Brooklyn. I nearly got my ass handed to me by some of the local hospitality industry bitches when I went into the village to pick up some additional flowers for the centerpiece at the entrance of the grand home. The florists at two of the shops refused to sell me anything, saying all of their flowers (down to the fucking carnations) were already sold for other parties.

The third florist, a woman, sold me a dozen white hydrangea stems and told me next time I planned a party in The Hamptons I would do well to at least use local vendors, even if I was from outside their community. It was no wonder Natalie Sommers, the third wife of Miles Sommers, had refused to use any of those condescending old biddies in town for her party.

Of course, Natalie was twenty-seven to Miles' forty-seven, but she wanted the party to be young and fresh. She attended the fundraiser I'd put on at The Bone Yard a few years earlier and loved the vibe. She called to explain what she wanted, and I accepted the job in a heartbeat because she was willing to pay my quoted price without negotiation. Bless her heart, she was a naïve young thing, but I liked her and gave her what she wanted.

Celeste Myers-Norman was the first wife of Geoffrey Norman, a name partner at Caswell-Norman, which was a stuffy, old brokerage house on Wall Street. Geoff, the husband, was caught with his mistress in a compromising position in an alley outside Rafael Bianco's flagship, Mangia con Me. The couple was engaged in a fellatio session, as I'd read on the internet when I went in search of the actual picture as opposed to the one printed in the papers with the black bars across the young mistress' ta-tas and her mouth on Geoff's wee-nee.

The gossip said Celeste had a clause in the prenup stating that if he committed adultery and got caught, she got a fifty-million-dollar kicker on top of half of the money he wasn't hiding in the Caymans, along with their three-thousand-square-foot apartment at Spires Tower. Mr. Norman had a run of bad luck that night because a wannabe-socialite saw them come out of the restaurant and head to the alley.

The girl took a selfie with the couple in the background, Geoff's Armani trousers pooling around his Ferragamo loafers as the girlfriend's small, perky breasts were on display for the world to see. It went viral when the socialite posted it on Instagram with the tag of *"I'm hanging with the upper crust while they get down! #SuckHimDry #NotTheNextWife."*

Geoff had chosen that exact moment to turn to his left toward the flash, making him easily identifiable and not particularly impressive in the penile region from what I saw when I finally found the damn picture. It was also easy to tell by the perkiness of the breasts it wasn't his fifty-nine-year-old wife on her knees in front of him. In my opinion, Celeste should give the socialite a kicker of her own. The young lady made the case of infidelity in living color for Celeste, including a fireworks filter, and it went viral on social media. No muss, no fuss, nothing left to discuss.

I cleared my throat and smiled at the woman. "Ms. Myers, I'd be happy to sit down and discuss your party at a more opportune time. Please, give your information to Toni and set up an appointment. We'll happily come to you at your convenience," I told her as I took her hand and kissed it, seeing a salacious smile on her face.

I turned to Toni and offered a smirk. "Get some ideas from this lovely woman, and we'll brainstorm tomorrow. Also, if Lawry Schatz calls me here, send him to my cell, will you? We've been missing each other." Of course, Toni smiled and nodded.

"Ladies, I bid you *adieu*," I offered as I left the office. I understood completely why Toni wanted to make me aware of the woman's identity because that party would be high profile. It would likely take place in Manhattan, and it would put us on the map. The heads-up was definitely appreciated. I'd need to really think about a plan because the opportunity to throw such a party brought with it a lot of pressure, but then again, pressurized was the environment in which I thrived. Manhattan would become my playground with that party, and I was always down to play.

Our little rooster *tête-à-tête* was enjoying coffee after finishing our lunch. Parker had been talking about the frequent disappearances of Rafael Bianco and how much he appreciated the man had trusted him with his restaurant in Brooklyn during those absences. Rafael had, on a few occasions, sent him into Manhattan to cook at Mangia over the last few weeks, and one time, Parker had unknowingly cooked for a food critic, receiving a glowing review on the woman's much-followed food blog. It was clear Parker was on his way to greatness.

"How does Shep feel about that? I mean, during the time I've spent with him, which has been considerable over the last few years, he's pretty shy, right? What does he think about you coming into the spotlight as you are?" Dexter asked.

Parker's face turned a little red, but he smiled. "He's okay with it as long as he's not standing next to me when the cameras are flashing."

Shay cleared his throat, looking more than a little pissed, which was a surprise. I didn't think the guy ever got mad about anything. "*What*? Is he embarrassed he's your boyfriend? Is he fucking embarrassed you're a couple? He's former military, right? Aren't they all macho assholes who never want anyone to know they like to suck cock?"

I immediately saw Dexter and Parker sit up to address the accusation, so I laughed to break the tension. "They're *gay* in the military, Shay. It's a whole different animal, I'd imagine. Anyway, I'm going to be planning a divorce party for the ex-wife of a certain Wall Street tycoon who was recently caught with his pants down in an alley outside one of Bianco's establishments," I teased, hoping to change the subject.

I could spot military men from a mile away. It was the way in which they carried themselves, much like my uncle who was gay in the military and beaten to death because of it when I was eight. There was no need to tread those waters. Every man had his own experience, and I was sure those men wouldn't appreciate the turn in the conversation during our weekly chin-wagging session. They were owed more respect than to become fodder for four gossipy girls. Those men had fought for *our* freedoms, too.

A stockbroker getting a blow job from a slut was exactly the level of dignity appropriate for our luncheons. It was common knowledge, having been blasted all over the *New York Times'* Page Six and the internet, and I knew everyone at the table had secrets they wouldn't want to share with the group. It was better to analyze the lives of strangers than scrutinize your friends, lest they do the same to you.

LAWRY

There was a knock on my office door before it opened without my invitation. It was Gabby, and he had that shit-eating grin on his face, which I was sure I'd come to hate. "Hey, Casper. How was last Saturday night?" Based on the smirk, I knew he'd seen my early exit from his birthday party and was prepared to give me shit about it.

Gabby had taken off the week after his party, in addition to Monday. He explained it was one of the kids' last day of school, and there was a school field trip he wanted to attend. I knew the man was a devoted family man and attended every recital, concert, and recess monitoring duty without hesitation. I always laughed when I thought about the giant of a man standing by the slide to ensure none of the little kids fell off sideways.

Gabby Torrente reminded me of Gene Schatz, my dad, though Dad wasn't carrying a Sig Sauer under his shoulder when he accompanied my class to the Magic House in Kirkwood. Dad was always there when any of us had anything going on, so I could appreciate Gabby's devotion to his son and daughter.

"It was okay. Honestly, it was a bit of a disaster, but it ended up working out, I think," I offered in as vague an explanation as possible. I hadn't spoken to nor heard from Maxi Partee since our breakfast date the day after the terrible encounter we'd had at the hotel. I was a little afraid to contact him because I was certain he'd changed his mind about forgiving me. I wasn't willing to find out.

Gabby laughed. "Okay, uh, I'll take your word for it. Are you working on anything right now? I've got someone coming in at one, and I'd like you to sit in with me on the briefing," he requested.

"Sure. Background?" I asked as I grabbed a pad to take notes.

"It's a soldier I met during the Howzer case. His name is Sergeant Kelly Boone. He testified at the courts-martial of two Rangers who were running a mercenary ring. They're in Leavenworth for a damn long time, but Boone was instrumental in putting them there. I told him I owed him one, and he's ready to collect.

"Anyway, it seems his thirteen-year-old sister has disappeared. She's been missing for a few days, but Boone isn't sure if she ran away or could have been kidnapped because their mother just called to tell him she's missing. Seems the girl and her mother fight a lot, and apparently, they had a huge fight over an older boy she'd been sneaking out to see. Boone's contacted the friends his mother had information on, and none of them have seen her. He's on his way up from Fort Lee, Virginia, where he's been stationed since his return from deployment, and not surprisingly, he's freaking the fuck out about his sister," Gabby explained.

"Okay, uh, where was she last seen? Does she have a cell phone, ATM card, credit cards, automobile..." I began before Gabby held up his hand.

"She's *thirteen*, so I doubt she has a car, but we'll get the rest of the information from Kelly when he gets here. You talked to Bull lately?" Gabby asked.

I glanced up to see the concern on his face. "Look, *Uncle* Gabby, I'm still going to meetings just about every day, and I've been sober since I got here. I'll take piss tests if it makes you feel better, *Boss*," I offered, diffidently. I didn't like being checked on.

I wasn't exactly attending the kind of meetings the man assumed I was, but I didn't have addiction problems like my brother had convinced his friend. I'd gone to a couple of AA meetings, but it just wasn't for me, so I found an alternative, which I felt suited me much better. I was attending morning meditation classes at the end of my morning run before work.

One morning when I'd been returning to the Torrente home where I'd been staying, I had headed through Carty Park. I'd seen a group of people—men, women, older, younger—meditating together, so I stopped to observe. Dex and Gabby meditated together in the early mornings, which was why I went for a run. It seemed very intimate to see them side-by-side on the living room floor, holding hands as they breathed together. What I found in the park was far different than the Torrente's routine.

The woman who had led the hour-long session had a very soothing air about her, and after noticing me standing off to the side more than one morning, she'd invited me to join the group as often as I liked. Through meditation, I'd learned how to center myself in the mornings, which had helped with my productivity and mental alertness as I'd faced my workdays.

Having fallen into the routine of meditating in the mornings, I'd found I had been able to better focus on many other things, aside from why I'd been so fucked up at having lost Julien. I hadn't had to talk about his suicide with anyone, and through meditation and exercise, I'd been able to put it completely out of my mind and do my fucking job, which was better than any twelve-step program I could be attending, or so I'd believed.

Learning to meditate had taught me to block out the questions constantly circling my mind and the interminable grief I couldn't seem to shed, which was what I'd needed the most. Throwing myself into work had helped as well. The late nights alone when I hadn't been able to sleep were my downfall, but I'd been trying to cope without the aid of drugs or alcohol.

"I'm sorry, Casper, but I feel very protective of you, that's all. I can remember back to when I'd be on missions with Bull. Of course, he'd be on his belly somewhere up high to keep an eye on our sixes and maintain a lookout for our marks. We'd get to eat and sleep while we were waiting to engage, but Bull stayed awake for seventy-two hours at a time to make damn sure we were safe. He always provided us with enough forewarning when we needed to prepare to confront the enemy, and he'd give his life for any of us.

"When we were working, your brother isolated himself to maintain his focus, which was hard on the rest of the unit because when we weren't on assignment, we hung out together and got along great. Bull was a hell of a lot of fun, if you can believe it. He was truly a brother, and I could actually talk to him about anything back then. Hell, maybe part of his PTSD is because he internalized all of our stress and fear and gave us support and encouragement in return. All I know is, he asked me to be here for you because he can't be, what with the issues he and Reed face with Brock. He needs to devote all of his time and energy to his son, so I swore on my mama's life I'd give you everything he gave me when I needed him.

"I guess what I mean is, I want you to get through the bad times and come out a happier person on the other side, Lawry. I want you to thrive. You're a genius, or so I've learned in the times you've helped us out when Johnny Chang was out of commission. I know your previous work was top secret and you maintained your distance from your colleagues, but here, we're a family. We've all held off asking for your help unless absolutely necessary because we aren't sure if your head's in the game. We're not an alphabet agency, but our clients depend on us, just the same.

"I want you to start working out in the gym with Nemo and Smokey so you can refine your field skills. I know the Spooks trained you in tactical maneuvers, but you were mostly in the office. This job won't be like your old job. You will spend time in the field, and you might run into altercations I want you prepared to walk away from unharmed.

"You'll have the same responsibilities as the rest of us—keep the primary asset safe at all costs. I will expect you to have the same level of marksmanship, hand-to-hand combat, and observation skills as all of the operatives who work at GEA-A. You don't get off easy because you have an additional gift of superior reasoning and technological skills the rest of us don't possess. It just makes you more valuable to our cause, and I plan to use you to your fullest potential, but you have to be prepared to protect yourself. You can't help me if you're dead, so don't get killed," Gabby explained. I felt proud of his praise and a little bit intimidated at the same time.

He then continued, "I'm interviewing a guy later in the week who was a drill sergeant at LeJeune. His name's Duke Chambers, and he left the Marines a few years ago. He's been traveling since he got out, but he claims to have heard of us through back channels, or so he said when we spoke on the phone a few weeks ago.

"I had Uncle G's geek run background on him, and Lotta claims he's squeaky clean with an impeccable service record. I'd like you to confirm it. Here's his info," Gabby told me as he handed me a file folder. I was taken aback they'd been holding off on involving me in cases, but it was probably my fault because I didn't talk to any of them unless forced. I had to get over that shit and soon.

Gabby stepped back and motioned for me to follow him, so I did. We got into the hallway and headed for the conference room we used for clients. "If Duke takes the job, he'll be running drills with all of you when he's not on a case. I'm going to implement some new training requirements I'm sure you're all going to hate, but I want every one of you ready to go at a moment's notice, and I won't stand for any dead operatives on my watch.

"I'm going to need you to meet with Miller Downing regarding the restructuring of GEA-A. We're more legally vulnerable than I'd like, so we need to tighten up a few things—licensing and permit registrations, additional aliases, and documentation, to name a few. We need shell companies to offer cover for our weapons licenses and keep us free from government scrutiny, especially if we're peeking into their tech sources for a little help, which I want you to do as infrequently as possible. I'll spend what I have to so we have the best tech available. I sure as fuck don't need Homeland Security or your former Spook bosses shining a flashlight up my asshole.

"I also want to ensure there's no direct tie from us to some of the things I suspect Uncle G undertakes in Italy. I don't wanna know for sure, but I have a feeling it's not exactly anything we'd find kosher. Anyway, let's meet with Kelly Boone. He's a decent guy, and I think we can help him," Gabe told me. I hoped he was right.

Kelly Boone was a good-looking guy, maybe twenty-six or seven. He had sandy blonde hair and hazel eyes. He stood about five-ten—about six inches shorter than me—and it seemed as if he was nothing but a raw nerve. I was guessing it was because of the crisis in his family, but what did I know? I was new to interacting with the public. I wasn't exactly great at reading people, but as Gabby took in his body language, I could sense he was worried about the man.

"Sergeant Boone, it's good to see you again. I sincerely want to thank you for your testimony in the courts-martial of Specialist Lance and Lieutenant Coffey. I hope you haven't suffered any repercussions from your fellow soldiers due to your involvement," Gabby offered as he shook the man's hand.

Gabby took off his jacket and hung it on a hall tree in the corner of the conference room. He was wearing his shoulder holster, but I noticed he wasn't carrying his gun. I was surprised, but maybe he didn't want to freak out the client? The info Gabby gave me showed that the guy was a mechanic in the Army, so I was pretty sure he was as used to carrying a gun as me—not at all. Those Rangers knew their shit when it came to handling people and putting them at ease in order to conduct a productive interrogation. The possibility of getting shot by the large man would be intimidating, I'd imagine. Not bringing his weapon into the room was a good call—one I'd remember for sure.

Gabby turned to me and smiled, so I did as well. "This is Lawrence Schatz. He's our resident computer genius. Take a seat, won't you? Can I get you something to drink?" Gabby asked as he picked up the phone on the credenza behind the chair at the head of the conference table.

I chuckled because I'd met Sierra, the receptionist, and I was pretty sure she was going to be pissed. "I'll have a mocha latte," I stated, seeing Gabby glare at me.

"Oh, that sounds great. Make it two," the Sergeant responded.

Gabby chuckled. "Might as well make it three if we're going to do battle with the devil herself." He punched in a couple of numbers and stepped away from the table, so I took my shot at getting some information from the soldier.

"Sergeant Boone, does your sister have a cell phone she's in the habit of carrying? I might be able to trace her whereabouts through it if she has it on her person. Also, how about access to cash? ATM card or maybe an emergency credit card from your mother? Where's her school? Any information you could give me on her friends would be helpful.

"If you have the names of her friends, I can get phone numbers and addresses so we can interview them," I asked, trying to get the investigation started, but also trying to keep Boone from hearing the argument Gabe was having with Sierra. I could hear her shouting over the phone *and* up the stairwell about how she wasn't a barista *and* didn't work for Grub Hub. I wanted to laugh like hell at Gabby's hissed responses.

When Gabby finally hung up the phone, he turned to us and put on that million-dollar smile for which he was known. "It'll be a few minutes. Let's get started," Gabe suggested.

Fifteen minutes later, Dominic Torrente, Gabe's nephew, came into the room with a big grin. "I, uh, took the liberty of getting the drinks for you, Uncle Gabe. Sierra is in the midst of doing a mailing for Dexter. Is there anything more I can do to help?" Dom asked as he took three mocha lattes off a tray and placed them on the table.

The handsome young man had been working at the agency since the first of the year, mostly driving our leaders crazy. Raleigh Wallis had been running things for a while to offer Gabby time with his family and mostly work from home when necessary. Nemo, as the other operatives called him, had been notified of a family emergency and was off to North Carolina without much notice, so the skipper was steering the ship full time once again. Gabby didn't seem to mind coming back to give Nemo the time he needed, which was nice to see. They honestly did have each other's backs.

Gabe smiled. "Maybe help Sierra with that mailing so she's not so stressed?"

Dom chuckled. "Yeah, you owe me because she's in a bad mood," he stated before he closed the door. I knew Dom was going to hear an earful from our receptionist for the rest of the afternoon, but the kid was a team player. Gabe was loyal to Sierra, even when she was pissed off, because she'd been loyal to him when they had the issue with Dexter's sister and the Mangello family who had broken into the Victorian a few years before I was working with them. I did admire the man for his allegiance to his employees.

"Okay, so tell us what you know about the day she went missing," Gabe suggested to Boone as he passed out the drinks and turned to look at our new client.

The handsome guy took a sip of his drink and whistled. I was pretty sure the drinks were hot as acid. I wasn't about to be the first to test them out because I wasn't sure what Sierra might have put in them when she made them. Since Dom had been the one to deliver them, I glanced at Gabby to see him taste his drink before he nodded and took another sip.

"My baby sister, Mia, turned thirteen last month, and she and Mom had a big fight about a sixteen-year-old boy she's been talking to online. See, my mom's a teacher at Van Wyck Junior High, which is also where Mia goes. Last Friday, Mom had parent/teacher conferences with the parents of the kids who have to attend summer school.

"Mia got grounded for sneaking out of the house to meet this older boy, Robby, so she was told to walk with the regular group of kids who go to Our Shepherd's House for afterschool activities instead of going to the mall with one of her girlfriends. Reverend Nate is the pastor at Shepherd's House, and my mother attends the church and believes the man to be a saint. I don't know him well, but Mom speaks highly of him. Sister Florence, she's the director of the community center, she keeps an eye on the kids who come to the center for an afterschool program that keeps them off the streets because the neighborhood's not so great.

"Anyway, the kids showed up at the center, but Mia wasn't with them. Sister Florence called Mom to see if my sister wasn't coming that day, because if she wasn't going to show, the parents are supposed to call so the folks at the center don't worry, otherwise, they get upset.

"Mom canceled her appointments that day and went in search of my sister, but she wasn't able to find her anywhere. Mom went to the police to report her missing, but they said they're gonna wait to really look for my sister or file a missing person report on her because they believe she ran away with that boy and she'll come back on her own.

"Mom just called me yesterday to tell me what happened, so I drove up last night. I was out in the neighborhood all day today looking for her, but she's just vanished into thin air," the young man stated, worry clear on his handsome face.

He handed me a photograph. "This is Mia's school picture. I don't know if it helps, but it was just taken back in October," he stated with tears in his eyes and his hands balled into tense fists.

"I'll get right on it. I can use facial recognition software to go over security tapes from all the traffic cameras near the school and the center. I'll be back," I told them.

I rose from the table but stopped when I heard Gabby get up from his seat. "I'll be right back, Sergeant Boone." He quickly escorted me out of the room and around the corner toward my office.

"We don't have that kind of software, Casper," he stated.

I hated to do it, but it was time to lie. "Yeah, we do, Gabby. When I revamped the system, I included facial recognition software, and I amped it up a bit. It's easy to get into the traffic cams in the area, and if necessary, we can canvas the neighborhood businesses to let us check their footage. Time's a-wastin'," I reminded him as I went into my office and closed the door.

Of course, we didn't have that software because only the Feds had next-gen facial recognition capability, which was nearly one-hundred-percent accurate in identification. Anything we could buy wouldn't be nearly as effective if it were even offered to the general public, and since the clock was ticking, I chose to bend the law a little bit. I could get in without alarming anyone because some agencies weren't as secure as they believed themselves to be. It was an emergency, after all.

It would take a while for the software at ATF to map the photo, so I turned to the other desktop and input the child's DOB, height, weight, hair and eye color, last seen location, and approximate time of the last sighting. I pulled up the missing person's database at One Police Plaza in Manhattan, hoping I'd get a hit on a filed missing persons' report after Mrs. Boone reported the girl missing to the LEOs (law enforcement officers) in Queens.

My other desktop chimed, so I turned back to it and found a hit outside Van Wyck Junior High. It appeared to be Mia Boone, and she was talking to a boy who looked to be more than a little older than her and might be the boyfriend. I watched the footage as the two of them headed in the opposite direction of the community center where Mia was to wait for her mother to pick her up.

I captured the images and tried to clean them up to get a sharper picture of the two of them. I printed those before I input another search through the traffic cameras heading northeast on 144th Avenue. I grabbed my laptop and opened the file with the footage before I raced down the hallway to the conference room.

Gabby was still with Kelly Boone, and I saw that Mathis Sinclair had joined them. He was the driver for Dexter, Dylan, and Searcy, Gabe's husband and two kids, though he worked cases as well. I knocked on the door and went inside when Gabby motioned for me. "Sorry to interrupt, and hello, Mathis. I picked up some footage from the traffic camera at 144th, and then the one at 150th. I've cleaned it up as best I can for right now," I told them as I placed the laptop in the middle of the glass table and clicked on the footage before taking a seat at the table.

Mathis scrambled around and stood behind me, looking over my shoulder as Kelly and Gabe moved their seats closer to me. "Here she is meeting up with someone who appears to be an older boy. They talk, and then Mia follows him up the street in the opposite direction of the afterschool center," I narrated.

"I'm familiar with *Our Shepherd's House* Church and Community Center because Reverend Nate is my dad, Nathaniel Sinclair. He's the pastor at the church, and Sister Florence is one of the elders and the director of the community center. We also operate a soup kitchen for the homeless in the area. I've never seen that boy at the center, but I've seen Mia a few times when I've been there helping out. Let me in on this," Mathis demanded, more forcefully than I'd ever seen or heard from him in the short time I'd been working there.

Gabe nodded, looking very concerned. "Sure, Mathis. Sounds like you know the area better than any of us, so I'll get someone else to look out for Dexter and the kids while you go with Sergeant Boone and see what you can find out by talking to people in the neighborhood. Talk to Sister Florence at the center to see if she knows that boy.

"Meanwhile, Casper can follow up with identifying the guy in the footage, because it seems as if Mia knew him and wasn't afraid to go with him. Maybe the guy's known in the neighborhood? He looks too old to be attending Van Wyck, so we can canvas the high schools in the area to see if he's a student elsewhere. Let's all check in tomorrow, okay?" Gabe instructed.

Mathis nodded before he and Kelly Boone left the room with a picture of the boy on Mathis's cell phone that he'd taken from my laptop. Gabby looked at me and smirked. "How'd you get that footage?"

"You really wanna know, or can you live with my assurances I won't get caught?"

"Could we buy that type of surveillance software on the market?" Gabe asked.

I shook my head that we couldn't. Gabby sighed. "Please, don't get caught and put us on the radar. You did well, Casper. I knew you'd fit in," he offered before he walked out of the room and left me alone. I appreciated his comments.

I returned to my office to find that Mia Boone and her companion had proceeded up 150th until they were picked up at the corner of 144th and Parsons Blvd. I froze the frame to see it was a black Lincoln Navigator, but I couldn't get the last three numbers of the New York license plate because there was a smudge on the camera, probably bird shit. That sucked because the likelihood of a match and an address for the registration was exponentially lower, but I was going to try. How could I not try? I had a sister just a little older than Mia Boone. I could imagine the hell Kelly Boone was going through at the time as I thought about Jewel, and if I could help find the young girl, I could maybe close my eyes to sleep at night. That would be a blessing.

I was tempted to hit the nearest bar to get that numbness I craved, but that would give credence to my dependence on alcohol, just as my brother had speculated, and I couldn't let the bastard be right. As I was leaving the building that evening at seven, I walked out to the sidewalk to see Maxi Partee leaning against his Nissan while speaking into his phone. It was still light out, so I'd planned to walk home. I wondered what he was doing at the Victorian.

"I'll pick you up in the morning, and we'll go meet with her together. George Michael's *Freedom*? Who knew? Yeah, I guess she's in the right age group to appreciate it. Kisses, kitten. Eight, and bring coffee. You, too. Night," he said as he shoved his cell into the pocket of his shorts and smiled at me.

"Bad day?" he asked as he reached for my messenger bag—which I willingly gave once I figured out what he was doing. He took my messenger bag and opened the trunk, placing it in the back before he walked around to the passenger side and opened my door. At his bidding, I hopped into his car, not sure why he was there but not really caring.

After a week of radio silence, I'd been pretty sure he never wanted to see me again. Our breakfast the day after Gabe's party had seemed to mend fences, but when he didn't call me after that day, I was sure we'd settle into being friendly acquaintances who ran into each other and were civil at Torrente-centric events.

"It could have been better. You?" I asked after he settled into his seat.

"Mine was pretty good. I've booked a job in Manhattan, but it's a rush. This Saturday. I can't even begin to tell you all the shit I have to try to do in a week, but my fee will more than make up for the long hours I'll be putting in. That's why I came to take you to dinner. I won't be available to talk for the rest of the week, but I want us to be friends. Pizza or Chinese?" he asked.

I thought for a second and decided. "Mexican?" I missed Dallas, so I was anxious to find a place to get my fix of Mexican food. It was something I could eat every day without a problem.

"Ah, yeah. Will it bother you if I have a margarita? There's this great mom-and-pop place near my house. We'll walk there, and you can drop me at home and drive my car to Dexter's house when we're done. I'll get it tomorrow," he suggested.

I glanced at him, seeing he was a bit nervous. "This car? This GT-R? You're willing to let me drive this beautiful, expensive car to Dex and Gabe's house?" I asked him.

He turned to look at me and offered a hard smile. I knew what he was doing because I'd taken some psych and behavioral studies classes over the years. He was attempting to show me trust, which I really didn't deserve. He wanted me to know he trusted me to take care of his possession in hopes I'd trust him and spill my guts. It was sweet, but it wasn't going to happen.

"I'll be fine to get home later, Maxi. So, a party?" I redirected. I turned to see a big, excited grin on his face, obviously happy to discuss the party he was planning.

"If I do it right, it's going to be my big introduction into Manhattan society. I've done some spectacular parties since I landed here in New York, but I haven't been able to land a big gig in Manhattan. I'm finally set to get my *slice* of the *big apple* pie," he offered with a giggle as if he didn't believe it.

"Where are you from?" I asked, hearing the slight tinge of an accent when he said 'pie.' He drew it out a bit, which was a surprise.

Maxi parked in the parking lot of a large building, and we proceeded to walk down the block, coming to a stop outside a colorful building with a string of small Mexican flags attached to the red, green, and white awning. The name of the place, '*Fiesta en tu Boca*,' translated to *party in your mouth,* and it made me laugh. I hoped to hell the food lived up to the name. I'd had damn good Mexican food in Dallas. My expectations were high, and I wasn't complaining about my dinner companion. I wasn't sure what he wanted with me, but I was happy to see him. That was a plus, for sure.

MAXI

Earlier in the day...

After our lunch that Tuesday, I took Dexter to pick up his kids so I could give them a ride home. While we were at lunch, Gabe called him and told him the SUV was in the shop for an oil change, and Mathis was on a case. Gabe asked Dex to get one of us to give him a ride to get the kids, so I volunteered. Of course, I didn't mind helping out because it also afforded me the opportunity to pick Dexter's brain about his house guest, Lawry Schatz.

I parked in front of the large home they had in a lovely neighborhood not far from the yoga studio. Everyone bailed out of the car, and Searcy immediately took my hand to lead me to the house while Dylan told Dexter that the babysitter, Mrs. Henry, wanted to take them into the city the next day to go to a painting class at The Drawing Center in SoHo. It was a small museum on Wooster Street, and they were offering a special class for kids, ages five to ten. Searcy had turned six back in April, and they were both anxious for the chance to learn to paint.

"Okay, I'll talk to Papa Gabe, and then we'll call Nana Irene and make sure you guys have a ride. I talked to Papa earlier, and Mathis is going on assignment, so he's going to assign us a new driver, probably Sherlock, but we'll see. That's why Maxi picked us up. Let's go inside so you can let your dog and cat out. Search the house to be sure nobody did anything ugly because if I find it first, they go back to the shelter," Dexter threatened, which surprised me.

"Searcy, you look for poop and fur balls. I'll take Magic out and then help you clean up. We'll do the litter box last," Dylan instructed as any respectable big brother would do. The sweet little brunette saluted before they ran in different directions once Dex unlocked the front door and we walked inside.

I turned to Dexter after taking off my shoes as he'd done. "You are positively cold-hearted, threatening to take their pets back to the shelter. I'm surprised and a little bit in awe," I teased.

Dexter laughed. "It's all bluster. They both know Gabriele would overrule me, but I have the remote to the television on a high shelf even Gabe doesn't know about, so they won't cross me. Come into the kitchen. You want a drink or a coffee?" he asked as he dropped a bag in the hallway and led me to the amazing kitchen they had in their beautiful home. It was a chef's dream, I was sure.

We settled at the large island with wine, white for him and red for me. Dexter was opening the mail, and I watched him, seeing absolute happiness radiating from the man. Something so simple as opening the mail actually made him happy. *Incredible!* "Can I pick your brain?" I asked, not sure what he'd think of the topic.

He nodded as he folded a bill and placed it back on the island, turning to look at me. "Sure. Hit me," he offered, which was the perfect lead for the route I wanted to take the discussion.

"Lawry Schatz. I slept with him that Saturday night after the party, and I gotta tell you, the man's fucked up. Seriously. He tied my hands and went to town on my ass without any discussion at all. He told me about his deceased boyfriend. The guy was into kinky shit, and he was the first guy Lawry was ever with, so he has some really screwed up ideas regarding sex. You know anything about it?" I asked, seeing the smirk on Dex's face.

"Gabe said he thought you two left together. What else did he do?" Dex asked.

"Shit I wasn't prepared for, but he did apologize to me on Sunday. He needs someone like you or Gabe to talk to him about sex, Dexter. I offered to help him out, but I'm not exactly sure he's comfortable with that idea since we already had a less than amicable encounter.

That guy, Jules, or whatever? He was into some fucked up shit, and Lawry thinks every gay guy is into BDSM. Someone needs to set him straight on that before some twink slits his throat because he crossed a line. He's looking for *Mr. Goodbar*, ya know?" I enlightened, referring to the old movie I'd watched a few weeks prior when it came on the retro channel. It was fucked up.

Dexter appeared surprised, but he was taking me seriously, which was a good sign. "Like what?"

I sighed. "Lawry tied my hands, flipped me onto my stomach, told me he loved me while fucking me hard before calling me by his last lover's name. I was pissed off, so after I got myself untied while he went and locked himself in the bathroom I got dressed and left the hotel without speaking to him. He didn't seem to give a shit about what I did or didn't want that night, and that's not exactly gentlemanly behavior. I don't know what the fuck he did with that guy, Julie, but he needs a little guidance, and I'm not sure he wants it from me," I instructed.

Dexter was lost in thought for a minute until Magic the dog ran into the kitchen followed closely by Sparkles, the one-eyed cat that slinked in with Searcy hot on its trail. "It's gwoss, Daddy. I cleaned it with toilet papewr, but it left a spot on the cawrpet," she stated as she went to the cabinet and threw away a wad of Charmin.

"Where?" Dexter asked as he held her up to wash her hands. After she had sanitized her little fingers, Dex placed her on the counter and looked at her just as Dylan came running into the house with his glasses in his hand.

"It's in you and Papa's woom. You didn't close the doowr," Searcy told him as she held up her hands for Dex to put her on the floor before she ran into the mudroom and grabbed a bag to clean the litter box. Those two kids were so adorable I could just eat them up.

"What happened to your glasses?" Dex asked as he turned to Dylan and reached for the two pieces of brown frames which had snapped at the nose piece.

"They slipped off when I was chasing Magic, and I accidentally kneeled on 'em. There's a hole under the fence between us and the Flynn's. I was pulling Magic back through the hole because Midnight was in the yard," Dylan explained. Midnight was the neighbor's trained Rottweiler, and that dog could eat a small child.

Dexter walked to a drawer and retrieved a pair of glasses from a brown case, handing them to Dylan with a smile. "I'll call Amy. I'm sure Midnight dug the hole because Magic doesn't like to get his paws dirty, crazy dog. I'll get these fixed tomorrow. Go help Searcy with the litter box while I make you guys a snack. Thank you for keeping him out of their yard where he could have been an appetizer for Midnight. You're a good man," Dexter told him as he scuffed the kid's dark hair gently, bringing a small laugh from the boy.

"Thanks, Daddy," he stated before he hugged Dex and ran off to the mudroom to help Searcy with the mess. Ten minutes later, the kids settled in the media room with carrots and ranch dressing watching some cartoon thing. Dex came back into the kitchen and poured me another half a glass of wine as he sat down, looking at me seriously.

"So, would you rather clean up cat barf and dog shit or be tied up?" he teased as he sipped his glass.

I chuckled. "Nope. You have a perfect life. The perfect husband, the perfect kids, and nearly perfect pets. You're the fucking greeting card for a gay family in 2019. You don't get to bitch about shit the rest of us envy like size thirty jeans. *Help meeee,*" I whined a bit.

Dexter put down his glass and looked at me with surprise. "Wait. Are you saying you're interested in Lawry Schatz? Is this why you're asking for someone else to talk to him? I can get on board with cleaning the guy up for you, but you have that pesky rule," he reminded, referring to my '*once-and-bounce*' clause.

I downed my glass of wine and placed the stemmed crystal in the sink. "I'm not asking for help with him because of *me*, okay? The guy is gonna pull some shit with the wrong twink and find a knife in his ribs or worse. I offered to help him out, but he hasn't taken me up on it. If y'all are looking out for him, you need to take steps…" I started to argue.

Dex held up his hand. "You seem more than a little invested, Maxi. Don't deny it. Take the first step yourself and talk to the man. If anyone can explain the etiquette regarding gay relationships and get through to him, *Glinda the Good Witch*, it's you. Don't wait for him to ask. Just call him and talk to him about things, honey. Lawry might not be receptive to anyone at his workplace having that sort of discussion with him, but at the risk of someone slitting his throat, I'll mention something to Gabe," Dexter told me.

I nodded and hugged him goodbye, heading to the Victorian to wait for Lawry. Maybe a no-pressure dinner was the answer? We could talk—maybe I could get a drink—and I'd get an idea if he was *really* worth spending my time to become friends. What could go wrong?

I stewed on Dex's comments as I drove to the Victorian, and I decided Dex had a point. I had offered to be the man's fairy godmother, so I needed to follow up on my proposition. I stepped out of Mona and stood at the curb in front of the Victorian, waiting for Lawry Schatz to materialize. When he came out, I was amazed at how easily I was able to get the guy into the car without any explanation at all.

I offered to take him to dinner as more of an apology because I'd sort of ghosted him for a week, but then again, he hadn't called me either, and he had my number, too. Also, it would be easy to dig for more info about his situation. I was pretty sure when Dex talked to Gabe, the big guy would confront Lawry about what had gone down that night between the two of us. I didn't want Lawry blindsided by his boss over something that wasn't his business.

I saw potential in Lawry Schatz, and I knew he'd been hurt deeply by his former lover. There was no need to pile on more bullshit, and I was coming to realize I should have kept my mouth shut with Dex, so I was going to talk to Lawry first.

We took a seat at a small booth in the back of the Mexican restaurant and proceeded with small talk, "How was your day?" "Busy. I got a new case." "That's interesting. What kind?" Finally, a waitress came over with a friendly smile and two menus, ending the painful, *polite* babble.

I ordered a small margarita while Lawry ordered a cola. We sat across from each other, not speaking for a moment as we perused the menu. Finally, he closed his and placed it on the table with a smile. "Tell me more about your new party." I saw it as the opportunity for an icebreaker, so I returned his smile and began explaining it.

"The Normans own a classic six in The Spires Tower, which is where she'll want to have the party because she won it in the divorce. I'm intimidated by the idea of the party and those who will attend if I'm honest," I offered. He looked at me and shook his head with a sexy grin.

"Why in hell are *you* intimidated? You throw awesome fucking parties. I heard about the party you planned for Dylan, and I was at Gabe's birthday party. It was fucking amazing. You've got this, Maxi," he stated as he sipped his soda.

I sipped my margarita and placed it in front of him. "You can have some, you know? There's barely any tequila in it," I offered. I kept telling myself it wasn't a test, but maybe I was lying? Maybe I *was* testing him, and that wasn't fucking fair.

I genuinely wanted to know if the man had substance-abuse issues because the problems that accompanied that baggage were ones I wasn't sure if I wanted to tackle. It was best to know up front before my feelings got ahead of me, as I feared they were doing without my consent.

The handsome man laughed. "I appreciate the offer, but as I said, I'm not that much of a connoisseur of alcohol. Well, actually, bourbon was my drink of choice, but I burned myself out on it over the course of about two years. I'm fine with just the cola. You go ahead, though. If you like tequila, have at it." He had a gentle look of honesty on his face, and it set my heart to pounding. I didn't want to continue to be attracted to him. I was just trying to get to know the guy because he seemed to need a friend. Anything else would end in disaster, or so I kept reminding myself.

We ordered food. I got the chicken enchiladas in Chile Verde sauce, and Lawry ordered something that included pork and rice in a mole sauce. He seemed to be happy with his choice when the waitress finished writing down our orders, so I stopped her before she left to order another margarita because the first one went down like water.

The fortunate thing about imbibing in tequila was I spoke frankly with those in my presence. The unfortunate thing about imbibing in tequila was I spoke frankly with those in my presence. "So, we need to talk about your skewed views of sex between men. Have you ever researched gay sex at all? There's plenty of porn out there for you to get a sense for it, I'd think.

"Have you ever bottomed for anyone? You don't just ram a hard cock into that small, tender space without really preparing your partner. God, you could maim a guy if he's never had anal. I'd think a little forethought, and maybe some exploration of your own body, would make that self-evident," I chastised, looking into his gorgeous eyes. *It should be against the law to look that good and be that stupid.*

His eyes were as wide as silver dollars at my comment, but after he cleared his throat, he leaned forward and whispered to me, a look of absolute contrition on his handsome face. "I'm so sorry, Maxi," he offered, seeming consumed with guilt, which wasn't what I was trying to bring out of him at all.

I held up my hand. "I'm not looking for another apology, Lawry. I'm trying to give you advice before somebody hurts you in retaliation if you point that big thing at them without a little prep first. There are a lot of crazies out there who would have reacted violently to you if you did to them what you did to me, and I don't want to see you get hurt. When was the last time you were teshted?" I asked, hearing myself slurring a bit.

The two glasses of wine at Dex's place and now the two margaritas were doing a number on me. I reached for my water, knocking over the saltshaker, which was a sign I was fucked up. I chuckled. "Look at me, preaching to you, while I'm not setting a very good example, am I?"

Lawry moved the margarita glass away from me, scooting my plastic cup of water in front of me as our food arrived. "Eat, Maxi. I'll get ya home," he told me. He had that sexy smile I found very attractive, and everything inside me was saying crawl under the table and rock his world. As I started to slink to the floor, he stood and grabbed my hand, waving to our waitress.

"We'll take these to go. My friend seems to have loved your margaritas a little too much," he teased as he pulled me up onto the bench and wrapped his long arm around me to keep me seated.

I knew I'd feel humiliated when I sobered up but feeling his arm around my shoulders was lovely. I wasn't one to enjoy PDA much, but feeling Lawry Schatz sitting next to me was too tempting. I couldn't dislike the man, which was a pity because it went against every rule I had. I never went back for seconds, though... *technically*, I never had a first, did I?

"Talk to me about your kind of man. What's your vision of the perfect partner?" I asked, having consumed a bunch of water once we got to my place. Lawry had driven us home, and I'd sobered my stupid ass up a bit, so I reheated our food and served him the meal he should have had at the restaurant.

Lawry was kind of inhaling his pork dish, revealing a healthy appetite before he wiped his mouth and took a swig of his water. "That's a really good question because I've never thought of a type, ya know? I mean, I know I've come to prefer being with men more than women, but I just fell for Julie without a lot of thinking about it. I've never considered what I might or might not like in a man because Julien was the first man I'd ever dated or had sex with. He just seemed to be perfect for me," Lawry explained.

I could see in his eyes he still loved the man, and I immediately wanted to dig that fucker up wherever he was and smack him around for how he'd hurt Lawry. The guy didn't deserve what his partner had done to him. Suicide was selfish, in case anyone cared to know my opinion on the matter. Those left behind could never make peace with the fact someone they loved would rather be dead than be with them.

"So, you're still at the deity stage? *He walked on water. He was perfect.* It didn't piss you off when he didn't put the cap on the toothpaste or clean the whiskers from the sink? All that shit never bothered you?" I asked him as I sipped my sparkling water.

Lawry chewed his bite of pork and chuckled a little bit before he swallowed and looked into my eyes. "Now, I never said any of that, but we just got along. It came so easy between us, and it sort of surprised me, because I wasn't physically attracted to him in the beginning.

"Don't get me wrong, Julien was a very handsome guy, but he sorta isolated himself from everyone and wasn't easy to get to know. He interacted with his staff as needed, but he didn't open up too much to any of us.

"One night, we were working on intercepts from a known terror cell in Malaysia, and it was just the two of us in the office. Something big was going down in a few days, so we had to analyze the translations to piece together who was saying what and how we could stop them. They were communicating with a group in Pakistan, and the chatter was that there would be an attack in Sri Lanka which would be simultaneous with an attack in Keren, Eritrea.

"Julien could translate Punjabi, which was the language spoken by the terror group in Sri Lanka. Luckily, the Pakistani group was also fluent in Punjabi which was the language in which they communicated. It was a break for us. As I picked up the messages I found on a site on the dark web, Julie translated them, and we began piecing together a terror network that hadn't been detected previously by US intelligence. We spent thirty-six straight hours together, gathering more information and communicating with our counterparts all over the globe before American forces, along with a NATO brigade, raided both compounds simultaneously and eliminated the threats.

"We'd stopped two simultaneous terror attacks on two different continents where they'd had cells planted for years before activating them. That definitely called for a celebration, so Julien and I went out for breakfast before we went our separate ways. We'd talked for hours while we were working the case, and I found myself totally attracted to him when we finished. Our relationship built slowly, but I believed myself to be in love with him within a few months. I guess he never cared at all," Lawry explained before he finished eating his meal.

My heart was breaking at what he'd told me. I pulled up all the empathy I felt for the man because he was telling me something very personal. It wasn't about me. "So, did the two of you begin dating right away?" I asked.

For the next hour and a half, we discussed his relationship with the man I was coming to believe was a self-hating gay man with sadistic tendencies. I could see Lawry Schatz was innocent in queer culture, and it made my heart bleed a bit at his predicament. His so-called boyfriend had fucked with his head mercilessly. A bright-eyed, naïve guy from the Midwest believed he'd found true love with the older, wiser, gay man? It was a sad tale, but unfortunately, it wasn't uncommon.

"Talk to me about what you like or don't like in the bedroom. You told me your partner wanted you to do things which made you uncomfortable, so tell me what you consider as comfortable," I suggested as we had some decaf and each ate a low-cal ice cream sandwich. I loved my evening treats, but I didn't want my ass to grow as big as a Thanksgiving parade balloon, so I went for ice milk sandwiches which really weren't that satisfying, but I told myself they were delicious.

We settled into my living room couch, and I turned on the electric fireplace, which didn't put out heat but offered a hell of an ambiance. I could honestly say that Lawry Schatz was the first guy I'd almost had sex with that I'd allowed into my home. It was a new dynamic I wasn't exactly hating.

"I don't like hitting or being hit at all. My parents didn't believe in physical punishment, so I never got spanked as a kid growing up. I got into a few fights in high school with a bully or two because that was just what happened, but that was it. I played baseball and ran track, but I didn't really fit in with the jocks. I wasn't afraid of anyone, but I never picked a fight. However, if one pops off, I'm not afraid to stand my ground. Ask my brother about his bachelor party in Dallas sometime.

"Anyway, uh, I've kissed a few girls in my younger years, and I found the experience pleasant enough, even if I didn't want to take it further. Julien refused to kiss me. He said it was too intimate an act, and gay men weren't really intimate with each other. They fucked and didn't make it personal," Lawry explained.

His behavior during our only encounter suddenly made sense to me, because the guy hadn't let me kiss his lips, nor had he tried to kiss mine. That theory needed to be corrected. I knew plenty of guys who loved to kiss. "Okay, that's just wrong. If you've ever seen Gabe kiss Dexter, or Shepard Colson kiss Parker Howzer, I believe that notion will fly right out of your head," I suggested.

Lawry seemed to consider my comment before nodding his head. "Fair enough, but I haven't seen any of that. What about you? Do you like to kiss?" he asked, the corners of his mouth tipped up in a sexy smirk.

"If a man won't kiss me, or I don't want to kiss him, he's not sucking my cock, and I'm damn well not sucking his. I know a lot of men feel sex is just sex, but at its core, it's an intimate act. You're trusting someone with your body. You're trusting that the person you're engaging in the act with won't harm you, and you don't mean to harm them. If you put your cock into someone's mouth and you don't know them very well, how do you know they won't bite it off?

"I've done the anonymous thing, but that was when I was young and stupid. I'm just fucking grateful I was a good enough judge of character that I didn't get maimed or killed, but it was what it was at the time. We trusted everyone until that one person breaks our heart so severely, we can't believe the hurt will ever heal and promise ourselves never to trust anyone again. That's where you are now, right?" I asked, trying not to sound like a fucking know-it-all, but I'd been in his shoes a time or two. Not quite so severely as a lover committing suicide but waiting by the phone for the call that doesn't come hurts pretty badly, too.

"Do you kiss the people you're going to fuck?" Lawry asked, drawing me from my memories of Sasha, a good-looking Ukrainian man I fell for a few years prior. He was a painter-cum-bartender I'd hired for a few parties, and we'd hooked up. I thought he could be the one, but he thought I was one with millions, and when I didn't become his benefactor, he pitched a fit and left. The rejection was hard to handle.

"I don't fuck people I won't kiss. You didn't even try to kiss me that night. Did it cross your mind as odd?" I asked.

"I didn't think gay men kissed, and I didn't want to upset you by trying," Lawry stated. I wanted to laugh at that one. God love his poor, innocent heart.

"Oh, you wouldn't kiss me, but you thought it was okay to tie my hands together with my tie and fuck me hard without any prep? Man, watch some fucking porn, okay? Sex usually isn't confrontational. It's something people do for pleasure, not pain," I instructed.

I looked to see it was nearly eleven o'clock, and I had a full day on Wednesday. "I guess you better get going. You probably have as busy a day ahead of you like me. As I said, you can take my car home with you. I'll get it tomorrow," I offered as I went to the counter and offered the keys.

"Thanks, but I can get a cab. You have that party in Manhattan on Saturday?" he asked, obviously having paid some attention to what I'd said earlier.

"Yeah. I'm assuming my client wants to host it at Spires Tower. Now, I just have to find a caterer, some waitstaff, and a magician," I told him, half-teasing. Toni and I had a meeting with Celeste the next morning at eight, and I needed my beauty sleep.

Celeste Meyers wanted a quartet to play Chopin during the party, and she only wanted the gathering to be a couple of hours, so I figured I'd get in touch with the Musicians Union in Manhattan and find someone who could fill the bill. The food would be easy enough. It was light hors-d'oeuvres and cocktails, so not a huge fête to pull off. I kept telling myself I'd be fine.

"Do you need any help? I'm free on Saturday, and I can fetch and carry like the next guy. I'm happy to help, and maybe we can have fun? Friends do that sort of thing, right?" Lawry offered with an exuberant grin as we headed toward the stairs.

We were standing at my front door, and Lawry looked so damn handsome, I reached up and pulled him down by the back of his neck, gently brushing my lips against his. I was surprised when he wrapped his arms around my waist, not pulling me closer, but deepening the kiss a bit, slanting his sensuous mouth over mine. It made my toes curl.

Lawry's tongue brushed over my lips, and I opened my mouth to the man shamelessly. His lips were soft and firm, seeking pleasure while offering it in return. I tried to rein in my desires, but I hadn't had a kiss that wonderful in quite a long time, so I was getting mine while I could.

I wrapped my arms around his neck and kissed him back just as eagerly, feeling the heat rise in my body. I had to stop myself before I crossed a line I didn't want to cross. I pulled away, pecking his lips a few times before I released my hold on his neck. I settled my hands on his shoulders and smiled at him. "See, the world didn't end. Maybe your boyfriend had that part wrong?" I suggested, not saying I thought the man he'd idolized was a fucking asshole. That wouldn't go well, for sure.

I saw Lawry contemplate my comment for a minute before he erased any emotion from his face. "Maybe," he stated as a horn honked outside my place. "Night," he called as he hurried out the door and off the porch to the curb where he hopped into a cab. I waved, but I doubted he saw it.

He was in a hell of a hurry to get away, so I brushed off the kiss as an experiment I didn't think he'd enjoyed. It was fine that he wasn't into it. We were working to become friends, after all, and I generally didn't kiss my friends with the passion I'd poured into the kiss with Lawry Schatz. I had to get a handle on that shit because it shouldn't ever happen again.

LAWRY

I walked into the office on Monday morning with a little pep in my step. I'd helped Maxi with his Manhattan party on Saturday so the guy could have a friendly face around because he was freaking out about the powerful people in attendance and the fact he was an unknown commodity on the Manhattan social strata. It had been a fantastic party, which was a surprise for me because I figured it would be stuffy for sure. At the end of it, I found the entire affair to be quite entertaining.

I'd worked the door for Maxi, checking the guest list Maxi had provided and turning away the riffraff who'd found out about the party through unknown sources and had decided they'd been accidentally left off the list and had deserved to be admitted. Maxi had instructed that no one else should be admitted because they were likely paparazzi or gossip reporters, unlike the friends of the hostess who were members of the press, so I'd adhered to his rules.

It had been a bit uncomfortable when the ex-husband, Geoffrey Norman, had shown up to collect the rest of his belongings while the party was still in progress. I'd wanted to laugh my ass off at the situation as I'd watched it unfold, but that would have definitely been in poor taste. It would have been worth the laugh, though.

"What do you mean, I'm not on the list? What fucking list? This is my goddamn apartment, mother fucker. I'm Geoffrey Fucking Norman," the slightly balding gentleman snapped as I'd greeted him at the door.

"Mr. Norman, I'd say it's in your best interests not to make a scene, sir. I'll alert Ms. Myers of your desire to collect the rest of your belongings, and she can get in touch with you tomorrow to set up a time. There are many friends of hers inside who have ties to the press, and I don't think you'd exactly be helping your social standing by causing a scene," I offered to the man.

I didn't know jack shit about the stockbroker, but I knew he'd be a fool if he thought going into that cocktail party was a good idea. Finally, he nodded and offered his hand for me to shake. "Thanks, I guess. I'm in the first circle of hell right now, but going into that party would be fucking suicide, I know," he told me before he left, heading toward the service elevator to take him down to the garage.

I sent Maxi a text to inform him the woman's ex-husband wanted her to call and offer a time when he could collect the remainder of his belongings. I wondered if that would have been something Julie and I should have done, me moving out under amicable circumstances instead of him killing himself to get away from me and then his parents evicting me? Hell, I didn't even know how he'd killed himself. The idea of it had me pissed off.

The rest of the evening went pretty smoothly, and I had the unhappy accident to meet a few of New York's elite. They were nice on a superficial level, just as I'd suspected they would be when I recognized them.

The few who stopped at the gutter to speak to me asked absurd questions… "Are you Celeste's boy-toy we've all been dying to meet?" "Mmm. Where did she find you, handsome? Do you make house calls?" "Actor or dancer? That's what all of you bouncers really do, right? I'm a Broadway producer. You're a good-lookin' guy. I've got a nice couch. Maybe we could strike some sort of deal, huh?" The last one was from a guy who was sporting a wedding ring, not that the behavior surprised me. They were all predators in one way or another, as I'd learned from the media.

Ms. Myers was paying me a pretty penny to stand there, run off the uninvited, and listen to her friends' probing questions about who I was with respect to the hostess, so I smiled and directed them toward the large living room where the party was taking place. It all made me laugh, because I was a guy from Washington, Missouri. The idea of greeting a Tony-winning actress of at least *sixty-five with a hot guy younger than me on her arm was nothing I expected, but I was learning that, even with all of their money and status, those people were really no different than me. They were just as insecure as anyone else.*

I saw Cyril Symington standing in the kitchen making himself a cup of coffee, so I walked in with a smile. We hadn't actually met, though when I spoke with Lasso, she gave me a rundown of all of the personalities in the office, save the new guy, Duke Chambers, who was yet to start at GEA-A. Apparently, the handsome Brit was the joker of the bunch. "Good morning," I greeted.

Cyril smiled. "So, you're another arse bandit? This place is fortified with 'em," the man said to me before he laughed and gently punched my arm. "Don't get miffed. I'm just taking the piss. You're a new bloke to the office, so I'm just checking if you have a sense of humor, s'all. We all get along, mate. No offense intended," the man explained.

I understood him perfectly, having been on more than one assignment in the UK. Taking in his body language, I honestly believed he wasn't showing me disrespect, so I smiled and nodded, extending my hand to shake.

"Lawry Schatz, queer computer nerd, and brother of Hank Bayless. I believe you know my brother and his husband, Reed? I'm not offended by your comments, but the next guy might punch you in your gob. You're Sherlock, right?" I asked as we shook hands.

Sherlock smiled and took an exaggerated bow. "That I am, and I'm also the resident odd-gent-out because I'm straight s'an arrow, but if I keep working with you bastards, I might end up polishing one of your mates' knobs after a few pints.

"Anyway, welcome aboard. I'm on Dylan and Searcy's detail while Sinclair is on assignment. You ever get bored in the office and want to have some fun, ring me. Those two ankle biters are hours of entertainment," the handsome man proclaimed before he headed down the grand staircase as he whistled a tune I didn't recognize. I was guessing he didn't know I lived with the Torrente family, but he was spot on about Dylan and Searcy. They were a lot of fun.

I checked the *Tor* browser, which was the key to surfing the parts of the internet where angels feared to tread. I'd accessed it through the FBI's encrypted database, which I was ghosting to hide my presence on their network. I'd scanned in Mia's school picture because the FBI had the best facial recognition software, and I found I'd struck gold with the query I'd planted over the weekend, though it wasn't exactly what I wanted to see.

Mia Boone, or someone who could be her twin, was up for auction on a website located in the pits of hell on the Dark Web where people could buy or sell anything they had the ability—or the insanity—to procure. The FBI had shut down *Silk Road*, a market for guns, drugs, murder, or trafficking anything one could imagine, but they didn't stop all illicit activities occurring over the parts of the internet where criminals and crazies met to wreak havoc on an unsuspecting world.

The profile picture of the thirteen-year-old girl made me want to throw up, but I got a screenshot and sent it to Mathis Sinclair's phone, waiting for further instructions. I tiptoed around the auction site to see there were many boys and girls, all of them under fifteen, for sale to the highest bidder.

There were countdown clocks showing the remaining time for each auction, but there wasn't any information about where the auction would take place, nor how the money would change hands, only a notice that the sellers weren't accepting bitcoin. There was a button to apply to bid, but I'd need a certifiable alias and confirmable backstory, neither of which I had.

After I swallowed the bile that burned in my throat and chest, I ran down the hallway to Gabe's office to find Nemo and Gabby inside discussing something serious. Based on the looks on their faces after I gave a quick knock and opened the door without waiting for an invitation. They were both upset, but I didn't have time for it. "You both need to have a look at this shit. It's related to the Boone case," I explained.

I turned and left them without waiting for a response from either man. When both walked into my office and looked at one of the two large monitors on my desk, seeing the picture of the beautiful young girl with tears on her face, one of them said, "Oh, fuck no." I agreed wholeheartedly.

"We only have a week before her auction. There are nineteen other kids, both boys and girls, who are available for purchase. Three of them are Caucasian. The rest of them are various ethnicities, but nothing hints at where they're being held. The opening bid for the white kids is twenty-five thousand, each. The other kids start between eight- and ten-grand, each. This... This shit is fucked up," I announced, as if they needed to hear it.

"Goddammit. That could be my kids. No. We have to stop this, somehow, and we don't have time for red tape. What the fuck..." Gabby trailed off.

"I didn't say I *couldn't* get a location. I just haven't tried yet because I need a fool-proof alias to create an account. I need a certifiable backstory because these bastards will check into it, and I don't have any allies at the Company who I can contact to provide it. We need someone on the inside of an agency, preferably the FBI, to find out if someone's already on this.

"We need to notify them that a little girl from Queens was abducted and is being trafficked. We have to talk to Mrs. Boone, Gabby. Somebody has to be looking for all of these kids, right?" I pleaded, unable to hold back my emotions. I had a sister, and I had a nephew. I couldn't comprehend that someone would try to buy children.

"Let me make some calls. Do what you gotta do to find out where this shit is supposed to happen. Get a location, and we'll formulate next steps. I'll set up a pseudo-account because I refuse to allow this auction to happen on my watch. Send out an all-hands alert to get everyone into the office, Casper," Gabe ordered. I did as he said. The ramifications of that shit going down had my head spinning.

I'd worked for the Company for years, but I'd never witnessed anything like I'd seen as I'd muddled through that fucking cesspool of an auction site. No, it couldn't happen. I'd give my life to ensure it *didn't* happen.

Where the fuck was the FBI on that shit? Don't they have entire divisions devoted to crimes against children? I had a hard time catching my breath as I looked at those fucking pictures. There was madness all around, and I had no idea how to handle it. Hell, I missed the days of dealing with terrorists.

I took a cab to Maxi's brownstone and paid the driver, offering a big tip because he'd gotten me there in record time. I pushed the bell several times, seeing my potential host was agitated when he opened the door, which was just fine with me.

"What the fuck, Lawry?" Maxi snapped at me. It was warranted because leaning on the bell was annoying, but I was so glad to see him, I teared up. I didn't know why, but I needed to see him.

"Can I come in?" I whispered as the tears fell, unbidden by me.

"Oh, sugar, what happened?" Maxi asked as he grasped my hand and led me into his home. He took me into the living room and settled me on the couch. "How about some chamomile?" he asked. I nodded, suddenly unable to explain my impromptu visit without calling first.

Maxi returned in a few minutes with a pot of tea and two cups, along with lemon slices, a bear-shaped jar of honey, and a small pitcher of milk. "How do you like it?" Maxi asked.

"Two sugars and a lemon," I replied. The idea of something so innocuous as having tea with someone reminded me of the time I'd gone to tea with Julien and a woman he'd known from one period of time in his life or another, Eliana Richard. Julie didn't explain their acquaintance, just telling me we were going to meet her at the *ZaZa Hotel* in Dallas, and I'd gone along without question, just because he told me to do it. Apparently, I was a fucking lap dog at the time, or so it seemed as I looked back. Those fuckers weren't wrong when they said hindsight was twenty-twenty.

Maxi handed me the saucer and cup, offering a sweet smile because he could tell I was upset. "Is it something you can talk about?" I could see he was honestly concerned, but what I had in my head wasn't something I wanted to tell him because it was too awful for him to even consider.

I took a sip of the tea, swallowing the warm liquid to feel it settle my nerves a bit. I placed my cup on the saucer and turned to Maxi. He was a stunningly handsome man, what with his sun-streaked hair and those gorgeous, azure blue eyes. He had the sincerest look of compassion on his face I believed I'd ever seen in my life—with the exception of my little sister, Jewel, who loved everyone and everything. If someone hurt, Jewel hurt. She was a one of a kind, to be sure.

"I came here because I don't want to talk about shit. I want to hear something happy about your life. You know how bitter and bitchy I am, but you have so much light, and I need something joyful to erase the negativity," I demanded, which wasn't a lie at all.

Maxi smiled at me as he sipped his tea. "Okay, uh, I don't have a lot of great memories from my childhood because my mother was a drug addict, but I remember one, when my grandpa, Jess, took me fishing. I was probably seven or so. He handed me a worm to put on the hook, and I freaked the fuck out, screaming and throwing my hands up in the air like a maniac.

"That's probably when Grandpa figured out I wasn't going to be his linebacker grandson who would be the pride and joy of Thibodaux, Louisiana," Maxi told me, as he glanced down at the nice rug under his coffee table. It was tan and brown, and it complemented his furniture perfectly.

He had a china blue, micro suede couch; a brown leather recliner; and a blue, brown, and yellow side chair. His home was extremely nice, and the fact it was so well put together reminded me too much of Julien and the townhouse.

"I bet you were cute, though," I offered, not knowing what else to say to him. He seemed a little sad, and I didn't want that for him at all. Maxi's light should always shine and never, ever dim from bad memories or painful experiences. In my opinion, the world needed more people like Maxim Partee. It was then I decided to take up another line of questioning.

"So, your name? *Maxim Partee*? Is that real, or is a pseudonym?" I asked.

The gorgeous man snickered as he sipped his tea again. "It's actually my real name. My mother was from Belarus, Maya, and her father's name was Maximilian, or so I was told by my grandfather when I was older. My father, Clary, met her somewhere and knocked her up. Grandpa told me she left me outside the front door of their home in Thibodaux, and my father raised me for a while before he took off as well.

"Jess and Tina, my grandparents, weren't thrilled at being saddled with a kid when they were in their early fifties and had worked hard and saved for early retirement. Jess worked for the Post Office where he'd been a mailman for a long time, and Tina worked for a local grocery store in town where she was a baker. Thankfully, they took me in and raised me.

"Trust me; I have no reason to complain about my upbringing. My grandparents didn't beat me. They fed me, clothed me, and put a roof over my head, and when I told them I believed I was gay, they didn't ship me off to one of those crazy camps or kick me out of their home. I left when I turned eighteen because it was better for all of us, and they were both dead within two years. They left their estate to the church they attended, and I have no ill will toward them for their choices. Me, in a nutshell," he offered.

I was surprised at his openness, but it was exactly what I needed to hear. The look on his face showed me that he'd survived his childhood, but he rose above it and pushed himself not to allow those memories to bring him down. He chose to live in positivity, and that was something I admired very much about him. "Tell me more about your experiences as a gay man," I asked, finally ready to honestly address my sexuality.

I'd always believed my sexual attraction to Julien was because of the man, not that I was gay. My attraction to Maxi told a very different story… I was a gay man, just like my brother. I needed to have more exposure to gay culture because Julie and I didn't have gay friends, and I was pretty much in the dark about it. Hell, we didn't even have friends in common, but I was coming to believe it was due to him being a self-loathing gay man, which I had no desire to become. I didn't want to follow his path of destruction because I knew where that trail ended, and I wanted no part of it now that I'd sobered up.

Max laughed a little as he finished his tea. "Lawry, what do you want to know, doll?" I looked down at the table in front of his couch, seeing it was quite nice. Cherrywood with leaded glass inlays, if I was guessing right, though I didn't know my trees as well as I probably should.

I slid closer to him on the couch, placing my left hand on his left knee and looking into his beautiful, sparkling eyes. "I need to feel warmth. I need to feel like I'm sitting in the sun's light and being around you makes me feel that way. This case? It's absolutely bone-chilling, and I need to be with someone who cares about others and radiates positivity and light. That's what I feel when I'm around you. I'm not trying to get you to sleep with me, honestly. I just need to feel something positive, and when I walked out of the office, I could only think of coming here to be around you.

"I can go. Maybe I shouldn't have come? You don't deserve to hear me complaining about my job," I offered as an apology.

Max touched my hand as I started to get up from the couch. "I think I know what you need. Trust me?" he asked with a gentle smile. I nodded because I did trust him. For reasons unknown to me, I believed I could trust that man with my life.

He took my hand and led me down a hallway to his bedroom and into his bathroom. He turned on the water in a large, jetted tub, squirting what I believed to be body wash or shower gel under the faucet. He turned to me and smiled. "You ever have a bubble bath?"

I chuckled. "Maybe when I was three or so. Mom used to put Hank and me in the tub together, killing two birds with one stone, I guess," I responded.

Max smiled as he ran a wet hand through his hair to pull it back from his handsome face. "I'd like to hear a story about that sometime," he joked as he reached into a cabinet under the sink and retrieved a large orange and blue bath sheet and placed it on the vanity.

"I'll step out so you can strip. I promise you this will do you a world of good," Max told me before leaving the room. The water was running, and the bubbles were growing, offering a temptation I couldn't remember experiencing. I quickly stripped, folding my clothes to place them on the counter before I put my naked ass into the most amazing smelling bath I believed I'd ever had. The scent was spicy with a hint of flowers. It was pretty fucking great.

I settled into the water and sank down a bit. The jets were relaxing the muscles in my body, and I closed my eyes in contemplation, just sinking into the water to only hear silence for as long as I could hold my breath. The warm water soothed my tired muscles and eased the tension in my lower back, threatening to make me feel boneless.

The door cracked open, so I sat up a little. "You settled? Can I come in?" Max asked. I saw a mug in his hand as it slipped through the crack in the door.

I laughed. "Max, I got nothing you ain't seen before, so please come in," I offered, remembering how awful our only sexual encounter had been. I'd been a total asshole to the man that night, and I felt horrible about it. He deserved much more respect and consideration than I'd shown him.

He came into the bathroom and plopped a towel on the floor next to the large tub, handing me another cup of tea. "So, tell me something," he urged, his gorgeous smile encouraging me.

I thought for a minute and decided to be honest with him about what I could. "I think you're amazing, Max. That party on Saturday was phenomenal, and you seemed to do it in your sleep. I admire that about you.

"Look, I'm going to be busy shortly, but I enjoy spending time with you. Do you think we can go out for dinner or lunch sometime?" I asked as I took a bath sponge from the deck of his tub and squeezed the warm, soapy water over my arms. It felt like I imagined a spa treatment would feel. Settling back against the jets as they pulsed over my body was relaxing.

Max blushed. "My grandparents called me Max when I was a little boy. I've missed hearing it, actually," he told me with an embarrassed grin. "We can get together sometime. I've got three weddings in the near future, so I'll be busy, but I have to eat, so if you're available at the drop of a hat, I'd like us to meet for lunch or dinner sometime.

"I'll be running around Brooklyn for the next two weeks with all of the weddings prep so lunch might be easiest. I'll be having some late nights, for sure, but we can have lunch. So, what's your case about, Lawry? I can see its impact on you, so maybe if you tell me about it, it won't weigh so heavy on your heart?"

I hoped he was right.

MAXI

I was awake all night, trying to digest what Lawry had told me about Mia Boone, a thirteen-year-old girl who had been kidnapped and was going to be auctioned off on a website on the Dark Web. He told me there were a number of other kids on the site being offered up, and he was working against the clock. I couldn't fathom what kind of monster would even conceive of such an idea as to kidnap children and sell them to God-knows-who to make money. How could one value money above the innocence of a child?

Finally, at four-in-the-morning, I gave up and got ready to start my day. I showered, slicked back my hair so it was out of my face, and fixed myself a soft-boiled egg. I reached for my laptop and pulled up my calendar, seeing what kind of day I had ahead of me.

I logged into the network at the office to double check nothing had changed that I hadn't been informed of. I was checking the group calendar against my personal calendar when an idea struck. I had money. Not millions, but I had money. I quickly pecked off a text to Dexter and hurried upstairs to my bedroom to dress for the day.

An hour later, I was at the office, checking the arrangements for the Hadden-Burk wedding, which was being coordinated by Key Gordon, one of my fantastic planners. Key had worked closely with the bride, Nina Hadden, and from what I'd observed, he'd been successful at seeing her vision come to fruition. The affair was set to take place at the Bronx Zoo, which was where the couple met.

Steven Burk, the groom, had his nephew with him at the zoo one day, and the little boy got away from him in the Congo Gorilla Forest. Nina volunteered at the zoo on weekends while finishing her degree in Veterinary Science, and she found the little boy making faces at one of the lowlands gorillas through the glass.

When Steven tracked his nephew into the building, he met Nina, and they hit it off immediately. They were planning to have their ceremony outside Astor Court where Indonesian peacocks roamed freely. Cocktail hour will be in the Gorilla Forest area, and then there's a sit-down dinner inside Astor Court.

The whole thing would take some maneuvering on Key's part because herding two-hundred guests between venues was a logistical nightmare, but the couple was going to have photos taken in various spots at the zoo, so they wanted to entertain their guests using the inhabitants of the Gorilla Forest to stave off boredom. It sounded fun to me.

I had every confidence Key could pull it off brilliantly without my assistance, so I gave him a few notes by email.

K – make sure to triple check the weather since it's an outside affair. Make sure you have a large enough clean-up crew on standby or the zoo will never allow us to host events there again. Take Monday off because you deserve it. Xoxo Maxi

I moved on to check the other two weddings which were the following weekend. Toni was handling the Zho-Pembrook wedding, which would be at Snug Harbor on Staten Island. The ceremony and reception would take place in the Chinese Scholar's Garden. The bride was Chinese American, and many of her relatives were coming to the US from Hong Kong for the wedding. The bride and her mother decided the gardens would give an appropriate nod to their Chinese heritage. I knew Toni was all over the arrangements, so I had no worries.

I sent an email to remind Toni to enlist enough help because it would be a busy day. Luckily, the garden had a large tent, under which the ceremony could relocate if the weather became inclement, so there were no worries there.

The Biggs-Dawson wedding was Fredrik Kulich's baby because the grooms were his friends, so I'd agreed Fredrik could offer them a courtesy discount, not charging for his time to plan the event, only pushing vendor charges through to them, allowing the couple the use of our discounts as well.

The couple were holding the wedding at the farm they'd just purchased in the Hudson Valley. Jarrod Biggs was an electrical engineer, and Jason Dawson was an architect. Fredrik had been working with vendors in the area to cut down on the grooms' costs because apparently, the farm had cost over two-million dollars, and the event was going to be a weekend affair, so the grooms were looking for ways to cut corners.

I'd told Fredrik I didn't mind if he was gifting them with his genius to plan the events, and he'd told me that he'd take along a lot of business cards to drum up interest in our services. I was thrilled with the arrangement and happy for him. I'd never planned a wedding for friends, but I'd been lucky to become friends with several of the couples I'd worked with in the past. Gabriele and Dexter Torrente were at the top of that list.

When I was confident I wasn't necessary for any of the upcoming events, I left copies of my notes for Toni and headed out to Dexter and Gabe's home to speak with Lawry Schatz. I glanced up to see Shay's shop was dark, checking my watch to see it was just seven in the morning. I stopped at the bakery down the street and grabbed pastries to take with me, including cupcakes for Dylan and Searcy and organic pet treats for Magic and Sparkles, which the bakery sold as well.

I parked in front of their lovely home and walked up the concrete-and-rock front stairs, knocking on the navy door instead of ringing the bell. I was sure Dex was up, but I didn't want to wake the little ones because I knew school was out, and I wasn't sure what their plans were for the summer. I heard small feet padding toward the door before there was a knock on the inside. It was Searcy's tell because she couldn't see anything from the short peephole Gabe had installed in their front door. I bent forward and waved to her. "It's me. Maxi," I offered in a sing-song voice, hearing her giggle.

"It's Maxi, Daddy!" she yelled because she couldn't reach the deadbolt, so Dex would need to open it for her. I heard the locks click, and the second the door opened, I had a little monkey hugging my leg before I could take a step. She was wearing yellow pajama shorts and a tank top with a Minion on the front. That was about as much as I knew about Disney culture.

"Hello, my little sweetheart. I brought you a treat if Daddy says you can have it. Let's go inside," I told her. Just as we were about to enter the house, I heard pounding feet headed in our direction from up the street. It was Gabe and Lawry, and they appeared to be racing. Dex stepped outside after he picked up Searcy, and we watched them both dive to touch the fountain in the front yard, knocking the statue of a little girl with a watering can off kilter.

"I swear, those two are worse than Dylan and some of his friends. Come inside," Dexter urged before he turned to Gabe and pointed, "Fix it. If the yard floods again, you're taking the day off to wait for the man to come and put down new sod. He looked at me like I was crazy last time," Dex snapped at his handsome husband. The huge Italian man blew him a kiss, which made Dexter laugh before he shot Gabe the finger.

We walked inside, and Dex closed the door. I could tell he wasn't in a great mood, and I was immediately concerned because those two men were so much in love it was sickening. "What's up? Tired of hosting Lawry?" I asked, knowing the guy had been there for nearly a month. In my opinion, houseguests were like fish—about three days before it all started to stink. Having Lawry with them for more than three weeks might have become a bit stale?

Dex smiled. "In all honesty, it's not Lawry at all. He's been great. He helps with chores, and he watches the kids one night a week so Gabe and I can go for dinner or to a movie. No, this is Gabe all the way.

"Mathis is on a case, so Cyril is driving the kids and me around and looking out for us. Gabe's now decided he's going to swap Cyril, who's a lovely man and great with our kids, out for a new guy we don't even know. Gabe said the guy's a former Marine but neglected to mention what he's been doing in the meantime, which is a big red flag for me. When my husband doesn't share details, I become concerned.

"The guy is probably nice, but the kids don't do well with change, and I only met him last night for about fifteen minutes when Gabe brought him home long enough to dictate orders to our children and me.

"Mr. Chambers has never been around children in his life, and Searcy's scared to death of him because he looks angry all the time. We fought last night after the Marine left, and Gabe's already brought it up again this morning before he and Lawry went for a run," Dexter complained.

I had a pretty good idea why the matter had come up in the first place. I'd met Cyril Symington at the three events I'd planned for Dex and Gabe, and the guy was quite friendly and entertaining. I knew, based on stories Dex had shared, that Cyril was close with the kids, and they loved him. Cyril Symington, however, wasn't going to be the guy to stop a kidnapping attempt if two thugs tried to take those precious kids. He was a smart man, but not quite one of the brutes working for that organization. He was civilized, but every now and again, one needed a thug.

In light of what I'd heard the previous night from Lawry, Gabriele had been alarmed by the auction situation involving the thirteen-year-old girl who was the missing sister of a client. It had upset me, as well, and as I watched Searcy cleaning out the litter box in the laundry/mud room, I understood why Gabe would want the most dangerous person in his employ to guard his family.

"I think you need to ease off a little bit, my dear friend. Who couldn't fall in love with Dylan and Searcy? I'll bet you a massage at DyeV Barr that if you give the guy a couple of hours with them, they'll warm up to him, too. Maybe you could gently suggest to the man that a smile might go a long way with Searcy? If the guy isn't used to being around kids, he's probably more afraid of them than they are of him," I suggested as we heard running up the stairs along with deep laughter. Gabe and Lawry must have finished righting the fountain and were off to clean up for work.

"Fair point. So, what have you brought?" Dex asked as he opened the large bag containing the box I'd carried inside. "Oh, my," he gushed as he looked at the Danish and cupcakes. I reached into the bottom of the accompanying bag, retrieving the pet biscuits.

"These are for the four-legged Torrente's," I offered with a smile.

Searcy returned to the kitchen and held up her arms to Dexter so he could hold her to wash her hands. "We've got to get a ladder or something. What do you do when I'm not here to lift you, you little punk?" he teased.

Searcy giggled. "I go upstaiwrs, Daddy," she responded as she soaped her hands and rinsed them, reaching for a paper towel.

Dex laughed. "Then why don't you just go upstairs instead of having me hold you up?" he teased her as he kissed her forehead. If I had ovaries, they'd be aching as I looked at the sweet little girl and thought about Mia Boone, the young woman Lawry had talked about the previous night. It made me want to die.

"Cause youwr hewre, Daddy. What's fowr bweakfast?" Searcy asked as she kissed Dex's cheek before he put her down.

"Eggs, sausage, and the surprise Maxi brought for you. Go upstairs and wake your brother. I'll get started on the food," he explained to her.

Searcy nodded before she walked over to me. "Come help me pick an outfit?" She offered her hand, and just like St. Patrick led the snakes out of Ireland, she led me up to her room and opened a closet burgeoning with adorable clothes. My insides were simply melting.

We settled on a pair of denim shorts with white, eyelet trim and a pink t-shirt with a magic wand on the front in glitter paint. She had pink sneakers with white soles, and after she was dressed, she had me put her hair in a ponytail with a big, pink bow. She looked adorable, but that wasn't anything new. She rushed to the jack-and-jill bathroom between her room and Dylan's, running into his room to wake him before stopping to wash her face and brush her teeth on the way back through.

The door opened as I was making the bed, and I heard a low chuckle I recognized. "You'll make that little girl mad. Searcy makes her bed so she can get her allowance." I turned to see Lawry standing in the doorway in a navy suit with a tie slung carelessly around his neck, untied.

I chuckled. "You tried it before and got burned?"

"Yep. You wanna talk about Miss Independent, that's her to a 'T.' What brings you by?" Lawry asked.

I walked out of her room and stepped into the hallway, closing her door behind me. "I didn't get any sleep last night. I have money, Lawry. I can go to that website and put in my information, which is true and totally verifiable. I can log a bid to buy that little girl, and maybe get her before some nefarious asshole has a chance? I wish to hell I had enough money to buy them all, but I can get that little girl for your client. Tell me the web address," I quietly demanded.

Just then, Gabe walked down the hallway with a smile. "That's very kind of you, Maxi, but we've got a plan. I see Lawry explained the situation to you? Can you try to talk some sense into Dexter regarding the new operative, Duke Chambers? He's a good guy, okay? He's a former Marine, and he's acclimating to civilian life, but I want him on point if he's watching my kids. When we get into this shit, we're going to have some people looking for us, and I want the cream of the crop watching the man I love and our two babies. I won't..." he explained before Searcy's door opened, and she rushed out, holding her arms up to Gabe.

"Hi, Papa. Can we go to the playgwound today?" she asked.

Gabe looked at the little girl with a parent's joyous smile as he smooched her cheek and blew a raspberry against her neck, making her giggle, which was like hearing music. "I thought you might want to go out to Nonna's and spend the week with her and Nonno. You can swim and go to the beach to hunt shells. I bet Zia Carmela will bring Bianca out. If Jimmy comes along, you'll keep him in line, right?" Gabe asked.

Searcy nodded, reminding me of a story Dex had told me about the first time they'd met Gabe's extended family. One of the cousins was a bit put off by the new family Gabe brought with him, and Dylan's glasses ended up broken in the process. I believed they'd hammered out their differences over time; at least, I thought so. I knew two of Gabe's sisters were in the process of getting divorced from the idiots they'd married. I certainly hoped it all went well and there could be peace in the family.

"Is Daddy coming with us, Papa?" she asked as she played with the back of Gabe's hair. She seemed to love the feel of his glorious mane, and as I looked at it, I noticed a little more salt in it than when I planned their wedding. He was hot as hell and only getting better looking, but my friend, Dexter, was no slouch either. Watching the two of them together was hard-on inducing.

"Probably not until the weekend, sweet girl. He's got classes all week, but Duke will be there, and I'm sending Sherlock along for a few days. If you get him to play tea party, take pictures for me. He has a birthday coming up," Gabe teased before he headed down the stairs with Searcy in his arms, her head resting on his broad shoulder.

I turned to look at Lawry who had a big grin on his face. "They're so cute."

He laughed. "I'm gonna have to take you back to Missouri to meet my sister. She's sixteen. She's a musician, and she's incredible. She has the biggest heart I've ever seen in a human," he told me as he took my hand and led me toward the stairs. We heard a door open behind us and saw Dylan walk out of his bedroom, adjusting his glasses. He had sneakers in his hand, and when he saw us, he smiled.

"I thought I heard you talking out here, Maxi. How ya been?" he asked, sounding all of his nine years.

"I've been good, kiddo. How was the end of the school year?" I asked as he stepped under my arm. He was getting taller, bless him, and he was certainly a handsome kid. He had just turned nine earlier in the spring, and I could see he was developing his own personality. It was just amazing to see him becoming an individual.

Dylan talked about the end of school field trip to Central Park which both Gabe and Dexter chaperoned, and how he'd been able to extricate a promise from Gabe that he'd talk to Dex so Dylan could go to soccer day camp over the summer. I wasn't surprised he wasn't going to a sleepaway camp because his fathers were too protective. Given what I'd learned about shit that went down when their mother was still around before she went into witness protection and never surfaced again, I couldn't blame them.

We all walked into the kitchen where Dexter was at the stove while Searcy was sitting on Gabe's lap, the two of them drinking orange juice. "Take a seat. Breakfast is almost ready," Dexter commanded as he stood at the stove in a pair of plaid shorts and a white undershirt. His hair was sticking up as it had been when I'd arrived at seven.

"How about I take over stirring the eggs while you enjoy your *toilette*?" I teased. He discreetly told me to fuck myself as he turned over the spatula to the scrambled eggs. I stirred them as Lawry and Dylan talked about going to an Empires game soon. It was almost like a picture-perfect scene. Everyone was happy and enjoying life. Every day should be so wonderful.

"When are we going to Mexico?" I heard Lawry ask quietly. I glanced over my shoulder to see Dylan was reading a book and Searcy was playing with Gabe's phone as she sat on his lap at the table.

"Just as soon as we get confirmation from my contact with a believable profile. You can get the equipment together today, right? I want us to be ready to go ASAP," Gabe ordered. Lawry only nodded. I stirred the eggs and turned off the burner when I was sure they were ready to serve. I poured them into a bowl and placed them on the table.

"Can I speak with you, privately?" I asked Lawry. I was feeling anger bloom in my stomach, and I wasn't sure why, but it was just at the edge of my brain.

"I'd like to have a hot…" he began.

I raised my eyebrow and saw him swallow. "Okay. I'll be right back. Don't wait for me," Lawry told Gabe as the large man was filling his children's plates. It was clear that Gabe Torrente didn't wait for anyone.

Lawry and I walked onto the back patio of the house through a set of French doors that were enviable. They were double paned and had intricate black designs that mimicked wrought iron between the glass. They were stunning.

We stepped to the side of the patio so we weren't visible to the inhabitants of the house, and I touched his forearm. "You're not going to Mexico for this auction thing, right? You're going to contact the Mexican police or Interpol or Europol or someone of authority somewhere, right? You're not going to try to do this on your own; please tell me you're not?" I implored, looking into his gorgeous, grass-green eyes, feeling my own begin to pool with tears.

Lawry pulled me into his strong chest and wrapped those long arms around me. It was then I knew I'd hit the nail on the head. They were going to Mexico without any support, and they were all going to get killed.

"Look, Max, I can't sit by and watch that little girl be sold to some crazy motherfucker who would do shit to her I can't even fathom. Hell, I can't sit by and watch any of those kids be sold into who knows what, so we're going to do everything we can to stop it. Gabe was able to get us a verifiable alias, and we used it on an application. We were accepted to bid on the girl's auction, so we're heading to Mexico as soon as we get more detailed instructions regarding specific place and time of the auction. The Mexican authorities are corrupt, so getting support from them for this sort of situation is useless. We have to rely on ourselves.

"I contacted my old boss at the Company, and he gave me the name of an agent he knew in the field office in Mexico City. He worked a case with the guy a few years ago, and he contacted him to give me an in. The guy was able to promise us two agents off the books for support when we arrive in Mexico.

"We placed a bid on Mia Boone that's yet to be topped, so we'll receive the coordinates for the location where we can pick her up unless someone makes a higher bid. Once we have a location, we'll do everything we can to take down the assholes who have all of those kids and keep any of them from harm. At this point, we have to follow through or we compromise the auction, and they'll either kill all of the kids or run with them. We won't get this chance again," Lawry informed.

I looked up into his eyes and felt a spark in my heart. It was one I'd never felt before, and while it was troublesome, I believed it to be the beginning of change. I wrapped my arms around his neck and pulled him closer. "I hope you don't hit me, but I'm going to kiss you before you leave, Lawry Schatz. You are a good and honorable man. Please stay alive so we can continue to get to know each other. Is there anything I can do to help from here?" I asked quietly.

He smirked as he looked into my eyes. "Can I come over and take a bath in your tub when I get back? That was unlike anything I've ever experienced before, and I'd love to do it again, but this time with a companion? The idea of it will satisfy me until I get back to you," he whispered against my ear as he held me close.

I didn't have to think about it. "Yes, and this time I'll pull out the whole shebang. I've got fizzy bath salts that will tickle your scrotum and smell like nothing you've ever smelled in your life. I didn't use them last night, but next time you come to bathe in the healing waters of Maxi Partee's magical bath, you'll get the full-on treatment. I have scented candles which will lull you into fragrant heaven, and I'll even wash your back," I teased him, though I meant every word.

Lawry Schatz was becoming important to me, and while I didn't want to consider it was something serious, I feared it might become so without my permission. I wasn't one who wanted to settle with the white picket fence, ivy-covered cottage, two-point-five kids, a dog, and a cat. It reminded me too much of Dexter and Gabe, who were currently fighting. If they couldn't make it work, then what chance did I even have?

LAWRY

In a moment of desperation, I'd called my former boss's boss, AD Ian Mallory, and given him the lowdown on what was happening with the auction. Mathis Sinclair had discovered that the boy seen on the security camera footage helping Mia into the van was a member of *Guerrillas Mayas*, a Latin gang which was well-known in Queens.

His name wasn't Robby, it was Roberto, and he was known in the neighborhood as an active gang member. The information made sense because it was where the Boone family lived, but it didn't explain how the young girl ended up in Mexico.

"Mallory," I'd heard over my cell phone. I'd called the man when I returned to the Torrente's home after my relaxing tub at Maxi's place. I'd known we'd need help of the official variety if we were going to Mexico on a suicide mission to rescue about twenty kids, so I'd used the only resource available to me at the time, not even sure if it would pan out.

"AD, it's me, Lawry Schatz. I uncovered something in my capacity as a private investigator and bodyguard in New York. It's bad, sir. It's a case that crosses borders, and I felt the need to alert you," I'd informed the man, surprised he'd even answered his phone when he'd seen my number pop up on the screen. I hadn't left the Company on the best of terms because I'd gone off my nut, but that was the past. I needed their help, and I'd play any chit I had left to get it.

"Go on," he'd responded, so I had.

"It's a kidnapping case, and there's going to be an auction of about twenty kids under the age of sixteen. Some of them are as young as six, sir. I found the website because an Army soldier approached my employer and reported his sister went missing about ten-days ago. The police in Queens aren't able, or maybe unwilling, to track her whereabouts at all, but I found the girl on my own. She's listed on an auction site for sale. The girl is thirteen, sir," I'd explained.

From then forward, Ian Mallory offered as much assistance as he could for an unsanctioned mission. He'd given me the names of two agents who he'd contacted, personally, and they'd agreed to meet us at a mom-and-pop hotel on Isla Cedros, a tiny island off the west coast of Baja California, Mexico. The town of El Morro had many abandoned warehouses which would have suited the kidnappers perfectly. We just had to ensure we got the building number correct.

The security measures the kidnappers had employed were first rate from what I could tell by the satellite photos I was able to collect through a stop at NORAD and a quick redirection of a weather satellite with a camera. I got in and out in three minutes. I had resources at my fingertips those fucking kidnappers couldn't fathom, and they wouldn't get the best of me.

We had landed at the small airport on Isla Cedros, and I glanced up to see Gabby, Nemo, Smokey, and Mathis were all staring at me as we taxied to the hangar. "I arranged for a driver to meet us and deliver us to the hotel I found outside El Morro. The auction goes live at nine o'clock tomorrow night.

"The compound where I believe the kids are being held is less than ten miles away. I can't tap into their security feed at the compound or their network because they have that shit locked down such that I couldn't get a RAT or a rootkit installed to take control of the auction and shut it down remotely. They've set up a botnet, so the InfoSec opens for a few seconds at random times to update bids and applications and sends out responses to the potential buyers. They want no distinct pattern for someone to capture and install malware or a worm to infiltrate. I found at least ten IP addresses, routed through about eight different countries, but we're physically closer to the location than we are technically," I informed the group.

Smokey unbuckled the flashy gold-plated seat belt of the buttery, tan leather reclining seat he'd slept in most of the flight and moved to take a seat next to me, glancing at the computer I was pounding to try to gain any updated information. He stilled my hands and pulled them from the keyboard.

"Casper, you're going to drive yourself insane. Besides, I only understood about ten percent of that gibberish, but take a break, man. Let's wait until your friends meet up with us at the hotel before we panic, okay? They might have more insight into this operation which they haven't shared yet. We're doing everything we can, but you can't take this on by yourself. We're all here to help you," he stated in a calm voice. I liked the man, and I loved his boyfriend's pastries. It was exactly what I needed to hear at that moment.

Mathis stood and paced the floor of the roomy Embraer Lineage 1000, the jet Gabby had at his disposal. Mathis was like a caged animal, anxiety dripping off of him like water. "We need to at least drive toward the area where Casper thinks he found the warehouse. We need eyes on the place, right?" he asked as he turned to Gabby for confirmation.

I cleared my throat. "There are sixteen buildings in that abandoned car plant. I don't know how the hell you'll be able to determine which one's the auction venue," I sniped, seeing he wasn't happy with the intel I had garnered. I had no idea what the fuck he'd been doing, but if he was calling into question my ability to do my job? I would fuck that guy up... somehow.

"No, wait, I'm not criticizing, but there have to be signs leading us to which buildings are being utilized, correct? Tire tracks to buildings that are still functioning, maybe? Electricity running to one of the buildings that's still active, perhaps? Trash stacked up outside?" he suggested.

I could tell Mathis was fully invested in finding Mia Boone, and I felt bad for jumping to the wrong conclusion. He wasn't questioning my skills; he was trying to find the girl. I got it. "Yeah, actually, but there may be security measures in place we haven't anticipated because, even though the compound is abandoned, the plant still seems to have security cameras on the exterior I saw when... I, uh, think I saw."

They were all looking at me expectantly, but I moved on quickly. "If the current inhabitants have reactivated the old system, I'll need to physically *dirty maid* the damn thing. There might be boobytraps set around the perimeter, so going in, we'll need to be triply cautious. Someone dying won't be helpful," I informed them as I considered options.

"What the fuck does *dirty maid* mean?" Nemo asked. I never remembered everyone didn't understand me when I talked about my job. I exhaled and pulled up my patience.

"I'll *physically* have to patch into their security system to get control of it on the property. I can't hack it remotely," I admitted. I hated to admit the weakness, but some things were unavoidable.

Since we were on the ground, I quickly got into the *Archivo* in Mexico City where all of the public records regarding land ownership were stored. I wanted to see if there was still a building plan for the complex outside El Morro. It had been a Japanese car manufacturing complex before they pulled out of the area. I understood why it worked for them because the climate was arid and weather-related issues didn't undermine their manufacturing process.

When the automobile industry began its revamp to manufacture driverless cars, the plant pulled out of Mexico because the South American market dried up, having sourced better deals in South Korea, India, and Indonesia, such that the Japanese could no longer compete.

I found what I was looking for and pulled up the blueprints that had been filed back in the early teens when the complex was being built. "Here's the footprint of the complex. I have no idea which building they might be using to hold the kids, but anyone is welcome to guess," I offered, feeling frustration burrow into my soul.

Gabby walked back from speaking with the pilot and sat down across from my chair, placing a beefy paw on my forearm and offering a squeeze of reassurance, I was sure. "Take a fucking breath, Casper. We'll figure it out. A few of us can take a ride out there and get a look before dark this evening," he stated before he stood and barked, "*¿Quién Habla Español?*"

I was surprised when Smokey stood and elbowed Gabby in the ribs, offering a smirk. "I do, ya jackass, and you know it." The two men grabbed their luggage and headed to the door of the plane, all of us following behind.

When we got to the hotel, we checked in, and everyone gathered in the lobby before heading to their rooms. I was sharing a room with Nemo, which was cool because I didn't know him very well. He seemed like a nice guy, and he didn't appear to be quick to temper, which was great. When we got to our room, we settled in, and I double checked my information to be sure nothing happened to fuck up the mission.

Nemo walked out on the balcony to take a phone call when there was a knock on the door. It was Mathis, and he still appeared to be a live wire. "Any news?" he asked, which made me chuckle.

"In the one-hundred, twenty-eight seconds since we went our separate ways? Not much. Nemo's on the balcony, and I'm about to go to the head," I offered, seeing the first smile I'd seen from the man since Kelly Boone darkened our doorway at the Victorian. I didn't know why I was giving him shit because I wasn't long on patience, either, which might go against me at some point in time.

When I returned to the sitting area between the two bedrooms Nemo and I would inhabit that night, I saw that Nemo had returned to the room and was sitting at the table across from Mathis. I finally took a look around the room and noticed the décor reminded me of a nineteen-fifties western movie set in Mexico. I was waiting for a mariachi band to come strolling through to serenade us gringos.

Nemo pulled out a chair at the table and patted the seat for me, so I sat down and watched him carefully, seeing he was just as on edge as the rest of us. "What's next? When do you expect your friends to show?" he asked just as my cell buzzed in the back pocket of my jeans.

I unlocked the screen to see Agents Marquez and Olmos were about ten minutes out, based on a text. "Seems they're on their way. They had to fly a fucking crop duster from Mexico City," I explained, based on the expletives in the text about the difficulty getting to the island on such short notice.

We all laughed, apparently in dire need of a reason to break the tension in the room. If we didn't get a bead on those fucking assholes who had those kids somewhere inside an old automobile manufacturing plant, the loss would be catastrophic. We needed a fucking break. I hoped to hell we got one.

An hour later, Gabby and Smokey returned to the hotel and called us to their suite. Field Agents Dario Marquez and Hector Olmos had arrived about thirty minutes earlier, and we all went down to the bar to have a drink while we waited for Gabby and Smokey. They'd gone out to the compound for some reconnaissance work but based on the disappointed looks on their faces when we arrived at their rooms, they'd garnered no significant information.

Sherlock and Duke Chambers had stayed behind in Bay Ridge to watch out for Dexter and the kids, while London St. Michael was on assignment with Mateo somewhere in Greece. The remaining five of us took up about half of the small hotel, but it was close to the site where we believed the twenty kids were being held captive. The place was off the beaten path, and the couple who owned it fell all over themselves to make sure we were comfortable.

We all took a seat at the large teak table in Gabe's sitting room, and I noticed Olmos signal to his partner, who then began to speak. "Let's remain cognizant of the fact this entire mission is unsanctioned by the U.S. Government. It's off-book, so if we get into trouble, there will be nobody to bail us out," Dario Marquez confirmed in his thick accent.

"Yeah, why is that? We're on foreign soil as far as I know, unless the U.S. has bought this little piece of paradise. Isn't the CIA involved in shit like this?" Gabby asked as he studied the two men who were sitting to the left of him at the rectangular table.

Marquez continued. "Actually, no. We are an intelligence gathering entity. It's right there in the name...Central *Intelligence* Agency. We've been able to gather very little intelligence regarding this particular situation, but we're still joining you as a favor to Ian Mallory, not because we give a fuck that you have a wild hair up your asses about something that's likely bullshit in the first place. If someone brought twenty minors through town, the captors would need to stock supplies for any length of stay out at that compound, and someone would have noticed.

"Hell, there's no running water out there because thieves have stripped anything worth salvage value from those buildings years ago. The only record of a large enough plane or boat coming to the island from the mainland is the plane you flew on that's sitting out at the airfield. Surely you've figured out there are only two ways on or off this island—air or sea?

"All we're doing is accompanying you to the compound so you can prove to yourselves there's no secret kidnapping ring holding twenty kids to auction off on the internet. If the local gang, *Guerrillas Mayas,* are using it as a storage facility for drugs or a lab of any kind, we immediately retreat and contact the DEA who will partner with the *Policia* and *Ejército Mexicano.* They'll handle that sort of situation, not us. We aren't authorized to do search and seizure on a large number of drugs.

"If it's being used as a warehouse or a lab, there will be a heavy presence of *Mayas,* and they'll be loaded with firepower. We have no desire to engage them because we'll be severely out armed. Unless there is proof of minors in captivity, we hold fire and retreat immediately. Otherwise, it's a fucking suicide mission, and I'm not going to die for you gringos. I don't give a fuck who you are or who you *think* you are.

"Now, in the event our intel is wrong, and there are, indeed, minors in custody at that compound, the time it would take to pull in all of the agencies who would try to claim jurisdiction over the bust would make it impossible to act with any efficiency, whatsoever. A quiet entrance onto the property will be the best bet to keep those kids safe if they're even there.

"We can breach the compound and send up a heat-seeking drone to cover the territory faster than we can clear all of the structures. If we find a building with a defined heat source that appears to be human, most of us can distract the captors while a few of us get the kids out. We can get a large farm truck with racks to wait on the road outside the fence to take them out of danger," Marquez explained.

His instructions left a lot to be desired because it seemed as if they had intel they weren't sharing with us, but I had no way to verify the information or the source, so we were at their mercy. I planned to check the website again when we finished for the night, but the air card I brought with me to remain anonymous while borrowing resources from federal agencies in Mexico City and anywhere with a strong signal wasn't working properly.

Olmos cleared his throat. "This territory is thick with *Guerrillas Mayas*. They are heavily fortified, *Señores*. Believe me, they already know we're here." His accent sounded even thicker than his partner's.

"I'd feel better if we had some backup on this," Nemo stated as he looked around.

They all turned to look at Marquez and Olmos, who chuckled and shook their heads. "You're not *federales*, friend. As far as anyone is concerned, this is a mercenary undertaking. The Company won't offer backup, so it's us or nothing. An unsanctioned mission is exactly as it sounds. Schatz resigned his commission, so we're here at the request of his former AD. Take us or leave us," Olmos taunted with a snide look on his face.

Gabby held up his hand. "We'll take you. The auction is supposed to take place tomorrow night, so let's get some rest. We'll meet at 0700 to finalize our strategy."

We all nodded and retired to our rooms. Nemo went into the room across the suite from mine and was snoring loudly when I came out of the shared bathroom adjacent to the sitting room after brushing my teeth. I set my alarm for 0500 to double back on my intel, taking a different path through the Dark Web to ensure nothing changed. Thankfully, I found the site again, and the clocks on top of the ads for each child were still running down. I checked our bid to see it was still the top bid for Mia Boone, and I sighed in relief. Things were still a go, so I went back to my bedroom to try to get some sleep.

We can't fuck this up. That was the only thought in my head before I dozed off. Twenty kids depended on us. Success was our only option.

My dreams were tumultuous during the few hours I was able to doze, and when I woke before my alarm at 0500, I opened my laptop sitting on the bed next to me to see the auction site I'd been following had been taken down. "Nemo, we need to go," I shouted as I hopped up from my bed and began dressing quickly, grabbing the Kevlar and the Glock I had in my possession.

I shoved my computer equipment into my bag to take along and rushed out of our room and down to Gabby's, pounding on the door until he opened it. "The fuck?" he asked.

"The site's been taken down. I'm afraid they're moving the hostages. We have to get out to the compound to stop them," I insisted before moving on to Mathis' room, scaring the fuck out of him as well.

A half-hour later, we drove to the compound to see all of the buildings were ablaze. If those children were still inside any of those structures, they were dead. If they weren't inside, they were lost to us. Neither was the desired outcome, and I wanted to crawl into a hole and pull it in over my head. As I scanned the looks on my colleague's faces, I saw none of them felt any different than me. We'd failed, and it was a painful pill to swallow.

I had no idea how Gabe would be able to tell Kelly Boone and his mother that the little girl they loved and cherished was either dead or moved to another location, but as I looked at Mathis Sinclair, I could see he was heartbroken. The tears rolling down his face had me crying some of my own. I was right there with him. It shouldn't have happened, but it did, and it fucking sucked.

When we returned to the hotel, I decided to wait outside for Olmos and Marquez, who had been unreachable when I'd called them five times on the way to the compound, to arrive. They showed up late to the party, and I needed to know why. When they strolled up to the front porch of the hotel, I approached them and steered them into the lobby which was empty so early in the morning. "Where were y'all? We coulda used your help," I asked.

"For what? Did you call us? Our phones didn't ring one time. Oh, wait. Are you using US cells because sometimes they don't get good reception down here?" Marquez asked with a smirk, obviously taking me for a fucking moron. I'd received their text the day before without one fucking problem. They were lying.

I took a deep breath because losing my temper showed weakness, or so Julie used to tell me. Something was fishy about the whole operation, and I didn't like it. "How do you guys know Ian Mallory?" I asked.

"He was assigned to the Mexico City office for a while. He's a friend," Olmos replied.

I took a deep breath and nodded. "Did either of you ever run into a field agent named Julien Renfro?"

When neither of them gave me any reaction, I definitely knew something was fucked up. Marquez looked at me, no humor in his face—and no accent in his voice. "Look, Schatz. This mission was fucked from jump, so it's best if you don't call in anymore favors because you're done with the Company. Your record is sealed, so let it go.

"Mallory was humoring you, because you went off the rails when you walked off the job, and he believed you might be suicidal, but after this colossal cluster fuck, it will be better if you just fade into the woodwork. You don't want a wet team stalking your ass because you've been deemed a danger to the public at large, do you? I mean, you put all of your coworkers in danger by mishandling information you obtained illegally in the first place. That's not the hallmark of a sane man, Schatz.

"Ian said we'll let this security breach slide but stay out of the Company's servers unless you want to see the inside of a TS/SCI penal facility that makes Abu Ghraib look like a fucking trip to Disneyland. That's your only warning," Olmos told me before he and Marquez left the hotel grounds.

I sat in the lobby for an indeterminable amount of time before I walked out to the pool and considered throwing myself into it to drown. The sad thing was I had strong survival instincts, as I'd learned from a psych test I had to take during my training to work for my former employer. I'd fight against drowning to stay alive though I had no real reason I could think of at the moment. Hell, I couldn't even kill myself properly because I didn't check the fucking revolver for bullets the last time. I was so completely pathetic it was… Well, it was pathetic.

I went back to my room to find Nemo on the couch in the sitting room. He looked quite upset as he sat with a bottle of water. "What's wrong with you?" I asked as I turned on the lamp in the room to see him crying.

"My baby sister died. She had a kidney transplant about six years ago, and everything was goin' well, but her body started rejecting the kidney a few weeks ago. I was with her in North Carolina when she started dialysis again and was put back on the transplant list, but I came back when Gabby called me and told me about this case. She died about an hour ago," he explained quietly.

Well, isn't this just the worst fucking luck in the world? What the hell have I done to the universe that it turned against me so fucking hard?

I had no responses from the heavens. I was on my own.

Later that morning, Gabby and Nemo took the charter jet to head to North Carolina. The rest of us were going to get a boat back to the mainland and fly commercial out of Ensenada to El Paso where we would get another flight to New York. Getting to Isla Cedros on a private plane was a hell of a lot more convenient than getting off that fucking eyesore.

"So, we're not leaving until tomorrow morning. What do we want to do today?" Mathis Sinclair asked as we all sat by the pool eating a late breakfast. A group of people from both offices of Golden Elite Associates were going to fly to North Carolina for the funeral, but I didn't know Nemo well enough to go, so I'd volunteered to stay behind and mind the store. I had a lot of decisions to make as I re-evaluated all of the mistakes I'd made in the kidnapping case of Mia Boone. Somewhere in my investigative research, I'd fucked up. I was sure I'd retrace my steps for years because I couldn't figure it out, and I couldn't live with failure.

Smokey finished his eggs and cleared his throat after he wiped his mouth, placing his napkin back in his lap. "I don't know about y'all, but I'd like to get back out to that compound and look at those buildings now that they're not still burning. I don't believe it's a coincidence they were set on fire and still burning when we got there.

"It's all a little too convenient for me, and those two douchebags from the Mexico Field office had no intentions of helping us in the first place. Something else is up; I feel it in my gut. I kept Popeye with me," the man stated as he held up a small pistol he'd retrieved from his boot. The remainder of the guns had been taken back to the States with Gabby and Nemo on the charter jet because the rest of us couldn't fly commercial with firearms on our persons.

Mathis looked at Smokey and chuckled. "How are you going to get that back into the country?"

Smokey exhaled and sat back, studying the Beretta Px4. "I've had him a long time, and maybe it's time to trade him for something a bit different. Anyway, let's rent a dune buggy and ride out there. I'd like to see what they left behind because every firefly leaves a trail," he told us.

We signed the check for breakfast and walked to the front desk to rent a dune buggy to take us to the compound without attracting much attention, or so we hoped. Smokey was a demolitions man from what I remembered, and if there was anything to find, I was sure he'd catch it. They all had skills that amazed me.

We approached the compound from the back where the fence had collapsed, whether it was torn down or had fallen due to lack of maintenance. In the light of day, it wasn't nearly as daunting as it had been that morning before the sun rose. We left the buggy outside the fence and walked onto the grounds, accompanying Smokey as he slowly meandered through the remains of the first building.

"What's he trying to find?" I whispered to Mathis who was standing next to me as we watched the man shift through the ashes, clearly looking for something. Every once in a while, he'd lift ash to his nose and sniff before he tossed it down and moved on.

"He's an ordinance expert—demolition man for Special Forces before he left the Army. If there's something irregular about the fires, he'll find it. He's probably sniffing for accelerants. Gabe says he's one of the best he's ever met," Mathis offered, watching every move Smokey made.

"How come you don't have a codename?" I whispered again as Smokey took a pen from the pocket of his shirt and moved debris around, picking up a small piece of something and slipping it into a plastic bag I recognized as the trash can liner from his room.

"I don't know. Guess I'm not cool enough because I wasn't in the military. Just a plain ol' cop," Mathis joked a little before sadness flooded his features again. I glanced to see Smokey was holding a piece of burned cloth as he squatted in the debris of one of the buildings and used his fingers to sift through some rubble. He came up with a partially scorched can and walked over to us, holding both things in his soot-covered hands.

I saw the can was a "Coke," and the cloth was a piece of singed knit material with small purple flowers stained with black ash. "Someone was here before they set these buildings on fire. They used an accelerant and sparked them individually. Not a bomb because there's no shrapnel. These buildings would have splintered if they were blown, but the steel roof and siding simply caved in when the wooden supports burned away. The fire was hot which made some of it buckle, but it's still intact enough that I can see there are no bone fragments in that mess. I'm guessing nobody died in these fires.

"I wanna check the other buildings to see if they separated the captives, then we can go. I believe you, Casper—those kids were here. I just want some proof to show Gabby. Let's get on with it and get back to town. I believe I wanna get drunk," Smokey informed us. I sure as hell wished I could do the same. If ever a time called for tequila, it was that moment.

MAXI

"Would you mind taking care of our place while we go out of town? Gabe's coming home from North Carolina to pick us up and go back for the funeral of Raleigh's younger sister. We're taking the kids with us for this one, but I need someone to check on the house and pets from time to time.

"It seems their last case didn't go well, and Lawry's really taking it hard. He feels like he let the team down by not having all of the information they needed to stop something bad from happening. Gabe won't give me details, not surprisingly, but I've seen Lawry moping around here enough since they got back from Mexico to believe he's teetering on the edge of the wagon. Hell, I'm not sure if he's even going to stick around here or if he'll hit the road again, so if you'd sort of house sit, I'd appreciate it," Dexter explained to me as I sat in my office on Thursday morning.

I'd been waiting to hear from Lawry when he returned from whatever he was doing in Mexico, but the call never came. I wasn't sure why, but having Dexter call me was honestly a blessing. "Sure. Of course. When do you need me?" I asked as I checked my calendar to see I was actually in the clear regarding that weekend and into the next week. My people had everything under control.

"If you could come by after work today, that would be great," Dex informed.

"I'll be there at—what time are you going to the airport?" I asked him as I quickly jotted down a list of things I needed to take with me. House sitting wasn't exactly my thing, but Dexter Torrente didn't ask for anything I couldn't do, really, and he'd entrusted me with celebrations which were important to his family and had raised my standard of living considerably, so I owed him. I would gladly repay my debt to my friend, especially with Lawry Schatz in the mix.

"We're leaving this afternoon at four. You don't have to leave work early. Wait until you're finished with your day. I'll leave you a note regarding Magic and Sparkles care. I'll change out Dylan's sheets so you can use his room," Dexter suggested.

"No, Dex. Of course, I'll be there to see you off. How about I drop by at noon so you can show me the routine for the mongrel and the feline. I've never had a pet," I informed Dexter, who laughed.

"Don't share that information with Searcy and Dylan because they'll demand to stay here to ensure you do it right. Anyway, that's perfect. It's not hard to care for them, but I'll feel better if you're around for backup. If Lawry's state of mind deteriorates any further, I'm not sure what we'd come home to," Dexter stated. His comments had me quite worried.

At five before twelve, I rang the bell at Dex and Gabe's home. Gabe opened the door and smiled at me, the sexy fucker. "Thanks for coming over. Casper's in a bad place, so I can't depend on him to care for the pets, and if something happens to Magic or Sparkles, the kids will hang me by my thumbs. We appreciate your help, Maxi."

The big guy took my duffel and invited me inside. "Dex is upstairs packing things for the kids to take along. Lawry's at a meeting, I think. I hate we're leaving this on your watch, but the shit that happened in Mexico hit the man hard. Fuck, Mathis has taken off as well, and I have no idea what the fuck to do about either of them.

"I'm not happy with the outcome of the case, but it wasn't our fault. We tried, but we were too late. The fucking FBI should have been all over that shit in the first place. It all fucking stinks," Gabe hissed as he walked into the kitchen and motioned for me to follow.

There were at least a dozen expensive liquor bottles, empty on the counter. I knew I had a look of confusion on my face at the sight.

"We got rid of the liquor because of Lawry, but if he gets out of hand and causes you any problems, here's Bull's number. Call him. I already left him a head's up voicemail to alert him there might be trouble, so he won't be surprised if you call him.

"Don't deal with Lawry on your own, Maxi. Call his brother and tell him to come get him because we have enough on our plate right now. We appreciate you stepping up on this," Gabe told me as running feet hammered down the stairs. We both turned to see Dylan and Searcy holding hands.

"I'll clean the litter box before we leave," Dylan offered.

I walked over to him and knelt down, taking his hands. "I've got it under control, I promise. I'll make sure Magic and Sparkles are just fine. You take care of your family, okay? Tell Mr. Wallis I'm sorry for his loss, will you?" I whispered to the boy.

"Thanks, Maxi. I feel better knowing you're gonna be here," Dylan assured as he hugged me around the neck. I went through the same discussion with Searcy and Dexter before Gabe finally shuffled them off to the SUV one of his guys was driving to take them to Kennedy for their flight to North Carolina. When I finally closed the door after they left, I sat down to await the return of the man I was most concerned about, Lawry Schatz.

Fifteen minutes later, feet were stomping on the front porch. I went to the dining room window with Magic hot on my heels as I glanced out through the curtains to see Lawry sitting on the steps, taking off his muddy sneakers. I put the leash on the dog and opened the door, stepping out onto the porch. "You should take him with you when you run. He needs the exercise as well," I announced as Magic wagged his tail inching closer to Lawry and licking the sweat on his right bicep.

The handsome man turned to look at the dog and smiled. "Hey, buddy. You think we should run together? Maybe I can get you run over by a car so I can totally devastate your family like I did the Boones?"

That didn't sound like the man I was so fond of, and it bothered me. The guy I'd spent some time with, before he ran off to Mexico in an attempt to save a teen girl, which apparently had gone all kinds of wrong, was actually fun to be around. I knew, however, the man had a dark side. I'd witnessed it first-hand once and never wanted to see—nor feel—it again.

I understood where Lawry was coming from with his self-deprecating comment regarding getting poor Magic run over, but I wasn't going to allow him to sink into a pit of despair. I hated that he wanted to blame himself for what happened. Lawry had told me that he had things in hand before they left for Mexico, and I believed him. Something got fucked up, but in my gut, I knew Lawry Schatz wasn't to blame. He was too kind and too intelligent to have made a mistake that brought the whole thing down. If he couldn't see it, I could.

"Now, that'll be enough of that bullshit," I instructed as I led Magic into the front yard and allowed him enough of the lead to sniff around the place. I felt Lawry's eyes on me, which was ridiculous, but when I glanced up to the stairs of the front porch, I saw him staring at me, concern evident on his handsome face.

After Magic left a healthy deposit in the side yard, I picked it up in the plastic bag Dexter had reminded me they kept in the kitchen pantry and disposed of the waste, trying not to gag. Cleaning up dog debris wasn't a favorite pastime for me, but it was a favor I owed to my dear friend, so I did it without complaint.

"I could have taken care of the animals just fine. Why'd they call you to come to the rescue and fuck up your weekend?" Lawry asked.

I took a deep breath and jumped off the ledge. I'd likely piss off the man, but there came a time when one had to commit to a course of action, and I was at that point. I did, however, choose my words carefully. "I think they thought you'd be too preoccupied with beating yourself up to look out for anyone or anything, starting with yourself. What happened, Lawry?" I asked, hoping he'd open up. Of course, it wouldn't go that easy.

"I fucked up and trusted the wrong people. I'm afraid I cost twenty kids their lives, one way or another. I'm leaving town tomorrow anyway so it's good you're here to take care of them," he explained as he nodded toward the dog and cat that had wandered outside on the porch.

After I had Magic in the house, I let him off the leash and watched as the cat ambled back inside, which was a relief because I knew Searcy would be upset if Sparkles ran away. I turned to look at Lawry Schatz who was standing in the open doorway. "So, what? Am I just trash by the road to you? You have no respect for me at all, do you? You once told me your boyfriend was a self-loathing fag. Are you one as well?"

I wanted to slap myself for admitting how much it hurt to hear him say he was leaving the next day. I wanted a fucking relationship with him, but apparently, I was the fool. He had no desire to stay around and make a new life for himself, which maybe could include me. He didn't want me. How stupid was I to even believe someone like Lawry Schatz could want a queen like me?

Suddenly, there were strong arms around my shoulders and a damp chest against my cheek. The smell of sweat, aftershave, and pure essence of the man caught me off guard. "I don't hate myself because I'm gay, Max. I hate myself because I'm not good enough for *you*. I wasn't good enough for Julien, and he didn't stay. I don't want you to decide to leave me as well. It's better..." he began before I pulled away and grabbed him by the straps of his tank top, slamming him into the hallway wall.

I looked into his eyes, not surprised to see so much sadness. "So, you're going to leave me just like people have always left me? Great. I keep my distance from people under most circumstances because I don't like being left behind. I find I don't want to keep my distance from you, but it won't matter, will it? Fuck you. Are you going to walk away like my parents? Like my grandparents when they died and left me with nobody when I was twenty?"

The tears were falling down my cheeks unbidden, and for the life of me, I had no idea I still harbored those pesky feelings of abandonment I believed I'd gotten over a long time ago. When had it ever felt good to have people you love walk away from you?

Love? WTF?

I reached up to wipe my eyes but before my hand could make

purchase, there were gentle fingers on my cheeks. I opened my eyes and looked up into those bright, green eyes to see they were watery, as well. "Please don't cry. I'm sorry, okay? You mean a lot to me, Max. You're the only person who really gave me a chance to be myself after all of that other bullshit. I guess I have some unfinished business that drags me down," he explained.

I swallowed and sniffled a bit, wishing I had a tissue. I was surprised to see Lawry Schatz produce a white handkerchief from the pocket of his running shorts. He offered it to me, and that was when I saw the small, blue "L" and "S" embroidered in the corner of the white cotton cloth.

I dried my eyes and wiped my nose on another corner, holding up the embroidered letters to him. "This is cute. Who did this?"

I looked up to see Lawry's face light up like I hadn't witnessed previously. "My sister, Jewel. She makes them for me for Christmas. Well, she makes them for me, Hank, Reed, and she made some for Julien, but he wouldn't carry them. He just tossed them into a drawer.

"I always have a handkerchief in my pocket because according to my father, you weren't a gentleman if you didn't have a handkerchief for moments just like this. Of course, my dad said it was for if you ever found a pretty girl who was crying, you should give her an embroidered handkerchief, so she'd want to get it back to you after she laundered it. Mom used to make them for all of us, but when Jewel was thirteen, she took over the task," Lawry explained with a grin, which touched my heart.

"Tell me about her. She sounds very sweet," I offered, glad to have Lawry talking instead of wallowing—or leaving.

"I believe you might have met her at Gabby and Dexter's wedding," Lawry offered.

I racked my brain for a young woman I might have met at that wedding, but I was running around like crazy that day and barely remembered any of the guests. "I'm sorry, but I don't remember…" I began before Lawry pulled out his phone to show me a picture of him with a little girl with brown hair and a huge smile. She had features that were common for people with…

"Oh, I remember her now. She wore the pale, pink dress and

managed to coax Searcy to walk down the aisle because that child was petrified to go out there alone. That's your sister?" I asked as I admired the picture on his phone. Her smile was huge and inviting. I definitely remembered her.

"She's a savant, actually. That's what they call kids with special needs who have unexplainable talents. Jewel can play the piano like Billy Joel, and she has the voice of an angel. She has Down's Syndrome, but she's high functioning. She attends a regular high school, and aside from math and science, both of which she hates, she's doing very well. She's on track to graduate with the rest of her class," he explained with pride.

I took a deep breath. "I'd like to meet Jewel again. Maybe sit down and talk to her about her music? She had the adorable cat-eye shaped glasses, right?" I asked, remembering her look at the wedding, which was fabulous.

Lawry laughed. "Yeah. She says they're 'statement eyewear.' She has a friend, Josh Griffin, who keeps her current regarding teen slang. She's a sophomore in high school, and Josh is a junior. They have a steady gig during the holidays at a Saks store in St. Louis. Jewel won an award from the St. Louis Symphony for a score she wrote with my brother-in-law's mentoring. She did it herself, but Reed helped her with technical issues," Lawry explained.

I smiled. "That's fabulous, Lawry. You should go see your family," I offered, unable to believe the words were coming out of my mouth. It seemed to me, though, if his sister meant so much to him, maybe seeing her and spending some time with her would bring him back from the edge of something bad, where I believed he was teetering. Someone needed to guide him away from whatever self-imposed hell he was putting himself through.

I was surprised to feel a warm hand on my cheek. "My sister has plenty of people around to stroke her ego, and after today, I believe I'm needed here more than back in St. Louis. I believe you might need me more than anyone else," he offered with a cocked eyebrow. God knew he was right. My tirade regarding being left behind seemed to have struck a soft spot in Lawry Schatz.

The tears began rolling again, and I didn't try to stop them. I simply nodded to Lawry before there was the gentle brush of his lips over mine. It was like a lightning storm overtook my body as Lawry kissed me. It was magical.

His soft tongue swept over my mouth, and I found I had no strength, nor will, to stop him from kissing me. I wrapped my arms around his broad shoulders before he pulled me into his body. It was absolutely the most amazing feeling in the world.

I had no idea how long Lawry Schatz worshiped my mouth, but I didn't even try to push him away. I knew in an instant that it was too late for me because, during *that* kiss, I gave him my heart. I had no idea if he even wanted it, but it wasn't mine any longer. Of course, that wasn't something I felt I could ever tell him, but it had happened, nonetheless.

After our tongues tangled in each other's mouths, he gently brushed his mouth over my lips before stepping back to offer me a cracking smile. "I smell like a locker room. I'll be back, and then we can get some lunch or make something here? The office is officially closed, but I might check in later. I—I'm glad you're here," he told me as he kissed me gently on the lips again, before he bolted up the stairs of Gabby and Dexter's home. I stood at the bottom of those same stairs, still stunned as his kiss lingered on my lips. It was remarkable.

⁀

"So, *wait*. You could have gone to any college in the country, Ivy League and all that other stuff, but you chose to stay in St. Louis to be near your family?" I asked Lawry as we sat at Dex and Gabe's kitchen island enjoying some nachos I made from the contents of their fridge.

After Lawry showered and dressed, we binge-watched a show about a motorcycle gang I'd never seen. Lawry had recommended it, already having watched all but the last season and loving it, so he was happy to sit through it again. I agreed without hesitation, which I suspected I would do with anything the man suggested.

"Well, yeah, I mean, my family was nearby, and I guess I wasn't ready to leave them behind. Hank was still in the Army, and I missed him a lot, but I knew Mom and Dad *really* missed him because he rarely came home. I didn't want Jewel to feel lonely for *both* of her brothers, so I decided to stay in state.

"Hell, Mom did my laundry when I came home on weekends, and I always went back to the city with lots of food," he explained with a sexy grin, which made me laugh. He seemed to have a very kind soul, and I was deeply attracted to him.

We cleaned up the kitchen from our nacho fest and then we walked Magic. I searched the house for Sparkles' *presents* while Lawry raided the litter box before we sat down on the large couch in their family room with a gallon of ice cream and two spoons as we turned on the next season of the show we'd been watching.

"Did you… How the hell did you get caught up with the CIA?" I asked. Dex had spilled the beans about Lawry Schatz being a Spook, as Gabe had called him, so that wasn't a secret. I was sure he had many secrets, but his immediate past wasn't one.

He chuckled as he fed me a bite of the vanilla-salted-caramel-swirl we'd found in the chest freezer in the garage. The Torrente's kept a well-stocked home.

"You shouldn't know about any of this, but the short story? I had an advisor, Dr. Davis, ask me to come talk to him after I turned in my Masters' thesis. He was an odd duck, which is to say the guy was weird as fuck, but I liked him. He wasn't big on talking, but when he did speak, he was one of those guys everyone listened to without question.

"I sort of looked up to him, much like I admired Hank and my dad when I was growing up. Hell, I still do to this day if I'm honest. Neither are big talkers, but when they open their mouths, people listen.

"Anyway, there was this woman sitting in his office when I stopped by one day to check in at his request. I remember she reminded me of Margaret Thatcher a bit, but it wasn't her. As I took in her appearance, I was shocked to see it was the former Secretary of State. Not the one under Bush, the previous one.

"I was totally freaked out because there I was, a kid from a small town in Missouri looking at a woman who had made history. She smiled at me and introduced herself, offering her hand to shake. I took a seat next to her because I was about to hyperventilate, but she touched my shoulder. 'Now, I'm not that great. Heavens, I was only as great as those I depended upon, and from what Dr. Davis tells me, you have a knack for information technology. Have you ever thought about being of service to your country?' she'd asked me. Until that moment, I'd dreamed of a life in Silicon Valley, working for a tech firm or maybe a gaming company if I got so lucky.

"I was provided a cover my family could accept, that I was a software engineer, and I went directly into training after I was conferred my degree. I worked all over the world for a while until I settled into the Dallas field office, which is where I met Julien. For four years, I devoted myself to the Company, and then Julien and I became serious. He transferred to another division when everything changed between us, and I thought I had my future at my feet. Well, you know the rest," Lawry told me as we continued to feed each other ice cream.

I nodded, offering a chuckle because Lawry had slid the spoon up from my mouth and had left ice cream on my nose. He laughed as well, and in that solitary moment, I had hope for us. He had issues, of course, but I believed him to be capable of moving forward. That was all I needed to know. There was that pot of gold at the end of our rainbow I never thought I'd find.

Later that night, I woke in Lawry's arms on the large couch, having fallen asleep in the middle of one of the episodes of the show we were binging. The ice cream had melted but thankfully hadn't leached out onto the beautiful rug under the coffee table. I'd replace the ice cream, but I never wanted to replace the feeling of Lawry holding me.

After I woke Lawry, the two of us went up to his room, and he wrapped those long arms around me while we laid on top of the comforter on the guest bed where he slept. In my heart, I didn't believe I'd ever felt so much contentment in my life. It didn't seem possible to feel so safe, but there I was, lying on my right side as the man's strong arms kept me tucked tightly into his body. It was pretty fucking incredible for me, little Maxim Partee from Lafourche Parish, Louisiana. I was afraid to wish for it for the rest of my life.

LAWRY

"Come on, dude! You should be able to lay me out flat. You've got the height advantage here," Mathis Sinclair complained as we sparred on the mats in the basement of the Victorian. The new guy, Duke Chambers, was working with us, and with the Torrente family still in North Carolina with Nemo, we had time on our hands. Mathis had taken some time off after Mexico, but he was back and eager to get to work. I was right along with him, all thoughts of taking a road trip gone like the wind. There was nowhere I'd rather be than in New York.

"Jackass, which is gonna be your codename as far as I'm concerned, I'm a lover, not a fighter," I told him as I swiped at my bloody nose with the stupid boxing glove on my hand. Sure, I had trained at Langley and went to the training base in southern Virginia for a month of hell, but I wasn't the guy who was going to beat anyone's ass in hand-to-hand. That was my brother, though I was a pretty good marksman as I'd proven the day before when we went to the shooting range out in Woodhaven where Gabby kept a membership.

Mathis chuckled as he untied the laces with his teeth before he shook off the gloves on his hands. We were both still suffering the aftershocks from the failed mission in Isla Cedros, I could tell. I wasn't sure what to say to the man because words weren't exactly my strong suit. The two of us working out some aggression on each other over the loss of an innocent little girl seemed to be the best apology I had to offer the guy.

I untied the laces as well and shook off my gloves, beginning to unwrap the cotton padding from my fists. "You talk to Kelly Boone about what happened? I've got an alert set on anything regarding those kids, an auction, or that gang. I feel like shit about that," I honestly offered to him.

Mathis nodded. "Gabe said he called him on the flight back to North Carolina with Nemo, but I went to see him in southern Virginia. He was in a bad way, man. He said his mother was fucked up about it, as well. If anything about it crosses your path, let me know, night or day, okay? I'm not holding you responsible because I know how this shit works, but if there's ever any information, contact me, will you?

"I'm taking some time off while we're on stand down to help my dad at the church in Queens. If you need me, just call or text, and I'll find you. Thanks for doin' this, today, Casper. I needed to blow off some steam," he informed as we fist bumped. I felt as if my knuckles were broken, so it hurt more than necessary, but the guy needed to get out the pent-up hostility due to a failed mission, and I supposed I did, too, once I thought about it.

"Check in with me, Jackass!" I called as he gathered his things. His loud laugh made me smile, which I needed to do more than anything.

Duke Chambers stepped onto the mat to retrieve the boxing gloves Mathis and I had left. "You need to work out more if you're going to be in the field. I'm glad to know you can shoot, but you're a big guy, and you could develop a lot of muscle, which would go in your favor against an enemy combatant.

"Sinclair is cut, but with your height, you *should* have had him on his ass most of the time," the man stated. The jury was still out with me regarding whether I liked him or not. Something seemed a bit shady about the guy, but who was I to judge? I wasn't exactly a pillar of integrity.

I'd basically walked away from my job at the Company without any notice or any concern about leaving all of my cases unattended. Maybe that was why Ian Mallory set me up with those two assholes in Mexico? I got the fucking message, for sure.

"Yeah, well, I'll work on it, okay?"

I hurried upstairs and took a quick shower in Gabby's office, because I was planning to do a little research after everyone left that night. I'd stopped using the Wi-Fi at Gabby's house, because as careful as I was when I went out on the hunt, I never wanted to implicate the Torrente's in my misdeeds. The network I'd revamped after Jian Chang had resigned was one I knew to be foolproof. I'd get in and out of places without a trace, much like a cat burglar, which was what I'd need to do if I was ever going to find out what really happened to Julien Renfro.

I was planning to hit the CIA's servers one last time before I gave up, because the last time I'd checked out Julien's file, there was a notation—Delaney Cartwright. I had no idea what that even meant, but I wanted another peek at the package. I needed more information regarding Julien because the fact he committed suicide still didn't add up to me. He tended to slant a little toward being sadistic, but suicide didn't fit the picture. The way things went down had driven me crazy for two years.

I called Mom and Dad to check in, and I had the happy opportunity to talk with my little sister. "I'm going to spend the summer with Reed and Hanky. Can you come visit?" Jewel asked, her sweet smile in her voice.

"I'll make time, I promise. What are Mom and Dad gonna do without you around to make trouble?" I asked her as a tease.

My sister giggled, which made me grin every time. "They'll miss me, but I get to spend time with Brock. He's so sweet, Lawry. You need to come home and get to know him better. Reed's teaching him sign language so he doesn't have to talk when he's uncomfortable with a bunch of people. I know how he feels sometimes.

"Brock likes learning new things a lot. He's also taking piano lessons. Oh! Hanky got a promotion at the Casino," Jewel explained. It reminded me I needed to call my brother to check in with him soon.

"That's great. How's your friend, Josh? Big plans for the summer?" I asked her, happy to hear her upbeat personality shine over the phone.

"His dads are taking him on a long trip to Europe over the summer. We'll still be able to talk on Facebook and email, but I'll miss him. He's excited to get away, though. When can you come visit? I miss you," she told me, which made my heart ache to see my family.

"I'll make time soon, I swear. I might bring a friend if you think Reed and Hank won't care," I offered, wondering exactly when I had lost my fucking mind. Maxim Partee was a wonderful man, but I seriously doubted he'd be down for the *meet-the-family* routine, especially since all we'd done was share meals and walk Magic together, while Gabe and Dex were still with Nemo in North Carolina. There I was letting my heart lead me into something too fast, just as I had with Julien. I needed to stop being so naïve and get my shit together before it was too late.

"What's his name?" Jewel asked without prompting.

I chuckled. "How do you know it's a guy?"

"Because you sound happy, Lawry. You haven't sounded happy in a long time. What's his name?" she pressed, *damn her*.

"Maxim Partee. You met..." I began.

"Oh, the wedding planner? He's pretty. I love his hair because it's like the sun. That's so great. Bring him home, please? I want to get to know him," she demanded before Mom took the phone.

"What's this, Lawrence? You've finally met someone decent?" Maureen Schatz interrogated. She wasn't nosy, really, but I knew she'd been worried about me for several years, and I owed it to her to provide proof I wasn't a fucking derelict. She had been there to see me at my worst because of Julien's harsh exit from life, so she had no love for the man any longer.

"I've become friends with Gabe's wedding planner, Maxim. He's a nice guy, and we hang out when we can. It's nothing serious, so talk Jewel into dialing it back before she starts practicing letters, Mom. It's not serious," I lied, twice.

I didn't know if it would ever be serious because we didn't broach the 'R' word, ever. Maxi seemed to have his own demons, and God knew I had mine. Pushing something between us seemed to be unfair to him. Hell, I didn't know if my heart would ever heal from the shit Julien had done to me.

Suicide. That's the gift that keeps on giving, and I was eternally grateful I hadn't been successful with my own attempt so my family would never have to feel how I sometimes felt when I allowed the awful shadows to invade my dreams. It fucking sucked.

"I'll call you next week, Mom. Love you. Hi to Dad," I offered in a quick goodbye.

Dad was getting ready to retire and sell his business to a rival, Franklin County Construction. Mom was grateful Dad was going to take time off and stick around the house more. She wanted someone around so she could smother… I mean mother them. Jewel was growing up and the fact my brother and I were nearing middle age didn't sit well with Mom. I was actually looking forward to seeing her with Brock. That would be a wonderful grandmother/grandson relationship to witness.

I thought about my parents, and I knew I'd never change one thing about them. They kept me breathing, after all. That was a gift many people didn't have. How could I hate it?

I sat on the floor of the media room in Gabby and Dex's home with Magic and Sparkles curled up on either side of me, both sound asleep. There was an old Robert Redford/Barbra Streisand movie playing on their big screen because I was feeling nostalgic. It was one I remembered Mom watching every time it was on television, and she cried at the end as if it was the first time she'd ever seen it. The ending didn't change. They didn't stay together, but they made peace. Mom always wanted them to get back together, bless her. Even in the movies, shit didn't work out perfectly.

I'd downloaded everything I could find on the CIA's server regarding 'Delaney Cartwright' before I left the office earlier in the evening. When I dug a little deeper into the files, I found an archive notation, "REDACTED," which wasn't helpful. It was indicative of an operative whose identity was removed from the Company records for undisclosed reasons, and that shit wasn't helpful to someone like me—someone who wasn't supposed to be snooping through their shit in the first place.

It was frustrating as hell to hit that roadblock, but it was another question in a long line of questions I had regarding the identity of Delaney Cartwright and why he/she was linked to Julien's expunged file. Nothing was ever really gone from the internet, and nothing was ever clear when one left the CIA.

Those thoughts prompted an idea, so for the hell of it, I typed the name into a public search engine to see nothing of interest on the regular web, really. There had to be a reason why the Company had that name annotated on Julien's file, and I needed to find out why. The name meant nothing to me, but those crazy bastards didn't make notations on files for nothing.

Much against my common sense and better judgment, I decided to hit the CIA server one last time. I was using several back channels, where I'd previously left breadcrumbs to get me back in, including a Russian marketing agency because it wouldn't be a surprise to the Company to find Russians trying to crack in again. Once I cleared the second level of security and was inside the network, I typed in 'Cartwright' to see what would happen.

The name *Eliana Richard* came up, which was of interest. I knew her to be a friend of Julien's. It was another piece of the puzzle, but I needed to know how she was tied to someone named Cartwright. I checked the clock on my phone to see I'd been in long enough, so I backed out and sent in a worm to drill holes in my path, just to be sure.

There were pounding footsteps on the stairs, and I knew who it was immediately. The door opened and bounced against the stopper. Suddenly, Dylan grabbed Searcy's hand. "*Shh!* He's watchin' a movie."

I hopped up and stalked toward them, turning on the lights in the room. "You interrupted my favorite movie," I growled out as I picked up Searcy and blew a raspberry against her cheek. Her giggle made life worth living.

Dylan laughed as I messed with his hair, seeing his bright smile as he pushed up his glasses. "How are you guys?" I asked as I placed my hand on his back and guided us downstairs to the living room where Gabby was sorting through the mail as Dexter was watering the few plants they had in the living room.

When he approached an orchid, I *tsked* him. "I watered. One shot glass, once a week. I'm good at taking directions, *Zen Master*," I joked, seeing my boss and his husband look at me with surprise on their handsome faces.

Dexter walked over and took Searcy from my arms, nuzzling her neck for a second before he turned her to look at him. "Go upstairs and get your shower, sweetheart. It's late, and Nana Irene is taking you guys into the city tomorrow. Thank Lawry for taking care of Magic and Sparkles," he instructed. Dylan and Searcy both hugged me and kissed my cheeks before they took off upstairs.

"Everything looks spotless," Dexter stated as he moved the luggage to the bottom of the stairs.

I decided to fuck with them a little. "Well, you can thank the crew I hired to come through and clean up the place after the other night. They patched the holes in the walls and matched the paint perfectly," I stated before I walked into the kitchen and grabbed myself a flavored tea from the fridge, waiting for both of them to process what I'd said.

Gabby started laughing as he watched Dex get wound up just as I'd expected. Before the *Zen Master* could get too excited, he looked around and giggled. "Fuck you, Casper," he teased as he walked over and hugged me.

"I got to give you a codename, Zen Master. Oh, I gave Mathis one. Jackass," I joked as the two of them continued going through their mail. They'd been gone for nearly two weeks. I was glad they were supporting Nemo as he coped with his sister's death and whatever family issues needed to be dealt with, but, honestly, I was glad they were home. I'd missed all of them.

"I heard from Duke that Mathis kicked your ass on the mats. Surely you can hold your own, Casper. He's about half the size of you," Gabby joked. I flipped him off and sipped my peach tea.

"How's Maxi?" Dexter looked at me with a cocked eyebrow, which I should have expected. The two men were good friends, I knew, and, after all, Dex had summoned the hottie to babysit me. The kissing we did and the talks we had were just bubbles in champagne, but I wasn't telling the two of them about it. Max and I would progress at our own pace without their help.

"I'm guessing he's fine," I offered, not telling Dexter that Max had been staying at their home, safe in my arms, until that morning. The conversations the man and I had shared were better than I could even imagine. I'd never had that type of chemistry with anyone—even Julien.

Dex turned to Gabby and smiled. "I'm going up to unpack and take a soak." I saw the large Italian man smile and nod, which I was guessing was code for the two of them.

Gabby leaned around my body and watched Dexter walk away. He shook his head and chuckled as he finished glancing through the mail, tossing a bunch in the trash after ripping it up. He looked at me and smiled. "You okay? Shit under control?" he asked.

Yeah, he had a right to ask because I'd been a fucking mess after Cedros. I still wanted to look into that shit some more, but I had another blip on my radar I was sure he wouldn't support. He'd asked me not to put his family in danger regarding how I got the information I collected to assist us, and I was trying my best to keep my word. I needed to do one last thing to keep my promise to myself—I had to know what Julie was working on that brought him to take his own life.

"I think I need to take a little time off. I have to try to find out what happened to Julien, Gabby. I'm trying to move on, I swear, but his behavior before he left for his last assignment? It makes no fucking sense.

"I'd like to go to Italy and use the cover of Giuseppe's organization to check into some things. I don't want any of you to get into trouble because of me, but Julien Renfro would never kill himself. Hell, he was too fucking afraid of his parents to even consider it." It was the God's honest truth. Julie would never defy his parents. He was too much of a Momma's boy.

"You wasted a lot of good liquor, Gabe. I'm sorry I haven't earned your trust that I'd live up to my promise of not going back down that road. I'm not an alcoholic. I guess I'll have to work a little harder to prove it to all of you," I observed.

I tried to keep the bite out of my voice because it really chapped my ass that people thought so little of my word, but I had to remind myself, I'd been drunk and high for two years. What else would they think of me?

MAXI

Friday mornings were always chaotic in my little slice of Heaven on earth—Brooklyn, to be precise. Most of our events took place on the weekends, so Friday was the day we checked our lists, loaded the trucks, and set up the venues. I was clearing invoices, ensuring the checks had been written and fees collected to be sure the bills were paid. It was a smooth routine we'd cultivated over the years, and it hadn't failed me yet.

"Maxi, there's a call for you on one. It's Lawry Schatz," Toni informed me as she stepped into my office. I reached for my cell, seeing it was dead. I'd meant to plug it into the charger when I arrived at the office that morning, but there was a minor emergency involving missing rings for one of the weddings that weekend, and Fredrik was losing his fucking mind when I walked in after stopping for my caffeine fix.

When it all washed out, one of the grooms' mothers had picked up the rings at the jewelry store in Manhattan while she was picking up her husband's tuxedo. It was a lot of drama about nothing, but that was Fredrik's specialty, bless him, so I assumed it bled into his friends' behaviors as well.

"Thanks, doll." I glanced at the phone to see the flashing light, but

I held back the smile. Lawry and I hadn't spoken since the morning Dex and Gabe returned from North Carolina. I'd fretted on it a bit, but I'd drowned myself in work so as not to become manic. If the man were really interested, he'd call. I wasn't going to beg. Maxim Partee didn't beg anyone for anything. *Maxim Partee needs to stop referring to himself in the third person before someone labels him as crazy and slaps his ass into a sanitarium.* Yeah, that was right, as well.

I picked up the phone and took a breath before I hit the button for the line. "Hi. How are you?" I asked, trying to sound calm, which was a fool's mission because my heart was nearly beating out of my chest.

"Am I interrupting you?" Lawry asked.

I chuckled a bit, trying to gather myself. "Interrupting me from *something*? Always, but it's fine. How have you been?"

"New day, same crazy. I'd like us to have dinner tonight. Can you make time? I know you're probably swamped, but I'd like to see you," Lawry asked, surprising the shit out of me. "You're going home tonight, right?" Where the hell else was I going? The man was like a jumping bean if those were even still a thing. From one idea to the next with no segue whatsoever. It took a lot of energy to keep up with him.

"Eventually. What's going on, Lawry? I know you're upset, and I'm willing to listen. I'm not the one who is keeping secrets." I wasn't trying to piss him off, but something was creeping around the edges of whatever was going on between us, and it had me worried.

"I need to look into something, which means I'm going to need to go to Italy. I'd like us to have tonight together before I leave. I'm not sure where things will lead or when I'll be back, but I want to spend time with you. Can we go out?" he asked, sounding quite serious.

Part of me wanted to give him hell for not calling earlier in the week when things were slower. I had so much going on at that moment, he could never begin to imagine it, but then again, if he hadn't called, I'd have been more pissed at him. I had the misfortune of falling in love with the man, and damn my hide, I'd make time for him.

If his trip was going to be the end of us, then we needed to give the brief affair a proper send off. Having him out of the country so I could grieve the loss would help. I'd lick my wounds after he left, and I'd bounce right back like I always did. I was fucking resilient, after all—and rather bendy, thanks to Dex's yoga classes.

I took a deep breath and plowed forward. "I'll be home by nine. I'll bring food. There's a key under the green frog in the garden. Let yourself in. Have a drink if you want one. I'm sure I'll need a few," I offered as I stood still and considered my options.

Every relationship I'd ever had ended badly. Actually, I couldn't call those brief encounters relationships, but being with Lawry Schatz had been what I believed a relationship should be, even though we refused to recognize it for what I hoped it could become. Hell, I was actually afraid to define it as much as him because I'd never had one that worked before, and it didn't seem as if he had, either. *Why the hell should things work out for us?*

"It's not goodbye, Max. It's just temporary," he offered. I heard the sincerity, which was believable. It wasn't that I didn't think he meant the words he'd said. It was that I knew he'd find someone else while he was gone, and I'd be a memory. *Not my first time at the party.*

"Okay. I'll see you around nine," I told Lawry before I hung up. "Fuck me," I hissed, knowing I'd be a wreck after it was all over.

I saw Key standing outside my office with a concerned look on his face, so I waved him off and sat down at my desk to double check the numbers and print the invoice for him to present to the family of the bride. We all had to pay the fucking piper, didn't we?

                        ~

I let myself into my home through the mudroom at about eight-forty-five. The lights were out, and I was concerned. I'd brought home two dishes—one for Lawry, and one for me. His was filet mignon with all the fixings, and mine was the eggplant parmesan. They were both easy to heat, but I didn't have an appetite anyway.

"Hello?" I called as I placed the containers on the counter in my kitchen. I heard music, so I followed the sound, surprised to see candles on various surfaces in my living room. Lawry was standing next to my fireplace which was lit with candles, thankfully, and not fire because it was fucking June. He was holding two glasses in his hands, sporting a sexy grin as he looked at me in the suit I was wearing. Of course, I'd gone to check on a rehearsal dinner, which was in full swing, before coming home. I had a business to run.

"Hello. I'm glad to see you looking so handsome. If you'd consent, I'd love to take that gorgeous suit off of you," Lawry suggested as he stepped forward and handed me a glass.

I laughed. What could I say? The man made me laugh, and it was one of the reasons I loved him. "Would you now, Mr. Schatz? To what should we toast?" I challenged. I saw a bottle of sparkling mineral water and a bottle of Torrente *Prosecco* in a bowl of ice resting on my coffee table with a towel under it, which was touching—and smart.

Lawry took my hand and pulled me closer. "Here's to what happens next. I'm not ending us, Max. I'm trying to clear the decks for our next step. You've shown me what I had before wasn't love. It was basically a co-dependent disaster. I just need to know what happened, okay, babe? I want to come back here to you. I want us to try to make a life together. I want to do it right, and until I've figured out what I don't know, I can't commit to you as I'd like.

"I'll get to the bottom of it because I want a future with you, sweetheart. We have a good shot at making a great life. I want it," Lawry told me as he touched his glass to mine and took a tiny sip, placing his glass on the table.

I sipped my glass as well, and then we proceeded to dance around my living room to an old song that was so romantic I nearly gagged. It was a moment I'd never forget, and I vowed to myself that if he broke my fucking heart, I'd hunt him down and kill him with my bare hands. One couldn't light up a lover the way Lawry Schatz lit me on fire and then douse the flame with sparkling ice water. It was terrifically unfair to even consider.

☙

"Fuck, Max," Lawry gasped as he gently pushed inside me from behind, wrapping his arms around my body as we both lost our minds. It was amazing. It felt incredible, but I wanted more.

"Harder. I need to feel you after you leave," I demanded as I looked over my left shoulder into his handsome face. He leaned over me and kissed my lips before he placed his hands on my hips and began pounding away, just as I wanted.

All plans to eat had evaporated like so much smoke as he flipped me onto my back and pushed into me again at a much slower and gentler pace. As we made love, which was all I could call it, I prayed the sexy man didn't disappear on me. I wanted him to be the man I believed he could be. The man I'd fallen in love with, not the man who would be shattered if he didn't get his answers or if he got the wrong ones from the wrong sources.

Lawry showed me love in every kiss, touch, nip, and mind-blowing thrust, though he hadn't articulated his feelings. It was fine. I could see it... feel it... absorb it. Unfortunately, I found myself *yearning* to hear it. I exploded between us, just as he exploded inside me. The swivel thing he did with his hips that pegged my prostate had me nearly unconscious.

"You're going where?" I asked as I tugged him closer after we were both spent.

"I'm going to Italy. Well, for my first stop. I'm not sure where my search might lead me, but I'll be back. I'm only going for a few weeks, Max. I'll be back before the Fourth of July. We can go see the fireworks together, yeah?" he asked.

Italy? What's in Italy? "Why? Why do you need to go to Italy?" I asked as I gently rubbed my hand over the soft curls on his chest. There weren't many, but it was sexy as hell. Lawry Schatz was sexy as hell, to be sure.

"Julien Renfro was not the kind of person to commit suicide. Ian Mallory told me he'd killed himself while he was on his last mission, and he made me think it might have something to do with me. I can't live with it, Max. I need to know the truth, because if I'm the worthless son of a bitch I believed myself to be after I was told Julie killed himself, then I'm nowhere near being good enough for someone like you.

"You're definitely levels above me, but for some crazy reason, I believe you might be falling in love with me, and I want to be worthy of that love, Max. I need to close one chapter before I open another,"

Lawry explained as he kissed my forehead. *He's right about that, but I'm not owning up to it quite yet.*

I bit his nipple, and he flinched, making both of us laugh, which was exactly what I was going for because things were too damn intense. The sex? It was other-worldly, to be sure, and it was precisely what I needed to keep me sane while he was gone. I didn't know what the hell he'd discover on his fact-finding mission, but if it was what he needed to do, then I had to let him go. If he never came back? Well, I had no power over his decisions, did I? We were all masters of our own fortunes, weren't we?

"I'll call you, babe. Don't let some guy slide in and sweep you off your feet at one of your events. I'll be back with a broom as quick as I can," Lawry told me the next morning while he waited for his Uber to take him to JFK. I'd made him a quick breakfast, poached eggs and bacon with toast, and he seemed to enjoy it.

I actually chuckled at his cheesy line, but it touched me as well. "I'm not a mouse. No need to set the trap with brie," I teased as he placed his dishes in the sink and pulled me into his arms. It was Saturday, but I wished he wasn't leaving until Monday. He was eager to get started on his quest, or whatever he was calling it. Based on the look on his face, he desperately needed closure regarding his ex. I just hoped I was his prize at the end of the journey.

Lawry laughed and gave me a kiss, a soft kiss worthy of an epic movie soundtrack. He gently peeled off the t-shirt I was wearing and smelled it. "I'm taking this with me. I left one of mine under your pillow. It's more than cheesy, but I will definitely miss you. Please miss me in return," he implored, which had me worried.

"Honey, I miss you already, so please, take care of yourself. Call me anytime, day or night. Be safe. If you need me, I can get on a plane, Lawry," I offered, feeling unease settle into my soul.

Lawry offered a sexy smirk in return. "I'll remember that, babe. You stay safe, as well. If you need anything and can't get me, call Gabby or Smokey. I—you know." His phone buzzed, and he grabbed his bag and rushed out to the curb where a car was waiting. After he tossed his bag into the trunk, he turned to me, smiled, and blew me a kiss. I took a deep breath and nodded before I closed the front door. If it was the last time I saw him, then it was a fitting goodbye.

⁂

Monday was a dreary fucking day. It was supposed to rain the entire week, and I hated the goddamn meteorologist when I heard the forecast. I stopped in front of the building I owned to see Shay's lights were on upstairs, so I dropped my umbrella and bag in my office. I made the two of us drinks and went upstairs. Shay was sitting in the chair at his station, cutting on his gorgeous hair. He was nearly bald, and I had to stop him.

"What the fuck are you doing?" I snapped as I placed his drink on his station and ripped the scissors from his hand. He had red eyes, and there were tear tracks on his face. Something wasn't right, and I needed to know what the hell had happened because the man I was looking at was a mere shadow of my beautiful friend.

"I met a guy. He was sexy as hell, and we fucked. I don't know his name because he didn't introduce himself, but I've seen him before. He said the sexiest things to me in French when we were fucking, and when I woke up, he was gone. No note. No number. I'm trying to shed myself of any pretense I'm desirable, so I'm cutting my hair. I'm just a convenient hole, so I need to…"

I grabbed Shay and held him in my arms, allowing him his breakdown. Hell, I was about five days away from feeling the hurt he was feeling. I knew that train was speeding down my tracks, and I was sure there was no way to prepare for it.

"No! You're not going to take that out on yourself. It's not your fault you hooked up with a guy who wasn't worthy of you, Shay. You had a one-night stand. We all do it. Hell, we need the release, so don't freak out, honey. It's his loss," I stated boldly. Unfortunately, I had a good idea of what Shay was feeling. Mistakes were like mile markers. We all made a note of where we were when the car broke down, but we never anticipated the breakdown to prevent it in the first place.

"I've got to change my life," Shay complained as he looked into the mirror. I could feel the pain inside him because I'd done it to myself more often than I could count on fingers and toes. Life could suck sometimes. It was why we needed friends to pull us from the muck. Otherwise, we'd drown.

"You're closed today. Let's go to my place and indulge in fatty foods, liquor, and Lifetime movies? Oh, we can get Parker to bring us chocolate. I'd say it's a good day to wallow. How about it?" I asked.

Shay finished cutting his hair, which now appeared to be a buzz cut from childhood, and then we swept up the salon. We locked the doors, and I led him out of the building to the waiting Uber I'd requested.

My heart was hurting as much as his, and taking the day to have a pity party seemed like a good idea. We were due.

When we left the building to hop into the Uber, I noticed a car sitting across the street. A man was sitting inside with the window open, and he was definitely watching Shay and me as we got into the Chevy.

The creep raised a camera and took some photos, though I had no idea why. Yes, we were hot, but we weren't camera ready. Having a stranger spying on us was annoying as hell, but when I noticed him speaking into a cell phone, I was pretty sure he wasn't just a random photographer.

The man had a more sinister look on his face that left me worried. I'd have to keep a keen eye on my surroundings. Something wasn't right, and I damn well didn't want to die. I had a lot of reasons to stay safe. Number one was Lawry Schatz.

LAWRY

I walked out of Rome Fiumicino Airport to see it was raining just as it had been in New York when I'd left earlier in the day. It was seven in the evening, and I'd been in contact with Giuseppe Torrente through Gabby before I'd left the States. Someone was supposed to pick me up and take me to their home in the city.

Gabby wasn't happy I was going over alone, pushing me to take Nemo with me, but he was busy clearing up his family affairs. I couldn't call him away from his personal business to help me take care of my own. I was sure I'd be fine.

I saw a man standing near the security exit after I'd cleared Customs. He was smiling and holding a sign with "Schatz" printed in black marker on white cardboard. I stepped to him and offered a smile. "Uh, Sono Schatz?" I offered, identifying myself as the person I believed he was seeking. I'd looked shit up on the flight, not sure how much English was spoken by Giuseppe's people. I was the ignorant Midwesterner, after all.

The man chuckled. "I'm Tommy Torrente, Mr. Schatz. It's a pleasure to meet you. I happened to be in Rome to meet with one of our distributors since Mateo is indisposed, so I agreed to pick you up. How was your flight?" the handsome man asked.

Tommy was definitely a Torrente. He was just as handsome as Gabe and Tomas, Gabe's father. The family had the most incredible genes, but my heart was still in New York with a feisty blond who had sex appeal to spare. Max was all I wanted. It was amazing that after two years, I still fell in love so fucking hard and fast for a guy who was nothing like Julien. That reminded me I had a reason to be there, so I got my head together. The handsome man in front of me had asked a question.

"The flight was long, so I truly appreciate that you came to pick me up. I've met Mateo. I've also met Gabe's whole family, but nobody else. How do you fit into the Torrente family tree?" I asked as we made our way out of the airport to the taxi cue.

The man had an infectious laugh as we hopped into a taxi. He'd circumvented the line, and nobody objected, which surprised me. "My father, Luigi, is the brother to Giuseppe, Mateo's father, and Tomas, Gabriele's father. I'm named after Tomas, my godfather. My father owns Torrente Vineyards, which is adjacent to Uncle Giuseppe's grounds in Siena, and I'm the vineyard manager.

"So, what brings you to Rome?" Tommy Torrente asked, his accent thick but clear.

What had brought me there? It was fucking hard to even remember after spending the night with Maxi Partee. We'd said goodbye that morning at his home after making love nearly all night, but I had vowed to get back to him as soon as I could because I'd left my heart there as well and without it, I was just a shell.

I exhaled as we sped through the streets. There were many beautiful buildings lit up across the city as we headed to Giuseppe Torrente's home in Rome, but I couldn't really appreciate their beauty because I was singularly focused on one thing—the need to find Walker Anderson.

"I'm looking for someone, and this is the best place to start," I told Tommy after several minutes of silence. It wasn't a lie. Walker had been in Italy, from what I'd found, so it would be easier to track him while in the country.

If I could pin him down, I could get to him a lot faster, or so I kept telling myself. I wanted answers to my questions so I could get on with my life. Get back to the States and go after what I wanted without anything hanging around my neck like a millstone. Max deserved all of me, not just the pieces I could duct tape back together and offer him.

The taxi pulled up in front of a grand home in the *Via dei Condotti* area of Rome, which was in the fashion district. When I looked out the window and saw the structure, I wished I'd brought Max with me because the area was suited to him much more than me. "*Grazie!*" Tommy called to the cab driver as he tossed Euros over the seat and stepped out of the car, retrieving my suitcase from the back.

I stepped onto the sidewalk in front of the magnificent building and took a breath, smelling the sweet fragrance of rosemary, narcissus, and lily that graced a beautiful, raised garden in front of the home. My mother loved flowers in the front yard as well, but what I was looking at as I stood on the sidewalk outside the ornate iron gate was nothing like the brick house my parents owned in Washington, Missouri. I'd traveled for my job in the past, but I'd never seen anything like I was facing. "This is..."

Tommy laughed. "*Zio* Giuseppe doesn't live here, really. He and *Zia* Teresa spend most of their time in Siena, but he's here to meet with you. Shall we?" Tommy asked in a beautiful voice which was much different than the one he'd used at the airport. There was just the hint of an accent, but it was obvious he was used to dealing with English speaking customers who did business with Torrente Vineyards. I felt a little better that he let down his guard with me.

I followed Tommy Torrente up the massive staircase from the street level to the front door, wondering what I'd set myself up for by deciding to request assistance from Giuseppe. I needed a base in Rome to track players outside of the U.S., but I was likely in over my head with the Torrente's. I should have stayed in Dallas. At least I knew what to expect back there.

I was taken to Giuseppe's office to meet him and his wife for formal introductions. Teresa Torrente was definitely a woman who didn't suffer fools, based on her quick handshake, where she just touched the tips of my fingers. She was quite striking, but she gave me no further attention after she handed me a glass of wine I only held, and the two of us had a very dull conversation about the weather.

Giuseppe Torrente was a bit of a surprise. He was smaller than Gabby in height and general build, but he had a mystique about him that spoke volumes. I had envisioned him as a stone-cold mafioso after overhearing some things from off-handed comments I'd heard around the office, but he looked like anyone's very handsome grandfather. It threw me off a little when someone didn't meet my predetermined notion, but I'd bounce back. Preconceptions aside, he did have a commanding presence, which reminded me very much of Gabby. To that, I could adjust.

Terresa had been reading a book as Giuseppe and I had chit chatted about my home in Missouri, but after his wife finished her glass of wine, offering a scathing look that mine hadn't been touched, the woman excused herself and left me with Giuseppe.

"So, you're the hacker Gabriele brought on board? I have to make sure you meet Carlotta, our IT guru. She is one of the best in Europe at her profession. She'd worked at MI6 with Cyril Symington and was able to clear his name before they both went underground. I was fortunate enough to talk her into joining my organization after Cyril came on board," the man told me, which had me a little confused, but I didn't really care about whatever had happened with Sherlock. I had bigger fish to fry.

"I'd really like to meet her. I understand she did a background check on Duke Chambers, our new operative. I might need her help with what I'm trying to do here. I hope you'll allow me to use your network. I'm not trying to cause trouble for anyone, but I have something I need to research, and being here is better than being in the States to accomplish my task," I explained.

Giuseppe nodded. "I explained things to Carlotta. She's been tracking your movements since you left New York because Gabriele was adamant regarding your safety. Also, she's been tracking your lover, Maxim Partee, at my nephew's insistence.

"It seems the event planner has acquired an admirer. There are inquiries regarding Mr. Partee's business and your relationship floating over back channels. Should we dig deeper into the identity?" *Signore* Torrente asked, which shocked me. I should have fucking known better than to leave Max unguarded. Of course I was being watched, and anyone associated with me was being observed as well. I was a fucking idiot.

"Why would anyone be interested in Maxi? Why would anyone even know about the two of us? We're not really official yet." I questioned, not really able to comprehend what the man was saying as the words settled on me.

Giuseppe smirked. "Official or not, you're not unknown in certain circles, *Casper*, even if you spend all of your time behind the keyboard of your computers. Some people want to put you in a position to provide them with secret information, and they will use anything or anyone they believe would sway you to their side—even an unofficial lover.

"They will want to use your talents for their benefit, to line their pockets, or assist them with hiding bad acts, and they will stop at nothing if they are being pressured for one reason or another. You should have anticipated such things when you left your former position and planned for your safety accordingly.

"When you left the Company and went underground, they tried very hard to find you from what Carlotta has uncovered while researching some unsavory organizations. Unfortunately, when you resurfaced and began working for Gabriele, then used the CIA network to launch searches or track someone as you were attempting to find your former lover, the activity alerted people regarding your emergence from hiding. At this point, we can't determine if the trackers are friends or foes. I'm sure even you don't know who would be on which side of that coin," the older man told me.

Of course, he was right. I should have anticipated nefarious forces would have tracked me from when I left the fucking Company. They would have looked for weaknesses and used them against me. I hated the fact I'd allowed myself to become so fucking singularly fixated. I had to get my head around more than the fact Julien was dead at his own hand. I'd put Max in danger without even considering the ramifications of him being in a relationship with me. I was fucking useless.

I was taken to the Golden Elite Associates-Italy offices in the heart of the city the next morning, and I was surprised to find Mateo and his brother, Rafael the restaurateur, working out with the trainers in the warehouse-style building. I was making my way to the second floor where the tech room was located, when I stopped to watch the workouts, and I hoped Gabby didn't resort to such harsh measures in our office.

We'd beefed up our training at GEA-A, but we didn't participate in bare-knuckle fights that intentionally drew blood as I was witnessing. I wasn't sure what combat discipline they were pursuing, but it looked fucking painful.

"Ah, Casper, it's good to see you," Mateo greeted as he wiped his bloody nose on a towel before he shoved a man standing in front of him. Smokey's boyfriend, Parker, was the head chef at Blue Plate, one of Rafael's restaurants. There were pictures on the wall of the restaurant featuring Rafael and the Mayor of New York, along with several sports figures and a rapper. Seeing the man in person didn't disappoint. Rafael and Mateo were nearly identical in facial features, and both men were fucking gorgeous, but I had finally found my *one*, or so I hoped, so I merely smiled.

Earlier that morning, I'd called Gabriele to confirm my Max was in Brooklyn planning happy occasions, just as I wanted him to be, and was under the watchful eyes of my colleagues. I wanted the fucking obsession I felt to know the truth regarding Julien over with as quickly as possible so I could get home to Maxim. I would shield him from any repercussions my actions caused, regardless of the personal costs. To me, he was worth every hurdle I, or anyone else, had to jump to keep him safe.

"Mateo, good to see you as well. I didn't know… Where are you headquartered?" I asked. He popped into the States from time to time without prior notice, but he didn't really hang around long, as far as I'd observed. He'd never asked me to help him with anything he might be working on, but that really wasn't a surprise after I spoke with Carlotta on the phone the previous afternoon. She was definitely no slouch when it came to finding her way through places other's didn't want to be penetrated.

We'd linked our networks before I left for Italy, establishing a secured line between the offices. I watched her work when I asked if she could find Walker Anderson, and she went to town on it. I was grateful and humbled by her willingness to jump into something that had nothing to do with her or her leg of the organization.

Mateo chuckled. "I'm a premier salesman for Torrente Vineyards part-time, and I work for my father as needed. My work for Uncle Luigi brings me to the States for meetings, but with Gabriele's business growing so quickly and him being short-handed, I offer to help out when he needs me. I spent five years in *Carabinieri* instead of university, so I'm not new to this work. Gabriele isn't the only specialized operative in the family, but he stayed with his military career longer than me. What do you think? You want to go a few rounds?" Mateo joked as he took a sip from the bottle of water in his hand.

I was aware the Carabinieri were Italian special police forces, because it was part of my old job to be aware of all the players, both good and bad, around the world. They were a highly trained, fourth armed force under Italy's military shield. I'd never met anyone from their ranks, but I knew the Carabinieri were tasked with public security, assisted with peacekeeping missions, and trained foreign police units. In other words, Mateo was as deadly as the rest of the family, not just a mild-mannered wine salesman. I also recognized his voice from the Sunday when I hid under my desk. He'd been in my office using my computer. Things made much more sense.

Out of the corner of my eye, I saw Mateo's brother point to his watch and roll his eyes. Rafael Bianco *Torrente* was also a handsome man. His hair was shorter than Mateo's, and he was leaner, but he still had a lethal look about him, always watching the surroundings and checking for alternative points of egress from the room. Of the two of them, Mateo struck me as the gentler beast. Rafael had the eyes of a cynical man, not trusting anyone who came into his orbit, and he was studying me, not saying a word or introducing himself at all. It scared the hell out of me. I'd seen eyes like his in the past, and no good ever came of the encounter.

I looked back at Mateo. "I'm here for some personal time, plus I wanted to meet Carlotta for the good of both offices since our paths may cross from time-to-time. Gabby's been making changes to our business model, and I believe it will be beneficial to both legs of the organization if Carlotta and I compare strategies so we can offer the operatives a united front. How about you? When is the harvest?" I asked.

"I'm not involved in that aspect of the business, thank goodness. I'm here to see Papa and Mama before I head to Sicily to pitch a new customer. While I'm there, I'll do some recon as I've always done in the past. A former friend of the family has taken some steps in a direction that is reckless. We like to stay ahead of such actions if possible, so I'll check on things to see what new developments have occurred since my last trip.

"Oh, we're having a big family dinner at the vineyard tonight before I leave. Tell me you'll drive out with us. Carlotta can set you up with passwords, and you can use the equipment Uncle Luigi has in the office at the tasting room. Getting out of the city will be nice. The air is sweeter in Siena," Mateo offered with that sexy Torrente smile, while Rafael stayed silent, still watching me.

"I appreciate the invitation, but I think what I need to do will require me to be here in Rome. If you'll excuse me," I told them as I shook Mateo's hand before heading off in the direction of the second floor where Carlotta's office was located. Rafael didn't offer a goodbye.

I knocked on the door and was stunned when an unbelievably beautiful woman opened the door and smiled at me. *"Entra?* You must be Lawrence. I'm Carlotta. Welcome to my kingdom," she joked. I liked her immediately. We settled into chairs at a long table housing several monitors showing various search results. It appeared she was working on many different things at the same time.

"So, tell me why you're pursuing this person?" the woman asked. Carlotta Renaldo was a woman who could probably kill me before I even saw it coming. She was as formidable as any of the guys with whom I worked, and she was a gorgeous woman with dark hair and beautiful features. I could only describe her as a goddess—sinewy muscles and a sexy demeanor. If I were into women, she'd be one I would go for without hesitation, though I'd probably get shot down before I'd even asked to buy her a drink. She definitely gave off a very stern vibe, much like Giuseppe, Mateo, and Rafael.

I sighed. "My former boyfriend reportedly killed himself on his last assignment. I want to know what he was doing because it wasn't his M.O. to do something so irrational," was my short answer. No need to fill her in on all the gory details.

"Ah, matters of the heart. I get it. Well, I've found Walker Anderson, but he's changed his name to Delaney Cartwright," Carlotta offered, showing me a screen with search results on Interpol's mainframe.

"How did you get into this? I thought they had…" I began, frustration mounting. I'd never been able to hack into Interpol while I worked at the CIA. I could call a contact and get a login if I was required to search through their records, but it was done with their approval. I'd never been able to acquire access on my own.

Carlotta giggled. "Mateo has contacts with some old friends, one of whom now works for Interpol. He got me an active password. You can't get into their system without one, though based on your face, you already know that fact. Anyway, Delaney Cartwright is *innnn*…" she drew out.

Suddenly, a map popped up on the screen, showing a ping from a cell phone in the country of Georgia. Carlotta typed in the coordinates, 47.762137, 44.704861, and hit the enter key. Another map popped up immediately with a pulsing pushpin symbol. "Tbilisi. His phone is pinging in Tbilisi," she informed me. I'd seen the name, Delaney Cartwright, associated with Julien's expunged file on the CIA network, but I assumed it was affiliated with Julien. I was even more confused by the new information, but I would follow the breadcrumbs.

"You can get a flight out of FCO to Tbilisi tomorrow at one-forty-five in the afternoon. Shall I book it?" she asked. It was then I noticed her British accent. I reached for my wallet and retrieved my personal credit card. Carlotta pushed my hand away, opening a drawer and retrieving a stack of credit cards and multi-colored passport folios.

"It wouldn't be smart to travel under your own identity, Lawrence. So, do you want to be, uh, Jacome? Anatoly? Wait, do you speak any foreign languages fluently? If you're not going to be American, you'll need to fake an accent convincingly," she instructed.

I laughed. "Nope. Midwestern boy from Missouri. I did spend several years in Dallas, so I can fake a Texas accent. I've dealt with enough southerners that I can pass," I admitted.

Carlotta laughed. "Give me a preview."

"All y'all are fixin' to get an ass-whoopin'," I joked. Lotta then cracked up in the most unfeminine way, which had me laughing as well. It was nice to joke around with someone under the circumstances.

"Okay. Uh, business? Oil is the primary source of energy for Eastern Europe, and it comes primarily from Russia. Do you know anything about the oil business?" Carlotta asked. It was a legitimate question. Texas was known for its oil business. I could learn enough about it to fake a discussion with a customs or immigration official. I'd never traveled on fake papers before, so I'd have to keep my nerves at bay. Even with the codename of Casper, I wasn't exactly comfortable with covert operations. It was obviously divine intervention that found me in the CIA in the first place.

The next morning, I took a taxi to Leonardo Da Vinci airport and boarded a flight to Tbilisi, Georgia. My name was Greg Turner, and I was the Vice President of an up-and-coming oil business looking for a market in Georgia. It wasn't anything that was being published because I damn well didn't need the Russians picking up on chatter regarding an American oil company trying to muscle into Russia's energy stronghold in their former states that had gained independence from the Motherland. It was just a slipshod cover to get me into the country without my old bosses noticing too much. I didn't need the extra scrutiny.

I tried to call Max that night before I left Italy, but his phone rang through to voicemail. I sent a text to Gabby who told me Max was fine, just busy. I was relieved, but I actually hoped he missed me. I sure as fuck missed him.

MAXI

Sunday morning dawned grey and gloomy. Well, actually, as I looked out the window of my brownstone, there was sunshine reflecting off car windows, but in my world, things were dreary. I knew it was because I was wallowing in misery since I hadn't spoken to Lawry since he left, only seeing a missed call from him a few days prior. I tried to call back, but it went right to voicemail. I didn't leave him a message either. I was aware he was working, so I tried to give him a pass on not calling me again, but it was getting harder with every hour that passed without any word from the tall dope.

I also kept seeing a scary-looking guy around the neighborhood, and he made me uncomfortable because he'd unexpectedly popped up in other places where I'd been. It seemed as if he were following me, but maybe I was paranoid? I just had a feeling he was up to no good, but maybe I'd watched too many government-intrigue movies of late, and my imagination was now fueled with espionage plots and the idea of a sexy secret agent coming to my rescue.

The recent weddings had kept me busy, which was actually a blessing under the circumstances. I was also asked to put together a small anniversary party for one of Celeste Myer's friends on Saturday, which I happily threw myself into to keep my mind off my loneliness.

It was a surprise party for Michael and Whitney Jayne, and I wanted to make it spectacular.

Michael Jayne was a Broadway producer, and his third wife was one of the younger *ladies-who-lunch* in Manhattan society. When Whitney Jayne was seen in all of the fashionable places wealthy wives frequented, she was seen with Celeste Myers-Norman and Natalie Sommers, two of Manhattan's doyens of the second wave of fabulousness. For Celeste and Natalie to choose me as the planner for the fifth-anniversary party for the happy couple was an honor. The weather in New York was beautiful that night, and we took a sunset dinner cruise aboard the *Destiny,* a beautiful yacht which easily accommodated the fifty guests.

The event was catered by Bianco Catering, Rafael Bianco's latest creation among his corporate holdings. He'd purchased a building next door to Blue Plate, his restaurant in Bay Ridge where Parker Howzer had been elevated to executive chef. Parker also planned catering menus for Bianco Catering, which was exactly what made the party so fantastic. Parker was a genius when it came to planning food for an event, and the night had been magical—and surprising.

The compliments and accolades regarding the success of the party had been gratifying, but the most amazing thing that happened that night was when Shepard Colson cornered me as the dinner course was being cleared. The couple would cut a cake, and there was a DJ who would take over for two hours of dancing before we docked at eleven. I was collecting dirty linens to move off to the galley when Shepard Colson walked up to me, a sheepish smile on his face.

"I, uh, I know I sort of bullied my way onto this boat, but I wanted to meet with you when we'd be able to talk. Parker's done with the food and headed back to the restaurant, so I know we won't be interrupted. I'd like to hire you," Shepard requested, *which surprised me.*

I'd probably only heard the man speak about a dozen words since I'd met him, so to have him ask me to help him, using full sentences, had been somewhat of a shock. "Sure, Mr. Colson," *I'd responded, not exactly feeling comfortable enough to have called him Shepard, or even his nickname of Smokey.*

I'd seen the man blush, which was a surprise considering his age. He'd chuckled a bit and smiled in that sexy, southern way I'd seen over the years from men who knew themselves but weren't too keen to let others know them. "Now, call me Smokey. Anyway, I want you to help me plan something for Parker. His birthday is coming up, and he'll be twenty-eight. We've been together for a while, and I believe it's time I show him off a little. I also want to ask him to marry me." I'd been quite surprised, but then again, I hadn't been. A blind man could have seen the love they had for each other just as sure as I could see my own face in the mirror. And, of course, happy events were my specialty.

We were meeting for brunch at Cactus, a place my friends and I loved to lunch at during the week. Parker was handling the Sunday brunch seating at Blue Plate, so he wouldn't learn of our scheming behind his back, which was exactly what I wanted for my friend. He deserved the best, and I was determined I'd help Smokey Colson give it to him.

I had just pulled on a pair of Bermuda shorts and a pink linen shirt when the doorbell rang. I walked downstairs and glanced out the peephole to see Parker's man standing on my porch. I was surprised he knew where I lived. "Hi, Smokey. Is something wrong?" I asked as I opened the glass storm door to invite the man inside.

"No, not at all. I just thought I'd pick you up since I was in the neighborhood. No need for us to take two cars. I had to drop Parker's phone off at the restaurant because he left it on the charger at home, so I checked his contacts list and got your address. I hope you don't mind," he told me with a smirk. He almost didn't strike me as sincere, but I didn't know him well enough to judge.

"No problem. Let me grab my keys and phone, as well. Is Cactus still okay? They have a great brunch," I suggested.

"Uh, Tex-Mex, right? I think Parker told me about that place, but we haven't gotten around to trying it yet," the man answered as he came upstairs to the main floor behind me. He whistled, which surprised me. I thought he was looking at my ass, and that was going to get him a knee to the crotch if he was planning to fuck over my friend, but when I turned, I saw him looking at my great room, and it made me smile.

"Yes, Tex-Mex. Look around if you'd like. I need to run upstairs to change shoes," I told him as I re-evaluated wearing tennis shoes when flip-flops were much more appropriate.

I ran upstairs and went to my closet, seeing some of Lawry's suits and shirts hanging there, which made me smile. He still had things at Gabe and Dexter's place, but he'd left stuff at my place before he went to Italy. It had made me deliriously happy to feel Lawry behind me when I woke in the middle of the night. I couldn't wait to feel it again.

I had decided the previous night, after returning from the party to an empty home that I was going to ask Lawry to move in, officially, when he returned from his fact-finding mission... if he still wanted to pursue something with me. I prayed he came home with the answers that would give him the relief required to help put the death of Julien Renfro behind him. I loved Lawry very much, and I wanted to tell him because not saying the words to him felt like lying, and I wasn't one to lie.

As I headed down the stairs, I watched Smokey walking around my living room with a black, plastic device in his hand, waving it over every corner of the room before he moved on. Suddenly, the thing made a loud noise, and the man froze, reaching under the china credenza in my dining area. He came up with a small device, and he examined it before he quickly placed it on the floor and crushed it under the heel of his cowboy boot.

He reached down with a handkerchief and picked it up, shoving it into the pocket of his jeans before he moved to the kitchen area. I slipped upstairs, wondering what the hell he was doing and why. I decided to stomp downstairs to alert him of my re-emergence and politely ask him what the fuck he was doing in my home, but when I arrived at the first floor, Smokey was nowhere to be found.

The front door was open, and he was talking on his phone, so I waited for him. He came inside, laughing. "Sure, man, hold on," he said before he handed me his phone.

"Hello?"

"Hey, Max. I'm sorry I haven't called you, but I've been busy, babe. How are you?" It was Lawry, and every other concern simply faded away.

"I'm fine, Lawry. I miss you," I informed him, stepping away from Smokey to have a private conversation. "You could have called my cell phone," I snapped, remembering how pissed I'd been earlier. It has been a week, damn him.

"I'm calling from a throwaway, and I didn't want to have your number connected to it because you use your number for business. I knew Smokey was going to talk to you about helping with Parker's birthday because he sent me a text to ask if it was a problem if the two of you went to brunch today to make plans. I called him to give my approval," Lawry told me, a laugh in his voice.

Of course, that comment pinged on my pissed-off meter like nothing ever had in my life. "I didn't realize I needed your permission to have a meal with anyone," I griped in return, actually stomping my foot in the process.

Lawry chuckled again. "I wish I could be there to see this little fit in person. You're damn sexy when you're mad. Don't blame me for this. Smokey's old-fashioned, and he just didn't want me to think you were creepin' with him behind my back. He's just being a good friend, Max. Anyway, enjoy brunch and don't give the guy too rough a time. He's in new territory regarding how he feels about Parker, so go easy on him. I work with him," Lawry advised, which made me giggle.

"Fine. How's it going?" I asked.

Lawry sighed. "I'm in Georgia. I'm close to finishing this," he told me.

"Georgia? I can come down. I can take a few days off and be with you. Toni has everything under control. I can be there for you," I urged, sounding a little too needy for my own ears.

"No, baby, not *that* Georgia. I'm in Europe. I think I've found what I'm looking for, and I'm going to confront him tomorrow. I'll call you when I'm headed home, okay?" Lawry informed me.

I felt tears in my eyes, but I blinked them away because I didn't want to ruin my eyeliner, which I never left the house without. "Okay, Lawry. Be careful, doll," I offered by way of goodbye. We hung up, and I walked back into the hallway, seeing Smokey coming downstairs with a smile.

"Sorry. I used your upstairs washroom. You ready?" the cowboy asked. His behavior was odd, but maybe for him, it wasn't? I hadn't really spent much time with the guy. I nodded and grabbed my Prada sunglasses before we left my house and made our way to Cactus for brunch. I was still wondering about whatever he'd stomped on in my dining room, but we had business to discuss. My questions could wait.

We parked on a side street and walked toward the restaurant. It was then I saw that creepy guy I'd seen around a little too often lately, and I felt a shiver up my spine. He was walking a bulldog, which led me to believe he must live in my neighborhood, and I was, once again, imagining things that weren't there. I turned to Smokey and smiled. "So, let's talk about your proposal and Parker's birthday because I think those things should be two separate occasions. I don't think you'd feel comfortable proposing to Parker in front of a huge group of people, would you?" I asked as we were shown to a small booth for two.

I saw the man's face flush, which wasn't a surprise, nor was it the first time I'd seen it. The fact he was asking for my assistance wasn't something I'd expected. The man was so private. Hell, I remembered when Shay Barr lost his shit over Parker and Smokey, questioning whether Smokey was embarrassed by his relationship with Parker. We all knew Smokey was shy. Proposing in front of a crowd didn't fit him.

"Well, no, but I'm not trying to hide the fact I love him and want him to be my husband," Smokey answered as our waitress approached our table wearing a brightly colored dress. She was carrying two glasses of ice and a pitcher of water, appearing very happy for a Sunday.

"I'm Leila, and I'll be your server. Have you—Oh, hey Maxi," she greeted with a big smile. She had waited on the guys and me when we came by for lunch several times, so she knew all of us.

"Hey, gorgeous. How are the kiddos?" I asked, knowing she had twin girls who were three. One got to know people when they frequented an establishment, plus I'd thrown some side work her way a couple of times when she needed extra money. She was a single mom, and I liked her. She was twenty-three, and she had nobody. I'd thought about offering her a job to work for me, but she seemed to enjoy her work at the restaurant, so I decided not to stir the pot.

"They'll be four in three months. I can't believe it," Leila told me, retrieving her cell phone from the apron pocket she was wearing to show me a picture of two little girls who were just too cute.

I showed it to Smokey, seeing the surprise in his eyes, which made me think of some things I wanted to drill the man on regarding his intentions with Parker Howzer since my friend no longer had family looking out for him. We—Dexter, Shay, and I—were his family now, and we'd watch out for him. "They, uh, they're cute," he offered as he took a gulp of water Leila had poured into our glasses.

"Thanks. So, can I bring you drinks? Tequila sunrises? Margaritas? Mexican Mulas?" she offered.

Smokey held out his hand for me to go first. "I'll have a premium margarita, rocks, salt," I ordered, turning to Smokey as a busboy dropped off chips and salsa.

"I'll, uh, I'll have a Modelo, please," Smokey ordered.

"Sure. I'll be right back," Leila stated as she bustled away.

I picked up my water and took a drink, studying Smokey's sudden unease. I decided not to wait for the alcohol to muster up the moxie to grill the man. "Have you talked with Parker about children?"

I saw the man gulp. "Children? What *about* children?"

"As in, do you want to be fathers? Do you want to have children? Does Parker want children? He'd be a great father, and you probably would as well after you loosen up a little," I explained, seeing the man squirm, which actually was becoming more entertaining by the moment.

"I, uh, we haven't... I mean, I don't... I've never thought about it," Smokey responded, seeming to pale in front of me.

"Well, don't you think you should know his views on children before you propose to him? I mean, what if you don't want children and he does? That's going to be a bone of contention going forward, right? I'd like to have a family because I didn't really have one growing up, and I'd be happy to adopt kids who were thrown away by people who didn't value how fortunate they were to have them in the first place," I admitted to him, seeing him gulp hard.

"Hell, I don't know. Are you tellin' me I shouldn't propose to Parker? Did he say somethin' to you when y'all had lunch?" I saw the man was scared, and I quickly deduced I was coming on far too strong and needed to pull back a little.

"No, no. I don't think Parker suspects you'd ever want to get married, which is why I brought this up, because I think you love each other so much, you'd both do anything the other wanted, even if one of you might not want it. I don't want you guys to… I think you should know where you stand regarding the important issues. Where to live. Children. Religion. I personally am more of a spiritual person than a religious one, so I wouldn't want to necessarily marry in a church, but what about you and Parker? Are either of you religious?" I asked as Leila brought our drinks and delivered them with a smile.

I really wanted to laugh, seeing fear on Smokey's face, but I also didn't want to fuck up Parker's future. "Look, don't mind me, Smokey. I'm just a nosey queen. Let's talk about Parker's birthday. When is it?" I asked before I took a sip of my drink, feeling it warm me all the way down.

Smokey took a sip of his beer and looked into my eyes. "No, you're right. It's too soon to propose. I need to talk to him about some stuff. I mean, my place is a shithole, and he deserves something much better, especially if he wants kids. We need to start saving money for a house, and God, with my job, how would… Do I even want kids? I never actually thought about it, but I wouldn't mind one, though I'd like it to be ours if possible.

"Hell, where would we even begin to look for a donor and a surrogate? I mean, that costs a lot of money, and sometimes, it doesn't work the first time, right? I saw something about that sort of thing on the news one night. I'm not starving, and I can support the two of us, but if we pursue surrogacy, then how much do we need to set aside, and how much will it cost for us to get a single-family house? You should have that with kids, right? Gabe and Dex bought a single-family place, but what if Parker wants to…" he spouted as he became more and more panicked. I wanted to kick my own ass.

Suddenly, he was breathing heavy and bending over the table, and I knew I'd gone too damn far. "Shit! Let me see if they have a bag. You're hyperventilating," I explained as I hurriedly stood from the table and started to rush away. I felt a hand on my wrist and turned to see Shepard Colson with a big smile on his face as he jerked me back into my seat, laughing at me.

Smokey had the most interesting, deep chuckle as he stared at me.

"You're a funny guy, Maxi. I don't go into anything lightly, but—and I mean no offense—I think those things you mentioned are between Parker and me. Not that I'm embarrassed to answer, but that's shit we're sorting out. I do, however, appreciate that you're looking out for him. He talks about you, Dex, and Shay all the time, and I'm glad he has friends like you guys. It's been hard on him, losin' Wes and Doreen, but I know having you guys to talk to has helped him a lot.

"I'm with you on not proposing to him at his party, so maybe help me plan two events. I wasn't exactly excited about the idea of such a personal thing taking place in front of an audience because I don't know if he suspects it, but my mom said she wanted to be there, and she and Parker are close. Hit me with some options. My family can travel for a weekend from Texas," he responded to me, which made me smile. I was coming to like Smokey Colson. He was surprisingly unpredictable, and I believed that was exactly what my friend needed.

※

Smokey dropped me off at my place a few hours later, and I could honestly say I'd had a good time with him. He was funny as hell, and he had stories about when Parker was in Texas with his family that had me in tears more than once. Smokey had mentioned how hard the time was for Parker, which I didn't doubt because I'd learned from talking with Parker how much he'd valued his relationship with his parents. Then Smokey told me about Parker bottle feeding little cows and ruining his shoes while tromping through cow shit which nearly had me falling out of my seat. The perfectionist chef I knew must have lost his mind with that mess.

"Give me a couple of days to think about it, and you consider where you think Parker would like to have his birthday party. We'll get this right," I told Smokey as I exited the truck where it was parked at the curb in front of my brownstone.

I turned to see that same guy walking down the street with a Doberman puppy, which surprised me. I watched Smokey following my gaze and study the man as well. "That guy must be a dog walker all over Brooklyn. I've seen him everywhere lately, and he has a different dog every time," I told Smokey without much more thought about it—though he had taken pictures of me and Shay once. Of course, we were good looking men, so maybe he was admiring how handsome we both were. Without another thought on the matter, I bid Smokey goodbye and closed the door of his large truck.

I made my way to my front porch and let myself into my house, locking the door behind me. I was a bit tipsy, but not really drunk. I decided to take a nap and then do some research regarding how to create the perfect weekend for Smokey and Parker. I thought the proposal could take place on Friday night, and then the birthday party could happen on Saturday where they could announce their engagement. That would leave Sunday for the couple to spend time with Smokey's family before they returned to Texas. I just had to figure out the logistics.

After my nap on the couch while music played quietly in the background, I decided to head upstairs for a soak, which was where I did my best thinking, especially on a Sunday evening. There was a knock on my front door, which startled me because I wasn't expecting anyone, especially anyone unannounced.

The sky was lit up with oranges, pinks, and purples as the sun was setting, so I flipped on the living room light and the hallway fixture. I went to the peephole, seeing the guy I'd seen earlier—the one who had taken my picture—standing at my front door.

I unlocked the front door and began pulling it toward me to see what the hell he wanted. Just as the hair stood up on the back of my neck, the man ripped open the storm door and pushed his way inside. This time, there wasn't a dog with him.

LAWRY

Two Days Before Sunday...

"Are you sure?" I asked over the satellite phone Carlotta had given me before I left Italy. We'd determined it was the most secure option for communication because something was totally fucked up with Delaney Cartwright. There was a link to Walker Anderson, but after I scraped my way through Russia and into the Company's mainframe, I saw Walker Anderson hadn't changed his name as we'd suspected. Something bigger was afoot.

"Yes, Lawrence. That's the right building. I can't narrow the signal to a specific apartment, but that's the building. Let me talk to Giuseppe and send backup. I shouldn't have allowed you to go alone," Lotta complained over the line, not for the first time.

"So, I just walk up to the door?" I challenged, feeling my mouth go dry.

"Oh, for the love of... Find your backbone and knock or get the fuck out of there and wait for backup. I can send Gunter. He's a German operative for us, and he's the closest to your location, but you'll have to give him a day to get there," Lotta suggested, which sounded more like *'man up or go home'* to me.

"I'll call you back," I informed her as I rang the buzzer on the first of six apartments, which were really more like townhouses back in the States. The door opened, though a little woman kept the chain engaged.

I held up the package, seeing the old woman with a cigarette hanging out of her mouth. She shooed me away and slammed the door, flipping several locks. Obviously, she wasn't my target, so before she came back with a pistol, I moved off her stoop.

Pulling down the orange cap I was wearing, which matched my delivery uniform, I went to the next apartment and rang the buzzer. I was holding a box in my hands, along with an electronic signature device as I stood on the porch, a little blue and orange delivery scooter I'd basically stolen from a courier service lot parked at the curb behind me. Between the sunglasses and the fake beard, I prayed I could pull off the ruse. The nerves were killing me.

As the locks began to click, I was hoping I didn't have to speak because I didn't know how to speak Kartvelian, which was one of the native languages used in Georgia. A woman opened the door, looking very upset. She was dressed in a red-leather, strapless dress, holding a riding crop in her left hand, which she was smacking against her boot-covered calf. That was unexpected.

I held up the box with the name, "Delaney Cartwright," on the slip. The box was empty, so I didn't release it. She looked at the paper and hissed, slapping her leg with the crop so loudly there was a cracking sound that echoed in the house. "*Suka! Zaydi syuda!*" the woman called out in what I believed to be Russian, not the native tongue.

The sound of someone scrambling to the door was loud, but when the man crawled into the room with a black, latex hood over his head, just to his nose, I was shocked. He had a collar around his neck, which was attached to a leash that dragged behind him. He kneeled next to the woman with his head resting against her fishnet-clad thigh. She swatted him on the back with the crop, and he curled up with his head on the ground near her stiletto boot.

"I'm sorry, Mistress. What can your bitch do for you?" The voice, which was American, was one I recognized easily, and I was stunned to hear it again.

"You have package. You may rise," the woman spoke in thickly accented English, which surprised me.

The man stood to his full height, which was familiar as well. When the woman removed the hood, I froze. It couldn't be, could it? "Delaney Cartwright?" I asked, offering my worst accent. I saw the shock on his face, and I nearly fainted.

"I ordered nothing. There's no return address. No thank you," Julien stated as he looked at me, trying to see through my sunglasses.

I scrambled for what to do. "We need confirmation you reject package, and phone number for confirmation to sender," I ordered, handing him a pen.

I knew Julien recognized my voice, and he knew I wasn't leaving without answers. He scribbled out a local number and signed his name before the door was slammed in my face. I walked back to the scooter and hopped on back, seeing he'd actually signed his real name, confirming he knew it was me.

I dumped the scooter on a side street near the delivery company, and I walked back to the hotel where I was staying in Tbilisi, dialing Carlotta Renaldo on the way. "It's Julien. He's alive," I informed her, feeling the tears come, not that I knew why. Was I upset because he wasn't dead, or was I upset because he'd faked his own death and tossed me out of the home we shared? He'd left everything to his parents while leaving me with a shattered heart and the reputation of a lush? Well, I suppose I'd earned the *lush* badge all on my own, though I didn't feel as if it actually fit me.

"I'm sending backup," Carlotta stated, leaving no room for argument.

"NO! I'm going to call him and set up a meet, then I'm coming back to Rome. He'll answer. He knows it was me, so it will be fine. If I don't call in tomorrow afternoon, send backup," I responded.

I heard her sigh. "I'll give you until five tomorrow night, local time. I'm making you a reservation out of Tbilisi tomorrow at six. Be on that plane, Casper," Lotta directed, which made me smile. I had people who cared about me, and I needed to get back to them—one in particular.

Later that evening, I was reclining on the bed with a bottle of

Chacha, a local type of moonshine, as best as I could ascertain. It was a by-product of wine, kind of like Italian grappa, from what I could find through a browser search, but it was touted as being a hell of a lot more potent. I stared at the bottle and willed it to open itself so I could say "wasn't me."

If I opened that bottle and guzzled it as I wanted to do, then I'd have to own the label... *Alcoholic*. I'd told myself I numbed up to forget about Julien, but if I found him alive as I had earlier in the day, could I stick with that lie? It was pathetic to try to deceive myself, wasn't it?

I placed the bottle in the bathroom and closed the door, walking out to sit on the small balcony of my hotel room. There were city lights, but none of them shined as brightly as when I was with Maxim Partee. The man was flamboyant at times, but I loved it because it brought levity to my mostly sullen existence.

When Max was happy, he was animated, and it alleviated all of my worries and infected my soul with positive feelings. That was something to consider because, for two years, I'd lived in the gutter, and I didn't want to live there any longer.

Max and I honestly had feelings for *each other*, unlike the way Julien had described our former relationship. I just had to let Max inside my walls, which were now useless to have, anyway, since Julien was alive, which confirmed he had never cared for me as I had cared for him.

I also had to realize my brother, Hank, was right. If I wasn't already, I had the makings of an alcoholic because I'd rather drown the feelings I felt after I was told Julien had killed himself than try to survive and rise above them. That would never do if I were serious about Maxim Partee. He deserved all of me, not just the parts that had to be soaked in alcohol to function.

If I wanted Max, I had to accept the flaw in myself. Those twelve steps would be hard to walk, but maybe with a supportive hand in mine, I could do it? It was worth a try.

The next morning, I dialed the number on the rejection slip from Julien. I found a burner phone at the liquor store where I bought the

Chacha—which I'd dumped down the sink at three in the morning after I made up my mind about a few things.

Soul searching wasn't a fun exercise, which wasn't a surprise. It was even worse when it was done soberly and in a foreign country. No hot guy to snuggle into after I reached some decisions was depressing as fuck.

I dialed the number from the fake delivery slip and counted the rings. "*Da?*" I heard answered in Julien's voice.

"When?" I asked.

There was silence over the line, and I thought he'd hung up, but then he cleared his throat. "Eleven. The courtyard outside Metekhi Cathedral. Near the statue of King Vakhtang Gorgasali," he told me.

"What?" I asked, unfamiliar with Georgian landmarks.

Julien sighed in that exasperated way I wasn't excited to hear again. "The horse statue," he stated before the line went dead.

I looked up the place to find it was an orthodox church of some kind, about which I knew nothing. I copied down the address and looked up a bus schedule on my laptop. I was going to be there to meet Julien and get some type of explanation out of him, come hell or high water, because I had to know what the fuck had occurred that had him leap from sharing a home with me in Dallas to faking his suicide and taking up residence in Crazy Town. I was sure the story Julien had to tell would be a doozy. Mother fucker owed me that much.

I stepped off the city bus I'd taken to the agreed upon meeting site—a beautiful church made of stone with a statue of a man on a horse, King Vakhtang Gorgasali, the founder of the city of Tbilisi and the once King of Iberia. He was probably a good guy, but he'd made bad decisions, which had me wondering if what I was doing was the right thing. In my gut, I knew I needed the truth, so I marched forward to conquer my fears.

I walked up the massive hill to the top where the church rested high above Tbilisi. The structure was from the twelfth century, or so I'd found during research, and it had a lot of history surrounding it, not that I cared. I had one purpose, and one purpose only. Get the information I wanted from Julien and get the hell home.

I watched carefully as people traversed the grounds, finally seeing a man ascending the hill in a pair of jeans and a t-shirt. His head was bald, where the day before he'd had short hair, but there was a different leather collar around his neck. He was gaunt, but I still recognized him as my former lover. Julien Renfro had always been thin, but looking at him as he trekked the grounds, I'd have called him emaciated. I wasn't sure if it was his choosing or his Mistress's, and honestly, I didn't really give a shit.

I stood and walked out of the shadows so he could see me. Our eyes met before he walked under the shade of a large tree, the type of which I'd never seen before, and he stood in front of me, not attempting physical contact. It didn't rip out my heart as I believed it should have, which was a good sign.

"Look, I only have a few minutes. Mistress is at the spa, and I have to get home before her. What are you *doing* here, Lawry?" he asked as if he was the aggrieved party, the fucking jackoff.

I chuckled in disbelief. "Oh, fuck no. You don't get to act all put out. You left me in the middle of the night and sent me a text to get out of our home. The home we'd shared—you remember that part, right? Your parents evicted me and left me with nothing, Julie," I snapped at him, seeing a bus full of tourists milling around the grounds. I took his arm and led him away from the immediate area to a shaded spot that was a bit more private.

"I'm sorry about that, but I left a will with my parents bequeathing you the townhouse and contents upon my death. We needed to separate our lives, Lawry. I'm defecting for real, not the way the Company believes I was to do as a double agent. I wanted you to leave me behind before you got caught up in the drama that would come in the wake of them learning my true intentions. I meant for you to get away from the job, not our home," he told me.

I laughed. "Aw, isn't that all self-serving of you. Did you really think your parents were going to abide by a will you left that gave me a fucking penny? No. They threw me out two fucking years ago... Wait, that's not the goddamn issue. You're defecting to where? Russia? Seriously? What the fuck, Julie?"

Julien took my arm and led me further away from the tourists, who were now perusing the grounds with a guide. Julien's hand on me felt all wrong. God, I wondered if I was dreaming he was still alive. Thinking about him being among the living made me angry and left a sick feeling in my gut. I'd mourned for him, uselessly, for two years, and all the while, he was walking around on some chick's leash? How fucked up was that one?

"I just… I didn't know… You always loved me more than I loved you, Lawry. I cared about you, but you wanted more from me than I was willing or able to give. I needed time, so I decided to get away for a while and get some perspective on what I was doing to you by continuing to lie about my feelings. That assignment came up when I needed it, so I took it.

"The Company had received information through some of our operatives in Moscow that Magda was in Cuba, which was where I was initially sent. She was there to ensure the Cuban dictator didn't get too cozy with the American president as he had in the past and switch his loyalties from Russia to the U.S.," Julian informed.

That definitely sounded like something the Company would do. There was always a method to their madness, that was for sure. "Who's this Magda?" In for a penny, in for a pound.

"Magda, she's Russian FSB… Russian Security Service. My mission was to get to know her and find vulnerabilities I could exploit to convince her to join our side, but it went the other way. Magda was in Cuba for an entirely different mission, and instead of me wooing her to join our side, she found my vulnerabilities—my needs—and she met them in a way you never could, Lawry. You weren't cut out to be the man I needed at all," Julie snapped. That was behavior I didn't miss. My Max would never act in such a fashion.

"So, faking your death was the way out, huh? You could have just fucking told me you wanted out. Surely you don't think I'd have put up a fight, do you? If you weren't happy, you should have said something," I snapped in return. Fucker had never seen me mad, but he was about to.

"You're clingy. You're docile. You don't... Look, let's not do this. There's no need for us to hash over what was wrong with you... uh, *our* relationship. I reported to Walker Anderson that I was unhappy with things in my personal life, namely our living situation, and I wanted out, but I wasn't sure how to do it.

"It had been his idea that I'd fake my death, so that's what I did in hopes you'd just move on and forget about me. Of course, I'd had no idea Walker had feelings for me, as well, which he'd attempted to act on when he'd arrived in Cuba to touch base. I rejected him when he told me how he felt. After I met Magda, I didn't want to be with anyone else," Julien added. By that point, I was really done listening. *Walk away...*

"So, what's your plan, huh? Are you a communist now?" I dared. He always had been a bit out there, so joining the Communist Party wouldn't be a stretch for him.

"As a matter of fact I... No, never mind. Look, when Magda and I left Cuba, we took diversionary measures to ensure Walker wouldn't find us right away, so I'm sure he's freaking out. Even if you tell him where you found me, which I fully expect you will, he won't get here fast enough to kill me. We're leaving in three days, and I'm never looking back.

"You fucked up by finding me. The Company will make your life hell if they find out you and I made contact. That's why I made sure Mallory notified you of my suicide. My parents, as well. I didn't want anybody looking for me, least of all you. I was never *in love* with you like I am with Magda, so leave me alone. I'm going to have the life I deserve. *You* should try to find that for yourself instead of pining over me," Julie concluded.

Well, that was it, wasn't it? My suspicions were confirmed. The son of a bitch had basically used me and walked away without a second thought. I'd wasted two years of my fucking life mourning the loss of that piece of garbage. What the fuck was *wrong* with me?

It was all I could do not to punch the fucker, but then again, what would that get me? I'd already established I wasn't a violent person when I refused to beat him while we were together, hadn't I?

I exhaled a shaky breath, trying to get my emotions under control. I wouldn't give the bastard the privilege of seeing how much of a mess he'd left behind. As I stood there in front of the most selfish man on the face of God's earth, I realized that I'd pick up the fucking pieces and put them all back together—hopefully with help from a beautiful blond party planner who was becoming the most important person in my world.

I nodded, not looking into his far too thin face and soulless eyes. "Okay, but what about Anderson? Will he accept that you're just *gone*? Won't he try to rescue you or something?" I asked. As the words left my mouth, I seriously asked myself why I gave a fuck. Julien had made his decisions, and the night before, I'd made mine. It was definitely time to close out that chapter of my life and start the next one, which I believed would be much happier.

Julien sighed with exasperation, something I'd heard far too many times. "Listen to me. Walker Anderson is completely unstable. I sent a report to the AD of Counterterrorism regarding Anderson's conduct before I left Cuba. Turn him in if he shows up because the fucker would rather kill you than look at you. You're not his favorite person," Julien warned.

"Why would he come looking for me if he thinks I believe you're dead? What did you say about me?" I reached for his t-shirt and shoved him against a tree. If the fucker was setting me up to get my ass shot off, I would shove him down that big fucking hill!

"The man's deranged, and he thinks he's in love with me. He'll do anything to find out where I am. Hell, maybe you two can relate to each other? *You're* here, aren't you?" Julien bated. I released his shirt, remembering how much of a bastard he could be. What the hell had I been thinking by coming here to look for him?

I turned to walk away, feeling disgusted with myself for how much of a hold the man had had on me for far too long. It was time to go home.

I turned to walk away, done with the whole fucking mess. "SCHATZ! Wait a minute," Julien ordered. I flipped the fucker off and continued on my path.

"Anderson is smart, Lawry, and he's deadly. If he shows up, contact

Ian. They need to neutralize him. He's too unhinged to keep around!" Those words stopped me dead in my tracks.

I thought back to the text from Smokey informing me that Max's house had bugs—listening devices—which was why I had called him on Sunday to see what the fuck was going on. The man also told me he was going to kick my ass for dreaming up the idea of the party for his boyfriend as a reason to hang out, but my Max was good at parties, and Parker did have a birthday coming up at the end of July. A party never killed anyone.

I didn't need to hear anything more. I came to the realization that Julien really was dead—or he'd never really been alive. The man I thought I loved had never existed, just a creation in my own mind. It was a shame it took me so long to see the fucking light.

I walked back over to him and looked at him for a moment, seeing a complete stranger. "Goodbye, Julien. I hate that you did this shit in the most fucked up way possible, but at least now I know it wasn't me. It was *you*. You're the one who is truly twisted, and I just didn't see it. Good luck," I tossed out before I walked away.

Julien called out, "How'd you find me, anyway?"

I chuckled. I turned around and smirked at the asshole. "I believe you've got a bug infestation. Something in your shit is traceable."

I headed to the bus stop to get back to my hotel and check out. I also needed to call Lotta to call off the dogs she had coming my way because I was headed home. I didn't need the backup.

I wanted the truth, and Julien finally gave it to me. I got what I came for, and it was time to get back to the reason I'd searched for the truth in the first place. I needed to get back to Max. We had a life to plan after all.

MAXI

Sunday…

"Hey! What the fuck?" I snapped at the man as he shoved his way into my home, his large hand on my chest pushing me further down the hallway. He appeared to be a bit crazed and nearly foaming at the mouth if I was judging right, and I wished to hell Smokey was still hanging around somewhere.

"Lawry Schatz. Where is he?" the man demanded as he pulled a gun from behind his waist. That couldn't be good.

"Who?" I asked as I backed into my living room and took a seat on my couch when the man shoved me toward it. I really needed to ask Lawry more questions when he returned to New York, but I was guessing the madman had something to do with his former career with the CIA, about which I really knew nothing.

I had an idea of why the man was asking, however. "What do you know about Julien?" I asked, not knowing the man's last name. Seeing the look in the intruder's eyes let me know I was on the right track.

"That son of a bitch is defecting—I just know it. Renfro fucked me over with a woman in Cuba and took off on me. He was supposed to run recon for us regarding a group of rebels we were watching, and he fucking took off. I know Lawrence Schatz has been looking for him for the last few months. Schatz disappeared off my radar, which means he must have found Julien and probably plans to join him. Where did he go?" the man rambled, likely giving away state secrets about which I knew nothing, nor did I care. What I cared about was that he kept that gun aimed at my head. I didn't think for a minute he wouldn't shoot me.

"I don't know," I admitted as fear enveloped my body. Suddenly, the lights flashed in my house before going dark, and the front door was kicked in. I quickly dropped to the floor and crawled behind my couch, praying the whole time I didn't piss my pants.

I heard a gunshot and a loud thump like something had fallen, so I froze in fear because I'd never in my life been exposed to violence of any kind. Hatred? I knew all about that one, but not physical violence. I had no idea what to expect, but I felt a strong arm around my shoulder as the lights came on. "You okay, Maxi?" I heard the drawl before I opened my eyes.

I turned to see Shepard Colson kneeling next to me with a gentle smile and a big six-shooter in his hand like the Old West cowboys carried in the movies. "I think I peed my pants," I offered, hearing him laugh and then an even deeper laugh join in as Gabriele Torrente walked into the room with that sexy grin.

"We've all done it at one time or another, Maxi. Put some shit in a suitcase and come stay with Dex and me until we can get this cleaned up," Gabe told me. I turned to see the man who had burst into my home with a bullet hole in his forehead and a lot of blood stuff I didn't want to think about was littered all over the beautiful rug under my coffee table—the expensive one I'd just purchased.

"How did you know something was going to happen?" I asked, not sure what to say, actually. I had no idea where the dead man came from or why he'd targeted me and asked after Lawry's whereabouts, which I didn't know much about in the first place. I couldn't find the country of Georgia on a fucking map if I had to.

"It's a long story. Pack some things and let's get home. We'll take care of this mess we made, I swear," Gabe reiterated.

I was stunned, but I could follow orders. I ran upstairs to take the fastest shower of my life before I grabbed a leather garment bag, loading outfits for a couple of days into it along with my toiletry kit. I grabbed my messenger bag and rushed downstairs to find Smokey rolling the dead man in my rug. It was only a few weeks old. "I guess that won't come out, will it?" I asked Gabe.

He relieved me of my bag and smiled. "I'll get you a new rug. That guy was a little too unhinged for us to wait until he left to take care of him. So, what did he say he was looking for?" Gabe asked.

"Lawry," I answered.

As we walked through the house, Smokey began turning off the lights and the music I'd had on before the man busted into my house. He followed us out the front door and pulled it closed, not locking it from the inside. "Should I lock that?" I asked.

"No need. I've got someone watching the house until the clean-up crew gets here to take care of it. I'll hang around in case a neighbor reported the shots. This is one the cops need to steer clear of. We'll return that guy where he needs to be, and I promise you there'll be no inquiry into it," Smokey assured.

I hopped into Gabe's big SUV, still stunned. He picked up his cell phone and dialed a number, looking at me with a cautious face. "Lotta? Gabriele. Can you get Lawry on the sat? Someone needs to talk to him. No, Maxi's fine. Thanks, sweetie. Hang on, man. Next time, cut it a little closer, will you?" With that, Gabe was laughing as he handed me his cell phone.

"Hu...hello?" I asked.

"Sweetheart, I'm so sorry. I had no idea what the fuck was going on, but when I talked to Smokey, he told me about the bugs in your house. I should have anticipated it," Lawry said.

That snapped me out of my terrorized daze. "Bugs? I'll have you know I don't have any bugs in my house. I have a contract with a pest control company to come out in the spring and spray for ants, and I have the house inspected for... Wait, you're not talking about insects, are you? That's what Smokey was smashing on the floor, right?" I asked, finally getting my head out of my ass.

Gabe chuckled, as did Lawry. "Yeah, that's it. You okay?" he asked.

Was I? How the fuck could one be okay when that sort of shit hits the fan? "I only peed my pants a little," I stated, looking at Gabe who smiled at me before starting the vehicle and heading toward his house.

"I'll be home on Friday. Giuseppe is sending in cleaners to put your house in order. Smokey or Jackass, uh, Mathis, will make sure everything's okay until I get there. I'm so sorry about this, Max. I had no idea shit would go down this way. I need to go to my old office in Dallas and talk to someone first, but I'll be home by Friday, for sure," Lawry promised.

I took a deep breath because I was tiptoeing out onto that limb without any knowledge regarding what had happened to him and whoever he found in Georgia. "I'll pack your things so we can bring them home," I stated boldly.

There was silence on the line, which felt like an eternity, before Lawry exhaled. "Good. You okay? Really?" he asked.

"I'll be fine with Gabe and Dex. Hurry home. I miss you," I told him before we disconnected the call. I wasn't really okay, but I'd survive. Lawry was coming home to me. Everything else could just fade into the background.

⁘

"And, we go to the beach to watch the fireworks," Searcy told me, surprising me with the sound coming out of her little body because she had the sweetest speaking voice in the world, but it had changed without my knowledge. Last time I'd seen her, she almost sounded like she was from Boston, pronouncing her 'R's' like 'W's.' It made me chuckle every time I spoke with her, but I knew she went to a speech pathologist because Dexter didn't want her getting teased at school when it started in the fall. I agreed. Kids were cruel.

It was Thursday, the Fourth of July, and the Torrente's were headed to Long Island for a family gathering. They were staying a few nights and coming back to Brooklyn on Saturday, and they were pulling out the big guns to convince me to go along—Searcy. Dylan had already left with Dominic, Gabe's nephew, to go out the previous day because Dom's mother and sisters were already there, and I told them to have fun and not worry about me.

I was staying in Brooklyn, and I'd decided to watch the fireworks on the big screen in the media room the couple had in their home. I wanted to be alone to sort of process what had happened, because none of the Torrente's had let me have a moment alone since the "thing we don't mention" had happened at my home. I was headed back to my house on Friday morning to survey if there was any damage I needed to repair, but that night I was staying put in the nice big house in Bay Ridge.

The last few days had been busy. I'd gone with Smokey to pick out an engagement ring for Parker, and I'd asked Gabe to speak with his cousin, Rafael, to secure Parker several days off. Smokey had decided there was a place at the ranch his parents owned where he wanted to propose to Parker, and the holiday seemed like the best time to do it.

We lucked out that the ring Smokey had picked out was available in Parker's size, which I knew because when I met the crew for lunch on Tuesday, I wore a ring on my finger I used to wear during my goth jewelry phase. I hadn't sported it for several years because it was tacky as hell, but I suffered through it to get Parker to try it on. I thought we wore the same size ring, and I was right. I'd given Smokey advice on setting the scene for the engagement, and I hoped he'd take it to heart.

"*There's this creek on the property where I took Parker when we were down there visiting my parents after Wes and Doreen were killed. It was the first time Parker rode a horse, as a matter of fact. It was the day we kissed for the first time, so it's special. I think that's the best place to propose. When we get back, we'll hammer out this birthday party thing, Maxi. Thanks for your help,*" he'd told me as he'd picked a white-gold band with rubies embedded between two braided yellow-gold strands. The ring was truly magnificent, and I was sure Parker would love it.

"*We will. Think about what you want while you're gone because the end of the month will be here before we know it. I'll make it perfect, Smokey, I promise,*" I'd agreed as I gave him a hug while we'd stood on the sidewalk outside the jewelry store on Wednesday afternoon.

Dexter came downstairs looking as if he'd stepped out of a J. Crew catalog. His dark brown hair was trimmed very short on the sides while the top was longer and swept to the right side. It made his pale blue eyes pop even more.

"Missy, did you pack a bathing suit for the pool? I know you have your stuff for the beach, but you know Nonna doesn't allow you to wear your beach suit into the pool. The sand ruins the filter," Dex stated as he put down the large duffel he was carrying.

"Poop!" Searcy called before she ran upstairs as the one-eyed cat, Sparkles, came slipping around the corner of the couch, eyeing the scene very suspiciously.

"You don't have to stay here with the animals. Momma and Papa are used to having them underfoot. It will be a lot of fun, so won't you come?" Dex attempted to coax, intent on convincing me to come along, yet again.

"It'll be a lot of crazy is what it'll be, but still you're welcome to come. The food will be incredible," Gabe offered as he came in from the garage carrying a cooler, which he put down on the kitchen island. The thud of it alerted me he'd already packed it with something, and it made me laugh.

"No, seriously, I'm going to pack up Lawry's stuff to take home tomorrow. I appreciate you guys letting me stay, and don't worry about the varmints. I'll come by and check on them a couple times a day. You'll be back on Saturday?" I asked to double check.

They'd been discussing whether they should extend their stay through the weekend, but I could tell Gabe wasn't into it. Two of his sisters had recently gotten divorced, and he said their constant man-bashing drove him up the wall. Laughingly, Dexter reminded him he'd called the men in question some very colorful names of his own in the past. Those were family stories I didn't need to hear.

"I'll call you. Lucia is here from San Francisco, so I think we should stay until Sunday, but it's an ongoing negotiation with this guy," Dexter stated as he pulled Gabe down for a kiss, which the big man didn't hesitate to heat up pretty quickly. They made me envious.

Searcy ran downstairs with a roller bag flopping on every step behind her, which had Magic the dog running after her and barking. I heard Gabe and Dexter laughing as they stepped into the hallway. "Come here, pumpkin pie," Gabe told Searcy, taking her suitcase and sliding down the handle to put it on top of the cooler as he carried them out to the SUV.

Searcy ran over to hug me, which I appreciated. "I have movies in the movie room if you get lonesome. My new favorite is *Coco*. You can watch it," she told me. She was so sincere, it nearly brought tears to my eyes. Yes, I wanted children. Would I get to have them? That remained to be seen.

I clamped a leash on Magic so we could walk the family out. Dex grabbed the duffel and placed a gentle hand on my back. "You can stay as long as you want, Maxi. I remember when we lived in the old apartment and there was a shooting. I had a hard time going back. Actually, that's the building we have where Nana Irene still lives, but I'm glad we don't live there anymore. Stay as long as you want," Dex offered again.

I kissed both of his cheeks. "Have fun with the family. I'll see you in class on Tuesday. Thanks for letting me stay here, Dexter. You're a wonderful friend," I told him as we hugged.

He pulled away and smiled, patting Magic on his giant head before Gabe opened the passenger door for his husband, pinching the man's tight ass as he hopped into the large vehicle. Dex jumped a bit and gave Gabe a sexy smirk over his shoulder, which made me laugh. I waved goodbye to them as they left Magic and me on the sidewalk. I decided to take him for a walk before I went into the office even though it was the holiday.

I needed to check schedules and prepare for the events we had looming in July. I'd closed the office for the long weekend, and we had no parties scheduled—not because I hadn't been begged to plan them, but because I needed the time to catch my breath after everything had happened in the recent past. I also wanted to give my employees the time off because they more than deserved it.

After I walked Magic, I put him back into the house and ensured he and Sparkles had water. I left the living room television on for them as I'd witnessed the family had done in the past, and then headed toward the front door to walk to my office and studio. It wasn't too far from where Dex and Gabe lived, and it was a nice day for the walk. It was in the high eighties, but the humidity was low, and there was a breeze, which made it pleasant.

When I arrived at the building, I saw Shay's shop was lit up, and since I hadn't sat down with him in a while, I decided to make us a couple of iced coffees and go check in with my friend. I turned on the large coffee maker before I went to my office, seeing everything was perfect. It was then I wondered if I had 'bugs' at my office like I had at my home. I'd have to ask Smokey or Lawry to bring that hand-held thingy to check.

I didn't like the idea someone had breached my home in the first place and planted them, but Gabe had explained to me how the CIA was capable of any number of sins, couching them under the umbrella of 'national security,' and I supposed he was right. I didn't like it, but I didn't really have a say under the circumstances.

After the coffee maker stopped hissing, I took the two tall, insulated glasses upstairs with me and knocked on Shay's door. He opened it and smiled at me, though I could tell it wasn't exactly genuine. "Hey, sugar," he greeted, kissing my cheek before accepting the glass I offered.

"Hi, doll. How've you been? What are you doing here today?" I asked him as he stepped aside and invited me in, closing the door.

"I could say the same for you. It's a national holiday, Maxi," he reminded as we took seats in two of the stylists' chairs which spun around. I loved those damn chairs.

"I've had a rough couple of days, so I closed the office to give my people time off after turning down parties for the holiday. Lawry's coming home tomorrow," I offered with a stupid grin.

Shay sighed. "*That's* still going on? I thought you two quit seeing each other."

I felt my brow furrow. "What would make you think that?" I asked. He was a bit hostile, which had me a bit worried.

"I saw you last Sunday with Shepard Colson at Cactus. You two were awfully cozy at brunch, enjoying cocktails and laughing a lot. I can't fucking *believe* you'd do that to Parker. He's so much better than that bastard he's with, and here *you* are, claiming to be his friend!" Shay hissed at me.

I shouldn't have laughed, but for him to think Smokey was my type of man? It was fucking ludicrous. No, the man wasn't ugly at all. He was definitely ruggedly handsome, but the man was totally smitten with Parker. If I were guessing right, as Shay and I sat there gearing up for a huge cat fight, Shepard and Parker were making love on a blanket by a questionable water source in Texas, Parker sporting that beautiful ring on his graceful, left ring finger. Outdoor sex wasn't my thing, but hell, more power to them if it was theirs.

"I'll give you the opportunity to take that shit back because I'd say you should know me better than that, Shane Barr. I'd never..." I retorted, feeling the offense all the way to my toes, which were in desperate need of a pedicure. I'd never go after another man's mister.

Shay sighed heavily. "I'm sorry, Maxi. I'm just bitter is all. I shouldn't have jumped to conclusions. What's going on?" he asked with the tone of contrition in his voice, which I appreciated.

"Smokey's asked me to plan a birthday party for Parker at the end of the month. We were having brunch to discuss it, and don't you dare mention it to Parker. It's a surprise," I explained, not mentioning the engagement. That was Parker's news to tell.

I saw Shay's cute smile. "Oh! My bad. I'm *so* sorry."

"What's going on with you, sweetie?" I asked him. He'd seemed off for the last several weeks or so, but I'd been too caught up in my own shit to give it a second thought. I had to get out of that habit. I cared about my friends. It wasn't like me to be self-centered.

"I'm having a hard time getting over that guy I told you about. I mean, it seemed like we had shit in common, and I can't stress how great the sex was between us. I can't get it out of my head because it's driving me fucking crazy. I've worn out a vibrator, for shit's sake," he snapped, which made me laugh. He scowled until he replayed his words, then he joined me.

"Hells bells. You feel like going to watch the fireworks tonight?" Shay asked. I had plans to watch it on television, but my friend was in a funk, so I'd scrap my plans and make a fabulous night for the two of us.

I pulled out my phone and sent off a text. "Okay, come to Gabe and Dex's at seven. *We* can have an early dinner and have a few drinks before they start. We'll have fun, I promise," I told Shay as I hugged him and headed downstairs. My phone rang when I opened the door to my office.

"Maxim Partee," I answered.

"I just landed in Dallas. I can't see my old boss until tomorrow, but after I do, I'm coming home. Should I go to Gabby's place or meet you at home?" Lawry asked. My heart skipped a beat for sure.

"Hello to you, Mr. Schatz. How was your flight?" I asked as I decided to skip any work I had planned that afternoon. I had better plans to make for sure.

"I'm sorry. How are you, babe? The flight was nerve-wracking because I wanna get home to you. What are you doing?" he asked.

"I'm getting ready to go back to Gabe and Dex's house to pack up your things. Come to their house tomorrow so we can figure out how to get your boxes home. They won't fit in Mona," I said.

"I'll be there before dinner tomorrow night. Can I take you out?" he asked in a sexy voice that sent my poor heart all aflutter.

I giggled. "We'll order pizza after we get out of bed," I told Lawry, feeling quite bold.

"That's the best offer I've had in a long time. I... I'll see you tomorrow evening, babe. Be safe," Lawry offered. I wished him the same. After everything, if he so much as got a splinter before he returned to Brooklyn, I was going into full-out diva meltdown. I deserved every good thing coming my way, but I'd damn well be grateful for it. I wasn't one to take the Universe for granted.

LAWRY

I watched the fireworks blazing over the East River on television as I sacked out at the Westin in Dallas. I'd left a message for Ian Mallory to call me, but the fucker hadn't. I was giving him the benefit of the doubt because it was a holiday, but if he didn't return my call, I'd hunt his ass down. It wasn't like I didn't know how to track the lying mother fucker.

I spent some time researching sobriety that evening, and I decided maybe I should seek out a therapist in addition to finding an AA group where I could be comfortable. It wasn't that I didn't trust myself not to drink, because I hadn't had a drop of alcohol in months, but maybe there would be one thing that would break me and send me back to the bottle, just as I'd almost done a few days prior. Max didn't deserve a drunk and having the man in my life was a very good reason not to drink. However, life didn't follow the careful plans we made, so I'd have to actually try to offer the man the best me that I could be because he was the man with whom I wanted to have a future.

Just as the first rockets' red glare appeared on the television in my room, my phone rang. I saw a number I didn't recognize, so I answered, but I didn't speak. I heard a laugh I recognized as Ian Mallory. "I guess you found out the truth. Meet me at Momma's

Kitchen, which is two blocks east of your hotel. Eleven in the morning. Let's get this done, Schatz," Ian Mallory told me before the line went dead. I hadn't said a word, but I wasn't surprised he didn't need the confirmation. I was pretty sure he knew everything that had happened, even down to the death of Walker Anderson. I'd have to wait to see what he wanted to do about all of it.

The next morning, I found an AA meeting at a church not far from where Julie and I used to live. I decided to give it a try to see what I was in for. and doing it away from where I wanted to make my new home seemed like a good way to test the theory that it would be a tool to help me remain sober.

I sat in the back of the room and watched a mixed crowd filter in as I sipped a cup of bad coffee. I wondered what Max was doing, but I'd find out soon enough. I planned to meet him at the Torrente's home by seven that night, or so I hoped.

I watched as people took their seats, surprised when a woman I knew stepped up to the podium and smiled a gentle smile. "Hello. I'm Paula, and I'm an alcoholic. I've been sober now for eleven years," Ian Mallory's assistant announced, which shocked me.

"Hi, Paula," the crowd responded.

"Twelve years ago, I made the ridiculously stupid decision to drive home after a birthday party for a good friend, giving her a ride as well. We'd both had a lot to drink, and I needed to get home because I was paying for a babysitter, so I not only drove drunk, I sped home drunk. We had an accident, and my best friend was killed. Surprisingly, it wasn't my fault because a man who was drunker than me T-boned us, but I pled guilty to drunk driving and was fortunate enough to be sentenced to only having my license suspended, probation, and community service.

"When I explained the situation to my boss, he petitioned our employer not to fire me because I was a single mother. My terms of remaining employed were that I undergo random urine testing, and I attend an out-patient rehabilitation facility. After I finished fulfilling the terms of my probation for the state and my employer, I began attending AA in my old neighborhood.

"When I moved here, there weren't any meetings, so I spoke with

Father Conant, and he agreed to allow us to use the church on Friday mornings. I'm grateful for the compassion I experienced when I needed it, and I continue to pray that those in need will find our group and allow us to hold them in our hearts as they walk the road to sobriety," she explained, shocking me.

I noticed she'd zeroed in on me and almost left, but after I thought about what the woman said, I could see she was actually reaching out to me, not judging me. That was a relief. I listened to several people tell their stories, and for reasons I was pretty fucking sure I would never understand, I stood and walked to the front of that room, taking my place behind the podium. "Hi. I'm Lawry, and I'm an... Wow, this isn't easy, is it? This is the first meeting in which I'm serious about this, but I'm an alcoholic."

"Hi Lawry," I heard in return. I felt a soft hand on my shoulder and turned to see Paula Gore standing next to me with a tender smile. She hugged me and dried my tears. She then stepped back and allowed me to turn to the crowded room.

"I haven't had a drink for about five months, but before that, I spent two years in a drunken, drug-fueled stupor. I thought I'd lost the love of my life, but I've since learned that wasn't the case at all. Once I sobered up, I actually *found* the love of my life, and I want to do everything I can to be worthy of that love.

"I don't live in the area, but I'm making the commitment that I'm going to walk the steps so I can be the best man I can for Maxi. Thank you for listening." I stepped away from the podium and was surprised at the applause. A lot of people offered hugs and handshakes, and I actually felt good about what I'd done. It was a place to start.

I sat down across the table from Ian Mallory, seeing him all tanned and relaxed. I wished to fuck I could say the same for myself. "How've you been, Schatz?" he asked.

I chuckled, not giving a shit what he thought of me any longer. He sat there and lied to my face about Julien's suicide, though that wasn't why I wanted to confront him. There was something else on my mind.

"Mia Boone. The little girl I called you about who went missing from Jamaica Queens? What the fuck happened with that mission? Those agents, Marquez and Olmos? What were they supposed to do? Did you allow those children to be moved and sold just to warn me not to call the Company again for help? That's one I'll be happy to tell the press," I told him, knowing I really had nothing concrete to tell anyone, but I could issue a threat just like anyone else. He'd probably shoot me in the head in the parking lot.

The waiter approached, and Ian ordered a beer while I ordered water. "Little early for that, isn't it?" I taunted.

Mallory chuckled. "I'm on vacation, and I'm not walking the twelve like you," he taunted in return. Yeah, he owed me that one.

I laughed. "Busted. It was an epic bender though. So, you lied to me," I accused.

The waiter brought over our drinks and a basket of chips with three different salsas. He left us with menus, and I turned back to Ian, seeing he wasn't exactly happy with the direction the conversation had turned. "I'm not going to explain that shit with Renfro. It's classified, and you're not working on our side any longer. Where's Anderson?"

I smirked. "Who's Anderson?" I asked. I could play the game, regardless of whether I still worked for the Company or not.

Mallory shook his head. "Those kids? We found them first and smuggled them back into the U.S. San Diego Children's Services took them into custody. It'll all work out, and that girl will find her way home," he explained.

I didn't think I could be angrier at anyone more than I'd been at Julien when I found out that fucker was still alive. I was wrong. When I stood from the table and swung my right fist into Mallory's jaw, knocking his fat ass onto the concrete floor of that restaurant, I'd never felt so much satisfaction in my life. Nor had I ever had a broken hand. I shook it, which was the wrong thing to do, but when a huge guy from the kitchen started toward me, Mallory held up his hand. "I deserved it. We'll go," he told the man who appeared to be ready to kick both of our asses.

I tossed a twenty on the table to cover our drinks and headed out the front door into the Dallas heat. July was fucking miserable in Texas.

Mallory walked out in his preppy shorts, holding his jaw. "We burned down that complex, Schatz. Olmos and Marquez were instructed to try to dissuade you from hacking us. I don't want to see you at Gitmo, you idiot. Those kids are safe, and we dealt with the gang. None of them lived to walk away. Those kids will find their ways home, I promise. If that girl doesn't turn up in six months, call Paula, but don't hack us again. I can't keep making excuses for you, Schatz.

"You left us for a good reason, so go have a full, happy life, Schatz. We don't want to have to find you again. Stay the fuck out of our network, and make a good life with your young man. I'm glad he's safe, by the way. Take care, Lawry. Hit up SDCS to track down that little girl," Mallory told me as he walked away holding his jaw. He knew where the fuck Anderson was the whole time. I was grateful he didn't push it, but that just meant someone else had to take out the trash, not the Company.

I wasn't at all happy to hear they'd dumped those kids in San Diego, but at least they weren't going to be sold. All I had to do was track Mia Boone. I could do it. I would do it. That little girl needed to be home.

I walked out of security at the airport to find the new guy, Duke Chambers, waiting for me. I'd called Gabe to tell him I was coming back to New York, but I hadn't expected anyone to pick me up. "Damn. What happened to your hand?" Duke asked as he stared at my new cast while relieving me of my duffel and messenger bag with my computer inside.

"I fear I have the bone structure of a bird. Hollow bones. I hit someone in the jaw, which left me with three fractured meta-some-things. I'm fine. Everything else okay? You need anything from me?" I asked as we walked out to the parking garage at Kennedy.

"Nope. How long before you're ready to get into the ring again?" Duke questioned.

I laughed at him. "Oh, no. I plan to spend my recuperating time in bed with my boyfriend. He'll be sympathetic, and he'll want to take care of me. Call me only in the event of emergencies until at least Tuesday," I instructed. I laughed as I climbed into the front seat of the Tahoe I knew to be one owned by GEA-A.

"Hey, man, I'm just following orders. How was Italy? Everyone okay?" Duke asked as we made our way out of the garage and onto the highway to head back to Brooklyn.

"The few I met were doing well. You know the Italy-based family?" I offered, making small talk.

"I do. We go *way* back," Duke responded, not appearing very happy about the question, which worried me.

I swallowed. "You were sent here against your will?"

"No, nothing like that. After I got out of the Marine's, I found other work. Some shit went down that was fucked up, so I was more than happy to leave that job and take a position working for Giuseppe. Now, I'm glad to be in the States again," Duke explained, which sounded a little bit shady, but I had better things to look forward to, and I wasn't going to allow anything to bring me down.

After that, he clammed up, increasing the volume on the radio as we drove to Gabe's home in Bay Ridge. I dozed off for a while, but he shook me awake when we pulled up in front of the nice home the Torrente family shared with anyone in need, including me.

"Thanks, man. See you next week," I offered to Duke. He nodded as I grabbed my shit and headed up the front porch, reaching for the bell when the door opened. There was my Max, engulfing me in a warm, much-needed hug.

"I've missed you so much, Lawry," he whispered as he held me in his arms. I dropped my duffel and wrapped him up as tightly as I could in my arms, enjoying the feel of his lean body next to mine.

Suddenly, he pulled back and looked at the cast, gently taking it into his hands. "God, what happened?" he asked.

I smiled at him. "It doesn't matter. It'll heal. I'm just happy to be going home with you. I *am* going home with you, right?" Hey, I'd been fucked over once. I didn't want to make a mistake twice.

"Yes, you are. If that's what you want," Max whispered as he kissed my lips softly. I couldn't have him thinking I was fragile because of my broken hand. A few fractured bones weren't going to keep me away from him, and my lips and dick were just fine.

"That's definitely what I want. You and food, in that order," I told Max as I picked up my stuff from the porch. I loaded it into his fancy car and went back for a box of my shit he'd packed from my room at Gabby and Dex's house. He had a leather garment bag he brought out and packed in the car before we walked the dog.

"We'll have to come by over the weekend to get the rest of your things. I didn't want to rent a car for it, so we'll just make two trips. Now... Tell me what happened?" he asked.

I nodded in agreement over my things in the house. I'd make as many trips as it took, as long as Max was with me.

I took his right hand in my left, which wasn't cast. "Julien is alive, and by now, he's living somewhere in Russia with a dominatrix. To tell you the truth, I'm not really surprised. He was always more than a little on the kinky side, and he says she fits the bill regarding what he needs from a relationship. I don't get it in the slightest, but it doesn't matter. I've got you, and that's all I care about. Let's get home and get naked," I suggested. We hurriedly took Magic back to the house, checked the water bowls and took up the food bowls before we hurried to his car, Maxim giggling the whole time.

When we arrived at the brownstone, I unloaded the car while Max went inside with my duffel. Watching his ass sway in those shorts was enough for me to get sprung. Being inside him was all I wanted at the moment. I had other things I wanted, as well, but feeling him around me was the priority on my list of needs, and I planned to need it for the rest of my life.

MAXI

Feeling Lawry's body behind me and his good hand on my hip was amazing. He stroked into me from behind as he reached around my body to tug on my hard cock. Much too quickly, I was losing my mind as my hands braced against the tile wall of my shower. We'd put a plastic bag around his cast, and he was fucking me hard. I was in heaven until I had a better idea.

I stepped forward just as he pushed into me again before slipping out. "Let's take this to bed. I want to ride you, Lawry," I told him as I slid the condom off him and pulled him forward under the spray to wash off the lube. I loved shower sex, but with the cast on his right hand, it wasn't as great as I wanted it to be because my mind was reeling with the potential for a fall and other broken bones.

I turned off the water and grabbed us large bath towels, drying Lawry first. I secured the towel around his waist and removed the plastic bag from his hand, seeing he looked quite worried. "Was I not getting it done? I'm sorry about the cast, but I think I only have to wear it for a couple more weeks. Tell me what you want, Max. I want you to enjoy our time together," he stated, panic edging his voice.

I dried his hair and stepped forward, cupping his handsome face in my hands. "It was fantastic, but we don't need you breaking any more bones in a slick shower, sweetheart. Especially not this one," I told him as I sunk to my knees and licked the mushroom head of his leaking cock, hearing him hiss at the sensation. I sucked him into my mouth and hollowed my cheeks, happy to feel his warmth again. That was until he pulled away and grabbed my arm, pulling me up.

I was stunned. I'd never had a man turn down a blow job from me before, and I felt embarrassed. No, we hadn't been together enough times for me to know what he liked, but hell? The worst head I'd ever had was still a blowjob.

"Was I not doing it right?" I asked.

Lawry shook his head as he wrapped my towel around me and pulled me close. "That's not it at all, baby. You're good at that, and I'm not dwelling on why. I haven't been given the opportunities to know what... you know this. You know I have a fucked-up view of sex because of my time with Julien, and I'm afraid I'm not enough for you. Julien told me I wasn't good..." he began.

I had to stop him, so I put my fingers over his soft lips. "No. Don't you let that asshole's justifications to *himself* regarding why he was so cruel to you make you doubt *yourself*. Look, for whatever reason, it seems the man was into pain and humiliation. Not everyone likes to be tied up. Not everyone likes to be hit or choked or whatever other shit he was into. Some of us just want to make love with the person we want to be ours for life," I told him, feeling my skin turning red because I hadn't told him how I really felt about him. I wanted to, but I was still sort of worried about it, coming off the heels of his meeting with that son of a bitch who'd broken his heart so carelessly.

Lawry's sexy smile surprised me. "So, you love me, Mr. Partee?"

I felt my throat start to close, but he'd called it right. I'd be a liar if I didn't admit it, and maybe he'd break my heart, but if one never took a chance, one would never know, would they? "I have a lot of *like* for you, Mr. Schatz," I admitted with a smirk, hoping to inch my way into a full confession.

Lawry took my hand and led me into my bedroom, pulling back the bedspread and flopping down on the bed, smiling at me after he tossed the large towel onto the floor. "How about you explain to me how much you *like* me while you settle on top of my pole so I can explain a few things to you?"

I didn't hesitate to do as he asked. I was already lubed up from the shower, so I quickly whisked another condom down his hard dick and climbed aboard. Lawry was resting against my headboard, and once he was fully seated inside me, he stopped my hips from moving and inched my torso closer, nipping at my bottom lip before kissing me softly. I could feel his heartbeat under my palm resting on his chest, and it felt as if my heartbeat synced up with his at that moment.

"I don't *like* you. You have many likable qualities, to be sure, but there's not one thing I *like* about you, Max. I don't *like* your soft lips. I don't *like* your quick laugh and happy smile. I don't *like* the compassion and kindness that oozes from every pore of your beautiful body. I don't *like* how much you worry about your friends and do your best to ensure that all of them, everyone in your orbit, knows they can always depend on you through good times and bad.

"I don't *like* the way my heart fills to capacity when I feel your body next to mine, and I damn sure don't *like* the fact that being inside you like this makes me feel ten feet tall. I love all of those things, and a whole lot more, but most of all, I love *you*, Maxim Partee. I want a life with you. I want to wake up every morning to kiss your beautiful lips while ignoring the awful morning breath you have," Lawry told me with a smirk.

I sat, still perched on his hard dick, and I felt completely bowled over by what he'd just told me, except the part about my bad breath, of course. Lawry had said those life-affirming words *first*, which wasn't anything I ever believed he'd do. I was just a country boy from Lafourche Parish, and I wasn't worth a second glance, though with the joy emanating from Lawry's face, I felt like the most precious diamond in the world. I looked into his beautiful eyes and held his handsome, stubbled jaw in my hands.

"I love you, too, Lawrence Schatz, your bad breath and all. I want a life with you, too, but right now, I want to feel you deep inside me. I'm gonna move now, sugar," I told him before I kissed his luscious lips. And, move I did.

Monday morning found us at Bay Ridge Health Center, both of us holding a cotton ball at the inside bend of our elbows. Lawry smiled as I stood and moaned a little bit at the sting in my ass, though it was well worth it. We'd had a hell of a weekend after we shared our "*I love yous,*" and every time we came together, Lawry poured his feelings inside me, though not directly, because we went through a box of condoms that weekend.

That was what brought us to the clinic that morning at seven-thirty. I wanted Lawrence Schatz to pour himself into me without anything keeping us apart. When I'd mentioned it to Lawry, his head nearly rolled off his shoulders because he was nodding so fast and hard, in much the same way he'd pounded into me with my legs over his shoulders. The ending had been explosive.

The doctor walked back into the room with a big grin as he saw us both smiling like fools as we remembered that glorious weekend. "I see Dracula's daughter is already gone. I'll call you when I get the results, most likely tomorrow. Take care, guys. Thanks for coming in."

We nodded and headed out to the front desk to make a donation in lieu of an actual payment. The tests were free, but a donation was accepted if one could afford it. I wrote a check for a thousand dollars to cover both of us because the center was doing good work, and I wanted to support it to keep it serving the community. It was well worth the money to me.

We stepped outside onto the sidewalk and kissed, preparing to go our separate ways for the day. Lawry had to track down a client's sister about whom he'd learned new information, and I had a party to plan for Parker Howzer's birthday. Just before I went to hop into Mona, Lawry stopped me and looked into my eyes. "Do you see yourself with children?"

I was stunned for a moment because I couldn't believe he'd asked so soon. I knew it was a conversation we needed to have, but it surprised me he'd ask so quickly after we just admitted we wanted to make a life together. I remembered my lecture to Smokey Colson about Parker's desire to have children, and I wondered for a moment if it was a joke, but looking into his eyes, I could see Lawrence Schatz was totally serious.

Having children was something I'd actually given a lot of thought recently, because when I'd stayed with Dex and Gabe, I'd seen firsthand the joy Dylan and Searcy brought to their lives. Besides, I didn't have anyone else in the world I could call my own, officially, and I wanted that feeling of having someone depend on me.

I believed it kept a person rooted in their life, and that was just what I wanted. Roots. I just hoped Lawry felt the same way about the issue, because if he didn't, I was in a world of trouble. "I hope to, someday. You? You think you'd like to be a dad in the future?"

"Definitely. Could you take off sometime in late-August to go to Missouri with me to meet the rest of my family? You met Hank and Reed at Gabby's wedding, but you didn't get to spend any time with them. I also want you to get to know Jewel and my parents. Plus, my nephew, Brock, is quite a kid, and I think he'd really warm up to you. Will you make the trip?" he asked, which had me in shock.

It took me a minute to formulate an answer. "I'd be honored to spend time with your family. I'm sorry I don't have any family for you to meet, Lawry," was my response.

He chuckled. "Don't worry about that. I have enough for the both of us. My mom loves to smother her family. This is your only warning on that count. I love you, Max. I want you to be part of my crazy family," he told me as he gave me a soft kiss before he pulled away as an SUV drove up to the curb. "That's Duke. I'll see you tonight, baby, and I'll go by Gabby's and get my stuff after I get off, so don't worry about it. I want to leave them a thank-you gift and an apology for what a shitty houseguest I'd been. You have a great day."

How the hell couldn't I have a great day? I was in love for the first time in my life. I knew it wasn't Lawry's first time, but his relationship with Julien Renfro was all kinds of wrong, or so he'd said in retrospect. We vowed we wouldn't let what happened with Julien ruin anything for us. That guy had fucked him up and fucked him over, and I'd sworn to help him through it. I'd be at his side as he walked the twelve steps he'd told me he wanted to commence. I'd support him regarding anything he ever wanted to do in his life.

When love finally found me, I wouldn't turn it away. I wouldn't question it, and I wouldn't gamble with it. I would accept it and be happy to finally have it. I'd waited twenty-nine years for it, after all.

Finally, it came in the perfect image of a wonderful man. That was a reason to be grateful and celebrate. That night, we definitely celebrated by doing the dance with no pants. It might kill me to continue having sex five times in one night, but what a way to go!

"Oh, no. That won't do," I told Toni as we were choosing flowers for a wedding. The summer had been a whirlwind, for sure. I'd planned many parties, none grander than Parker's birthday party where he and Smokey Colson announced their engagement. The party was held at Tomas and Graciela Torrente's home on Long Island at Grace's insistence—with a little encouragement from yours truly.

The Colson family came to Glen Cove, New York, from Paris, Texas, which was where Parker and Smokey actually got engaged in their private spot by a creek in a clearing on the family's ranch. Smokey's parents held a small barbecue at the ranch in celebration, or so Parker gushed at our usual Tuesday lunch when they returned, and he beamed as he flashed the ring. I didn't believe I'd ever been happier for anyone than I'd been for Parker that Tuesday.

The birthday party was the next weekend, and it had been wonderful. The happy couple had decided to wait until the next spring for the ceremony because they couldn't decide whether to have it in New York or Texas, but to look at them, anyone could tell it didn't matter. They were both so happy at that moment, they didn't even worry about when they'd make it official. I was thrilled for them, and I'd plan the event wherever they wanted to hold it, free of charge.

"Well, we're limited regarding what we have at our disposal, thanks to someone dragging their feet regarding an answer to the proposal. Having three days to plan the damn thing doesn't leave a lot of time for one to be choosy," Toni complained with a frown. I laughed as I turned to look at the florist. Yes, it was a rush job, but life threw challenges at us every day. There was no need for a bitch fit about it.

"I'm sure you have something in the back, right?" I challenged the man, offering a sickeningly sweet grin. The proprietor waiting on us was in his late fifties, but I'd seen a portly man moving around the counter by the cash register, and based on the matching rings they both wore, I was sure they were a couple. Besides, most businesses always had *something* in the back they were saving for the right person. Who was to say we weren't the right people?

The man, Chester as he'd introduced, smiled at me and offered a wink. "I happen to have deep red calla lilies, white gardenias, and a selection of specialty colored roses. Come take a look and let's see what tickles your fancy," he offered, making me laugh.

"Thank you, Chester. I truly appreciate it. The couple is very special," Toni offered before I could open my mouth. I shook my head and followed them to the back room. I started to go into the walk-in with them when Toni turned to me and pushed me away.

"I've got this, Max. I've learned from the best, remember? Why don't you go find your man or check on some other things? We'll connect later," she ordered. I knew it was time to turn over control to her because I'd asked her to plan it in the first place, so I could just enjoy the weekend with our friends. I kissed her cheek and held out my corporate card for her to use. She pulled her matching card from the pocket of her navy dress and smirked at me. The woman knew me too well.

I walked back to the hotel to check in with the on-site event planner to see if there were any issues about the reception space he'd been trying to find for us on the second floor. It was short notice for such a gathering, but there were unforeseen circumstances, though they were happy circumstances. A baby was always welcome news, and hell, Las Vegas had some really beautiful places for a wedding. Besides, we were throwing a lot of money at that hotel, and if we had to hold the fucking reception in a hallway outside one of the huge ballrooms, so be it.

As I was strolling through the lobby of the massive hotel on my way to the catering office, I caught sight of Lawry standing at the lobby bar with a glass in his hand that he appeared to be gripping tightly. He was watching one of the TV's mounted on the wall behind the bartender, and my handsome man looked positively pale. I walked up to him and, judging by his demeanor, I could see he was quite upset. It was the weekend before the Labor Day holiday, so the shiver of his body couldn't be blamed on the weather, because it was damn hot outside.

I stood next to him and touched his empty hand, feeling it cold and clammy. When he loosened his fist, I saw crescent shapes on his palm from where his nails had dug into his skin due to how upset he seemed to be. Lawry turned to glance at me, and I watched as he pointed to the television before he handed me the glass to offer a drink. It was seltzer with a splash of lime juice as I'd expected, which was what we'd both started drinking in social settings. I wasn't worried about him drinking, anyway.

Lawry had attended AA meetings every day at lunchtime since he returned from his godforsaken trip to Europe. He was dedicated to maintaining his sobriety, so when I could, I attended with him in support. He was yet to find a permanent sponsor, but the woman who facilitated the group offered her support until they could find someone to step in for her. I thought it was damn nice of her.

I took a sip of the drink and glanced up at the television to see five blurred figures hanging from ropes fastened to a metal beam on an elevated platform that had been constructed in Red Square with the Kremlin and St. Basil's in the background. The closed captioning crawl across the bottom of the screen offered more than I really wanted to know.

"Russian news agency TASS is reporting five members of the so-called 'Novoye Vosstaniye Ordena,' or New Order Rebellion, were tried and hung yesterday for treason and other crimes against the Republic. The Kremlin has vowed to beat down the rebellion after learning factions were reportedly gaining popularity in both Moscow and St. Petersburg. It has been rumored the rebellion was launched by former Federal Security Service operatives who organized in Cuba before returning to St. Petersburg. Among those reported dead is one American counter-intelligence agent. The U.S. is denying any participation in the plans for assassinating the Russian president or aiding the NOR with its plans by covertly providing weapons or financial support.

"The Department of Defense has put all U.S. military installations in

Europe, Africa, and Asia on DEFCON 4, given recent events, because it is unclear if the administration had any knowledge or was offering any support to the rebellion through back channels in the attempt to stage a coup of the Russian government. The State Department has issued a statement denying the allegations, but unnamed sources within the DoD have admitted it has become clearer the two countries are on the brink of war due to the lack of trust after the retaliation for the 2018 Syrian chemical attacks.

"The existing suspicion between the world powers seems to fuel the current instability in the global economy, contributing to the ups and downs of the Dow Jones index in America. It is rumored an emergency meeting of the Federal Reserve's Federal Open Market Committee has been called off-cycle to discuss the feasibility of lowering the overnight discount rate to stabilize the market. There has been no confirmation from the Federal Reserve of any such meeting.

"The identities of the operatives put to death have yet to be released. Stay tuned for more news," the crawl stated before a commercial for erectile dysfunction pills came on the screen.

I turned to look at Lawry, seeing a tear on his cheek. The news was bleak, to be sure, but I wasn't certain what had him so upset. Shit was bad all over, as far as I was concerned. "What's wrong, love?"

"The second one from the left was Julien. The one next to him was his lover. At least he died with her by his side," Lawry whispered as he wrapped an arm around me and hugged me tightly. I felt awful for him. I knew he'd come to terms regarding things with his ex-partner, but he'd cared for the man deeply before it all went to hell. It would still hurt even if they no longer had any love between them.

I felt a tap on my shoulder and turned to see my new friend, Johnny Chang, looking all wild-eyed. "Where's Abby? Was she with you? Have you seen her lately?" he asked, seemingly freaked out.

"She's with Dexter and Parker at the spa getting the full treatment. Man, you need a drink," I joked with the man. He was jumpy and wringing his hands as if he was about to claw off his skin. It wasn't my place to say anything, but I wanted to remind him that having sex tended to lead to babies between hetero couples. Vivien, their oldest child who was just as adorable as Searcy, was with Johnny's parents upstairs taking a nap after lunch.

Lawry chuckled next to me as he ordered the kid a whiskey on the rocks and ordered the two of us another seltzer and lime. Gabe Torrente and Smokey Colson both strolled up to us, having gone to a shooting range outside the city after the group lunch so they could shoot some sort of gun they'd reserved. It was one that was used during the Spanish-American War, or so I thought that's what Smokey had said that morning at breakfast. The man was actually giddy because it was some sort of an antique machine gun. I knew nothing about that sort of thing, and I pitied poor Parker for having to listen to that crap.

Gabe was rolling a hundred-dollar poker chip over his knuckles, that sexy grin on full display. He wrapped a large arm around Johnny Chang and kissed his cheek. "You need to calm the fuck down before you have a goddamn heart attack and leave Lasso as a widow with three kids... You are having twins, right?" he asked with a taunting chuckle in his deep voice.

The blood drained from the young man's face, and we all laughed. It was cruel to tease him regarding what had been such a shock to his system that he was expecting twins with his iffy-girlfriend, but I was happy we were all together, and I didn't feel like an outsider. I'd planned an amazing quickie wedding for the couple, and we were in Vegas for a long weekend, all of us excited to enjoy the occasion.

The number in attendance would be thirty-five because I'd brought along a few of my people to ensure the wedding and reception the next day went smoothly. Some grandmas and grandpas were watching the kids so the adults could hang out at night, and the whole thing was damn near perfect.

Maybe someday I'd have something as grand with my Lawry, but for now, we were in a good place. There was no reason to rush into anything. It was better to savor the incredible things life had to offer, and that was exactly what Lawry and I were doing.

Everyone's life had ups and downs, but if one held on long enough, the grand times would outweigh the bad. That was what I believed, and I dared anyone to challenge me because I'd experienced it firsthand.

I'd met a man who had been dealt a harsh hand, but he'd hung on and rode out the storm, though not always gracefully. He was human, after all, even though I had a hard time always seeing it.

Lawry and I had grown to depend on each other for love and support, and we'd come out on the other side of heartache. I vowed I wouldn't let him traverse his path alone any longer, and I didn't plan to allow it for myself, either. Those days were long behind us. We had a bright future ahead of us, the hacker and me. I wasn't taking off the rose-colored glasses any time soon. The world looked too beautiful through that flattering lens.

EPILOGUE

Lawry

Johnny and Lasso's wedding had been pretty incredible for something so quickly put together, yet in a very tasteful way as Max told me when we sat in the pew behind Johnny's parents and little Vivien, their daughter. Apparently, when Abby found out she was pregnant with twins just eighteen months after Vivien made her debut, Johnny ran out and got the ring, as he told the group at the rehearsal dinner when he gave his speech to thank those in attendance for flying to Vegas to celebrate with them.

"I couldn't take the chance the shock would wear off after the news of the twins, and Abby would come to her senses and get as far away from me as quickly as she could. Three kids and our business together make us about as committed as anyone can be, but my wife-to-be can be a bit stubborn. This way, I get to stick around because we have too much at stake for her to decide to leave my dumb ass in the dust."

Everyone had laughed, but I could see the sincerity in the kid's eyes as he watched every move the beautiful woman had made as she interacted with the crowd while Johnny had sort of lurked behind her, only speaking when Abby had taken his hand and had literally pulled him into a conversation. It had been kind of beautiful to watch them.

Poor Johnny was truly head-over-heels in love with the woman, but as I'd observed Abby's behavior when she laughed at his speech, I could see she'd had no intention of getting away from him anytime soon. It might take him some time to see it for himself, but I knew that feeling too well.

How Max could want to be with me after all the shit he'd learned over the three months we'd known each other was very much a surprise. Hell, having fallen for him so quickly had been another surprise, but the more I'd learned about the man, the more I'd believed things between us were more than I could have ever imagined I'd get in this life… Or the next if there was one.

I'd moved in with him after that shit in Georgia, and we'd been getting settled. My Max had bitched when I'd left my underwear next to the hamper instead of inside, and I'd complained that I had no room for my stuff in the bathroom because his shit took up the whole counter of the single-sink vanity.

A compromise had been reached. We'd gone to a store and bought a cabinet to mount over the back of the toilet where I'd been able to house my stuff because I was taller and could reach the top shelf, unlike Max. We'd also stocked the house with lots of lube because we were now condom-free and loving every minute of it. Unlike my previous relationship, Max and I had learned to actually communicate with each other and talk out differences, and life was full of beautiful possibilities.

The life I'd had with Julien and the aftermath of his actual death had taught me a very important lesson. If a person wanted something badly enough, they'd have to work hard to achieve the goal. Julie had gone so far as to fake his own death to seek out another life he wasn't willing to share with me, but that stunt had taught me an important lesson about our relationship. Julie and I, *we* didn't want it enough. Not just him, but me as well.

Everything, including bathroom counter space—because Julie and I hadn't shared a bathroom—seemed to have come easy for us. We hadn't worked at anything, and we'd both become complacent, or we'd been too convenient for each other to care that we hadn't been building a relationship. We'd simply been coexisting.

Neither of us had put any effort into our relationship at all. When the going had gotten tough, Julie hopped a case that had taken him to Cuba and points northeast after that, finally leading him to his real death. I had hoped Julie felt even one fleeting moment of happiness with his Magda the way I felt with my Max. If he hadn't, it had been a wasted life.

Maureen and Gene, my parents, had loved Max as much and as fast as I'd thought they would, and my sweet sister Jewel had had monogrammed handkerchiefs waiting for him as a 'welcome to the family' present when we'd arrived in Washington, Missouri, on the Friday before Labor Day.

"These are truly gorgeous, young lady. I don't know how to thank you for such a wonderful, personal gift. I've never had anyone actually make me something this special before in my life, and I'll cherish them," Max had told my sister after tearing off the white tissue paper in which she'd wrapped the cotton squares with the bright gold initials in the corner. MP.

"I'm glad you like them. Lawry told me your smile felt like sunshine on his skin, so I had to make them the color of the sun. You wanna come listen to a new song I'm working on? Maybe you can inspire me so I can get my friend, Josh, to write some lyrics. It's a song for Brock's birthday in October when he turns thirteen. You'll come to the party, right?" Jewel asked.

Max had looked at me with concern about planning something in the future, but I'd just laughed. *"Try to keep us away. Max plans parties as his business. If Reed or Hank need any help, have them call us. We'll come back for sure,"* I'd offered, seeing the relief on Max's face. That was when I knew things needed to move just a little faster, because I couldn't have him unsure of our future. I wanted things hammered out as well.

I'd been aggravating Charlene Devaney, the caseworker I'd tracked down in San Diego who'd directed Mia Boone's placement with a couple stationed at Camp Pendleton. It had been a month after Mia had been rescued in Mexico by the CIA. That had been nearly three months earlier, and I couldn't imagine what the hell was holding up the process of returning Mia to her mother and brother in Jamaica, Queens.

I decided to call Ms. Devaney, yet again, before I called it quits for the day to see if there had been any progress on finding the family who seemed to have just disappeared from the Naval Station.

I walked down the hall to where Mathis Sinclair was in the conference room with London St. Michael, the two men pouring over a schedule regarding the upcoming school year and the division of their duties regarding Searcy and Dylan, or so I believed until I opened the door and heard the Mangello name mentioned.

"Giancarlo Mangello's head was found outside the Palazzo Vecchio in Florence, or so the *Florence Daily News* had reported. *Just* the head. How the fuck did the rest of his body end up here in New York?" Duke asked as he pointed to a map of Florence, Italy, anger evident on his unusually red face. It wasn't what I wanted to discuss that morning, to be sure.

"Oh, ick," I snarled as I stood at the door. "It's too fucking late in the day for that shit, guys."

Mathis chuckled. "It's a new hobby of ours. We're trying to track all of the pieces of Frankie Man's middle son, Giancarlo. I've got a buddy at the coroner's office in Manhattan who told me they were finding parts of him all over the state of New York.

"So far, his head was found in Florence, but an arm with one identifiable fingerprint was found here in Bed-Stuy outside a crack house, and a tattooed leg was found in Red Hook. There's a hand from Bushwick they're trying to identify at the moment. Pictures were confirming it was Carlo's leg, apparently. Frankie Man is shitting himself from what I've heard, screaming the cops aren't even trying to get to the bottom of what happened to either of his sons, Dino or Giancarlo. I'd say the man's just unlucky."

London St. Michael offered a laugh. "I could give Frankie a tip about what happened to Dino, but that might start World War III. The cleaners didn't even tell me where they put the bodies. Probably in an unmarked grave somewhere, who knows.

"The DEA takes to heart the reasoning that dead men tell no tales. Glad I got the fuck outta there when I did," London stated. I'd heard about what happened with Dexter's sister and the results of his kidnapping. I decided the less I knew about shit, the better off it was for me.

"Jackass, I'm gonna call Ms. Devaney with SDCS. You wanna sit in on it? I got nowhere with my inquiries at Pendleton, and I can't go through some of my old routes to get into the California Department of Children's Services to try to hack the file. I can't go through Russia anymore, either, considering the fact the world might blow up if I do. I've been planting breadcrumbs through other agencies, but security is cracking down in light of last year's midterm elections disaster, so I'm trying to use legitimate sources for a while," I offered.

London laughed. "Oh, is that what we're calling Carlotta Renaldo these days?"

I laughed with him. Lotta was a lot gutsier than me when it came to making use of certain channels to obtain information. I'd used her trail several times, with her permission of course, but I wasn't having any luck with finding the identities of the foster parents where Mia had been placed, and it was pissing me off.

Ms. Devaney sure as fuck wasn't any help in the matter. The woman had asked all sorts of questions regarding how Mrs. Boone had lost track of her daughter in the first place and how the child had ended up in San Diego. Unfortunately, that wasn't anything Mrs. Boone had easy answers for because Ian Mallory offered no explanation regarding where the girl had been before being dropped off at a hospital with nineteen other kids, most of whom had no traceable identities.

To make it worse, Kelly Boone had gone AWOL after the police had refused to look into his sister's disappearance. They'd chalked it up as a runaway situation after they'd seen the footage Mathis had provided from the CCTV feed near the school that we'd combed from hacked files, and they'd determined the girl had clearly gone willingly.

With all the missing kids in New York alone, the cops had refused to devote any time to follow up leads from unknown sources, namely *me*. It was frustrating as shit, but we were still building the manpower necessary to be able to follow those leads on our own. There were only seven of us, what with Nemo being out on leave to handle personal business. An investigation like Mia Boone's disappearance required a lot more people than just the seven of us.

"I don't need to sit in, but let me know what she says, will you? I need to go get the kids from school and drop them off at Irene's until Gabe gets off. I'll be interested in Devaney's next excuse for not trying to track that foster family," Mathis stated. I agreed with him one hundred percent that there had been some shady shit going down, and I was definitely eager to get to the bottom of it.

I nodded and waved to the men in the room as I headed back to my office to finish out my day. My desk phone was ringing when I walked inside, so I grabbed it, caller ID unseen. "Schatz."

"Casper, there's a delivery for you down here," Sierra stated.

I looked at my watch to see it was three-thirty, and I still had a lot to do before quitting time. "Can't Beaver bring it up?" I asked, referring to Dominic, Gabe's nephew. Nemo had nicknamed the kid *Eager Beaver*, and the rest of us picked up on it. I got stuck with being named after a fucking cartoon ghost who was friendly, and I'd survived. The kid would live through it, as well.

"He's running an errand for Gabby, and I'm busy. Come get this shit off my desk," she snapped, friendly as ever. I wondered if she just hated me or was she so curt with all of us. I really wondered how Sierra got along with Lasso when the woman had worked at the agency because she hadn't taken shit from anyone as far as I'd heard, but it didn't really matter.

I walked down the grand staircase to see a huge bouquet of roses—red roses—on the end of the receptionist desk. Smokey, Gabby, London, Duke, and Mathis—Jackass—all came thundering down the stairs as I rounded the corner to see Max standing at the bottom, looking all kinds of nervous.

He was wearing a new suit, which looked incredible on him, and he had that beautiful smile that made me weak in the knees when I saw it on his face. I almost couldn't believe the guy with the beautiful blond hair standing in front of me wanted to be in a relationship with me, but he wasn't a liar.

"Hey, babe. I didn't know you were coming by," I greeted. I gave him a gentle kiss before remembering most of my coworkers were milling around behind me, which was weird.

Max stepped back and smiled. "I feel the need to take some drastic steps, Lawry—or at least one. Life has been... Hell, it seems like things have been going along at breakneck pace, and as much as I want to savor every moment, I find myself wanting to secure one very important thing in my life. I want to have something concrete before I become really, really busy over the holiday season.

"Next Thursday is Halloween, and I'd like to make a suggestion for our costumes when we give out candy," he stated nervously.

"You're all coming over to our place to take the kids out, right?" Gabby called behind me as the others gave up the pretense that they were even doing anything except butting in.

I turned to him and laughed. "Yeah, whatever," I stated as I turned around to see Max with a silver wig on his head, along with a pair of gold, wire-rimmed glasses. He was on one knee, and I was completely stunned.

"I want us to go as a couple celebrating our Fiftieth Wedding Anniversary. That won't be possible unless I can ask you this one important question right now. In 2071, will you agree to celebrate fifty years as my husband? Will you marry me now so we can make that happen?"

I was stunned, and the fact the room was silent except for the door opening at Dex's yoga studio and a group of men and women had padded out in bare feet barely fazed me. "Will I what?" I damn sure never thought Max would propose to *me*.

My sexy boyfriend suddenly looked worried. "Okay, I've planned this for a lot of couples, but I never knew I'd fuck up mine so much. What I'm trying to ask you is if you'll do me the honor…

"*Yes!* Yes, Max, I'd be so fucking happy to marry you," I responded as I joined him on my knees and kissed the man who had come to mean so much more to me than I ever imagined. At the end of the day, I guessed I liked that mouth on him for more than one reason. He was truly what my heart had sought, and I'd finally learned to trust my heart again. It wouldn't steer me wrong.

Maxi

When Lawry said yes, my heart lept into my throat. It was better than I imagined it could ever be to hear that one word—*Yes!* Yes to me. Yes to our life together. Yes to the idea of having a family. Yes to weathering the storms with me.

Lawry stood and pulled me up with him. "I love you." He then turned to those gathered and offered the biggest grin to his colleagues. "I'm taking the rest of the day off. *I just got engaged!*" Everyone laughed at his pronouncement, and out the door we went.

I drove us home, and after the two of us made dinner together, we toasted to our engagement with sparkling apple cider, and then we made love on the new rug Gabe had bought for me. It was more beautiful than the one I'd had that ended up being the final resting place of a crazy man.

One thing I knew as I rested my head on Lawry's chest after round two—our life would never be dull!

♥♥♥

If you enjoyed "Hacker Lawry," I hope you'll look for the rest of "The Lonely Heroes Series." Next up—"Positive Raleigh!"

ABOUT THE AUTHOR

I am proud to say I grew up in the rural Midwest until I was fortunate enough to meet a dashing young man who swept me off my feet and to the East Coast. Recently, we moved to the desert Southwest where we are beginning a new chapter of our lives. I greet each day with a tremendous amount of gratitude for the life with which I've been blessed.

I have a loving, supportive family who overlook my addiction to writing, reading, and the extensions of my hands—my computer to write, or my Kindle Fire to read the stories others write. I'm old enough to know how to have fun but too old to care what others think about my definition of a good time. In my heart and soul, I believe I hit the cosmic jackpot with the life I have, and I thank the Universe for it.

Cheers!

If you enjoyed this book, I'd appreciate it if you'd leave a rating and/or a review at Amazon.com, BookBub, and/or Goodreads. If you have constructive criticism to help me evolve as a writer, please pass it along to me.

You can find me at: https://linktr.ee/SamE.Kraemer
Facebook Profile: Author Sam E. Kraemer
Facebook Reader Group: Kraemer's Klubhouse
Goodreads: Sam on Goodreads
Amazon Author Page: Sam's Amazon Page

BookBub: Sam E. Kraemer, Author
Newsletter: Sam's Newsletter Sign-up
Website: Sam E. Kraemer Website

Whew! I'm everywhere (even on Insta and Twitter. Go to Linktree profile). I'd love to hear from you!

ALSO BY SAM E. KRAEMER

The Lonely Heroes
Ranger Hank
Guardian Gabe
Cowboy Shep
Hacker Lawry
The Lonely Heroes Box Set Volume 1

Weighting...
Weighting for Love
Weighting for Laughter
Weighting for a Lifetime

Single Novels
The Secrets We Whisper to the Bees
The Holiday Gamble
Unbreak Him

May-December Hearts Collection
A Wise Heart
Heart of Stone

Elves after Dark & Dawn
My Jingle Bell Heart
Georgie's Eggcellent Adventure

Men of Memphis Blues
Cash & Cary
Kim & Skip